Honolulu Play-off

Bibliography

The Alan Saxon Mysteries
Bullet Hole, 1986
Double Eagle, 1987
Green Murder, 1990
Flagstick, 1991
Bermuda Grass, 2002

The Merlin Richards Series
Murder in Perspective, 1997
Saint's Rest, 1999

The Nicholas Bracewell Novels (as Edward Marston)
The Queen's Head, 1988
The Merry Devils, 1989
The Trip to Jerusalem, 1990
The Nine Giants, 1991
The Mad Courtesan, 1992
The Silent Woman, 1994
The Roaring Boy, 1995
The Laughing Hangman, 1996
The Fair Maid of Bohemia, 1997
The Wanton Angel, 1999
The Devil's Apprentice, 2001
The Bawdy Basket, 2002

The Domesday Books (as Edward Marston)
The Wolves of Savernake, 1993
The Ravens of Blackwater, 1994
The Dragons of Archenfield, 1995
The Lions of the North, 1996
The Serpents of Harbledown, 1996
The Stallions of Woodstock, 1998
The Hawks of Delamere, 1998
The Wildcats of Exeter, 1998
The Foxes of Warwick, 1999
The Owls of Gloucester, 1999
The Elephants of Norwich, 2000

The Christopher Redmayne Series (as Edward Marston)
The King's Evil, 1999
The Amorous Nightingale, 2000
The Repentant Rake, 2001

The George Porter Dillman Series (as Conrad Allen)
Murder on the Lusitania, 1999
Murder on the Mauretania, 2000
Murder on the Minnesota, 2002

As Martin Inigo
Stone Dead, 1991
Touch Play, 1991

Honolulu Play-off

Keith Miles

Poisoned Pen Press

First Edition 2004

10 9 8 7 6 5 4 3 2 1

Library of Congress Catalog Card Number: 2003108661

ISBN: 1-59058-071-0

Poisoned Pen Press
6962 E. First Ave., Ste. 103
Scottsdale, AZ 85251
www.poisonedpenpress.com
info@poisonedpenpress.com

Printed in the United States of America

Chapter One

For once in my life, I was in the right place at the right time. When the call came, I was also in the right mood. I was sitting on the balcony of my hotel room, sipping a glass of superior white wine, enjoying a very special view and congratulating myself on a job well done. I felt exhilarated. Basking in the Californian sunshine, filled with pride and satisfaction, I was surveying the golf course that I had helped to design and realizing that it actually *worked.* Officially opened the day before—I had the privilege of hitting the first ball off the tee—it was now swarming with golfers of all ages and abilities, eager to play a debut round on the new course and ready to curse the name of Alan Saxon when they encountered the various hazards that I'd cunningly incorporated.

San Diego had been a lucky place for me. From the start, everything had gone well. Generous employers, rewarding work, perfect weather. No delays, no disasters. The course was completed bang on schedule. I had reason to be very grateful to the city. There was a cordless telephone at my elbow. When it rang, I picked it up to discover that San Diego had blessed me with even more good fortune.

"Al?" said a familiar voice. "Is that you?"

"The very same," I replied, delighted to hear from him. "And that sounds like my old sparring partner."

"Donald Dukelow—at your service!"

"In that case, I'll have another glass of wine, please." We shared a laugh. "How did you know where to find me?"

"I have my spies."

"They must be well trained," I said. "I'm only here for a few days."

"That's why I rang. I read in the golf press that you'd designed a new course down in San Diego so I figured you had to be there for the opening. Congratulations, Al!"

"Save them for my partner, Peter Fullard. He's the real course architect. I just ride shotgun with him. Peter's a genius when it comes to landscaping and he knows more about grass than anyone still on the healthy side of it. He does all the fancy stuff. I just chip in with my name and my know-how."

"Don't be so modest," he chided with his easy drawl. "What you give is hands-on experience and there's no substitute for that. We had a vacation in Bermuda earlier this year. I played one of your courses."

"The Blue Dolphin?"

"Yeah. It had Alan Saxon written all over it."

"Is that good or bad?"

"Terrific!"

I was touched. Donald Dukelow was one of the best golfers I'd ever come up against in my long and erratic career. To have his seal of approval was nothing short of an honor. My work at the Blue Dolphin Hotel was not only my first venture into the mysterious world of golf architecture, it was very nearly my last. Someone did all they could to sabotage our efforts. The dead body found hanging from a cedar was not in our original specifications, nor was the attempt on my life and all the other perils that we had to survive. Pushed to the limit, Peter Fullard, a neurotic man at best, came close to having three simultaneous heart attacks and a complete mental breakdown. Bermuda had been a continuous nightmare. San Diego was the antidote.

"Bring back memories, Al?" asked Donald.

"Memories?"

"Being so close to La Jolla again."

A hollow laugh. "I try to suppress that particular memory."

"But you were on great form at Torrey Pines that day."

"I know," I said, ruefully. "That's what made it so maddening. The trouble was that you were on even better form. During the play-off, you did everything but get a hole in one."

"I guess that Lady Luck smiled on me."

"She only stuck out her tongue in my direction. I tell you this, Donald. From that day on, I've never been able to listen to an Andy Williams record."

"Why not?" he teased, gently. "You were—Almost There."

It was a private joke. Fifteen years after the event, it still rankled. I was so convinced that I was going to win the Andy Williams Open on that occasion that I was rehearsing my acceptance speech as I walked down the 18th fairway after the sweetest drive of the day. It was in the bag, I foolishly thought. Then I heard the explosion of delight from another part of the course and realized that I had competition. Seven strokes behind me at the start of the final round, Donald Dukelow had crept up slowly on me and his brilliant eagle was cheered to the echo. When he matched my birdie at the last hole, we tied for the lead. In a sudden death play-off, there would only be one winner. It was his domain. Donald was the Prince of the Play-offs and it gave him an enormous psychological advantage. I lost the chance to win and Andy Williams lost a hitherto faithful fan. A mention of one of his most famous recordings—"Almost There"—only served to rub salt into my wounds.

"It's not like you to gloat," I complained.

"Sorry, Al."

"You were unbeatable that day. End of story."

"Full stop."

"So where are you speaking from?"

"Rochester, New York."

"Oh, no," I said, bracing myself. "I hope that you haven't rung to remind me of the time you trounced me in that play-off at Oak Hill. My one opportunity to sneak the PGA Championship and you ruined it."

"Did I?" he asked, feigning surprise. "Forgot all about it."

"I appreciate your discretion."

"To be honest, Rochester is not a place that inspires any golfing memories at the moment. It's winter here and there's six inches of snow on the ground."

"So what are you doing there? Building an igloo?"

"Staying with my mother for a few days."

"How is she?"

"Still angry with me."

"Why?"

"I'm coming to that, Al."

There was a long pause. He took a drink of something at the other end of the line. I had another sip of wine. Being called out of the blue by Donald Dukelow was a real treat. He was a very private man, not given to idle chatter on the telephone, preferring the company of a select few rather than the legion of fans he had built up over the years. I counted myself fortunate to be part of his inner circle. Beyond the game of golf, we had little in common yet we somehow hit it off. Notwithstanding his tendency to rob me of title after title on the American circuit, I liked and admired the man. He was a true friend. I sensed that he wanted something from me.

"You still there?" he wondered.

"No," I quipped. "I just popped out for a round of golf. Of course, I'm still here. This is the first time we've spoken in ages. I wouldn't let go of this phone if a tidal wave suddenly hit the hotel."

"Ah," he said, seizing his cue, "I'm glad you mentioned tidal waves. Do you, by any chance, surf?"

"Very poorly."

"Then you need some practice. I can arrange that."

"How?"

"By inviting you to Hawaii for a week."

I goggled. "Are you joking?"

"Never more serious, Al. I want you to be there."

"Whatever for?"

"I'm getting married," he announced.

"But you already *are* married, aren't you?"

"Not any more."

"You and Janine have split up?" I said in astonishment.

"Things didn't work out. I had to let her go."

"How on earth can you afford it? I only have one ex-wife but the financial implications of divorce were horrendous. Rosemary came out of it so much better than me. I pity you, Donald," I said with feeling. "You now have three ex-wives."

"No, Al. Just two. Heidi and Janine."

"What about the ravishing Esmeralda? You were hitched to her when I first met you—or has that skipped your mind?"

"We were never technically married," he admitted.

"You gave every indication of being so."

"That was Esmeralda's idea."

"I thought that you divorced her to marry Janine."

"We came to an amicable parting of the ways, that's all."

"I wish that I'd done that with Rosemary," I sighed. "Unfortunately, she wasn't very amicable. She preferred to have a ferocious legal battle with me. I still bear her tooth marks to this day—and her love-bites, for that matter. I treasure those. Anyway," I went on, "that was enough to put me off the whole idea of marriage. In a curious way, I still love Rosemary but I could never live as man and wife with her. Or tie the knot with any other woman. I think it takes a very brave man to walk down the aisle for the third time."

"Wait until you meet Zann."

"Zann?"

"Short for Suzanne. That's her name," he said with undisguised affection. "Suzanne Kaheiki. She's the one, Al."

I was about to point out that he'd said exactly the same thing to me about both Esmeralda and Janine, but it didn't seem like the appropriate moment. When talking to a man who is deeply in love, never try to introduce cold reason into the conversation. It has absolutely no place there. My friend was getting married and it was my duty to feel happy for him.

"I'm sure that she is, Donald," I reassured him.

"She's looking forward to meeting you."

"Hey, hold on. I haven't agreed to come yet. I have plans. I can't just drop everything and shoot off to Hawaii."

"Yes, you can," he said, confidently. "Now that your commitments in San Diego have been fulfilled, you intended to some take time off in the sun. I'll meet you in Honolulu. Don't argue," he continued as I tried to disagree. "I took the liberty of ringing your pal, Clive Phelps. He's the one person who always knows where Alan Saxon is. Clive told me what your movements were. He's the real reason I was able to get through to you today." A note of pleading sounded. "You *must* be there, Al. I'm counting on it. Zann and I shifted the date of the wedding to accommodate you."

"Why? Am I the best man or something?"

"More of a key witness."

"In other words, you won't be getting married in a church."

"Not exactly."

"So where will the venue be?"

"In the sight of God."

Given the range of the Almighty's vision, it opened up all sorts of possibilities. I knew that he'd married his first wife on a golf course in South Carolina during an ill-timed thunderstorm and Janine, I recalled, had become Mrs. Donald Dukelow while cruising around the Alaskan fjords. What strange location did he have in mind for his third wedding? An extinct volcano? An abandoned lighthouse? The belly of a whale?

"I know," I said, triumphantly. "You're going to Waikiki Beach to get married on a surfboard built for two."

He chuckled. "That's not a bad idea."

"But you had a better one."

"More romantic, anyway. I'll let Zann tell you all about it."

"Don't rush me. I need time to consider your invitation."

"What is there to consider?"

"Whether or not I can make it."

"You *have* to make it, Al," he said with quiet authority. "The only thing you need to consider is how to get to the airport tomorrow. Your flight leaves at 11 a.m. There'll be a first class ticket waiting for you at the United desk. Our plane reaches Honolulu about half an hour earlier so we'll be there to give you a real Hawaiian welcome."

"*Our* plane. Are you traveling with Zann?"

"No. She's at home on the island. I'll be bringing Mom and Heidi."

I gulped. "Your first wife is coming to your wedding?"

"Sure. It was the only way to get my mother there."

"I take it that she doesn't approve of your new bride."

"Mom can be ornery," he confessed. "*Real* ornery. She didn't approve of Esmeralda either and she sure as hell had no time for Janine. If it were left to Mom, I'd still be married to Heidi. In fact, in her eyes—my mother's, that is—I still am. She's got this crazy idea that, when I run out of alternatives, I'll get back together with Heidi."

"How does your first wife feel about all this?"

"Oh, she takes it in her stride."

"Won't she *mind* seeing you get married to someone else?"

"Not at all. Heidi will be the first to congratulate us."

"I don't think my ex-wife would do that," I said. "Rosemary would be more likely to ruin the whole event out of jealousy. She'd be the Specter at the Feast. In the most exquisitely polite way, of course."

Everything that Rosemary did was exquisitely polite. That's what made her so impossible as a wife. She'd always polish the knife to a high sheen before she slipped it between my ribs. Yet we'd been so happy at first, and I still had fond memories of that time. Heidi was clearly cut from very different cloth. Compared to my ex-wife, she sounded like a saint. But even saints have sexual urges.

"Did Heidi never get married again?" I asked.

"No, she preferred to stay single."

"What about significant others?"

"They come and go," he said, casually. "Heidi just makes sure that none of them are in sight when she's around my mother. Mom would take a dim view of that. She prefers to think that Heidi's carrying a torch for me." He chortled to himself. "Heidi would sooner carry my golf bag. That's how we met, as it happens. She caddied for me."

"A wife as caddie. Sounds like an ideal arrangement."

"It was for a while," he said, wistfully. "But that's all water under the bridge now. Anyway, it's one more reason why I want you there, Al—to keep an eye on Heidi for me. She's no mean golfer and you used to be one of her idols."

"Used to be?" I echoed. "I'm not a museum piece yet, Donald."

"I know. Neither am I."

"We're both still well short of the Seniors Tour."

"We always will be." He suddenly became tentative. "So what do you say? Will you be on that flight tomorrow?"

"Do I have any choice?"

"Nobody's holding a gun to your head."

"Then why do I feel cold steel against my temple? I just wish you'd given me a little more time to take it all in."

"Yeah, I'm sorry that it's such short notice. Truth is we only decided to get married a fortnight ago. Been something of a whirlwind relationship. Then I discovered that you were in San Diego. That has to be more than a coincidence, Al. I call it Destiny."

"Who else is coming from the golfing fraternity?"

"Nobody. This is the original quiet wedding."

"That rules out Clive Phelps then. Nothing is quiet if he's involved. Be warned though," I added. "Clive's got a journalist's intuition. He knows that you wouldn't try to track me down on a whim. He'll pester the daylights out of me until he gets a blow-by-blow account of the Secret Marriage of Donald Dukelow."

"Fine by me. When it's all over, the whole world can know."

"And meanwhile?"

"It's a very private affair. Keep it to yourself."

"Will do."

"That's it, then? You'll come?"

"On one condition."

"Just tell me what it is."

"If you so much as mention Andy Williams, I'm on the next plane out of there. Agreed?"

"It's a deal," he promised. "I'll make sure that his songs are banned from the airwaves during your stay on the island. The only entertainer whose name will pass my lips is Bob Hope. Say," he went on, artlessly, "don't I remember you once winning the Bob Hope Classic by a margin of five clear strokes?"

"See you in Honolulu," I said, luxuriating in a cherished memory of a tournament in which I actually beat him. "You've talked me into it."

Chapter Two

It was only when the plane lifted off the runway on the following morning that I began to question the wisdom of my decision. In responding to the unexpected invitation, I had to leave my business partner much sooner than I'd intended and forgo the pleasure of meeting old friends on whom I'd promised to call in San Francisco. Peter Fullard was understandably upset about my change of plan and the friends would be deeply disappointed that I'd pulled out at the eleventh hour. I still couldn't work out why I'd done it. Was it because of my affection for Donald or had I been betrayed by a lack of willpower? Simple curiosity had a definite part to play. Who could miss an all-expenses-paid wedding at a secret venue in Hawaii, attended by a first wife of the groom and a diehard mother who hated the whole idea of her son marrying anyone but the bride of her choice?

For any golfer with red blood in his veins, going to Hawaii is akin to a true believer making a pilgrimage to Mecca. The islands are replete with the most wonderful courses imaginable. They're almost too beautiful to play on, full of stunning vistas and sensual contours and greens that have been manicured to perfection. If I had been returning to the Waialae Country Club in Honolulu to play in the Sony Open, then I'd be tingling with excitement. Instead, I was assailed by doubts and troubled by guilt. On the strength of a single phone call, I'd cancelled my arrangements without a second thought. Peter Fullard and I had worked together for over a year on designing the new course. Now that our brainchild had been successfully launched, he was entitled to celebrate with me. Peter had a right to my time. So did the friends in San Francisco whom I'd warned of my arrival. They deserved better than a short e-mail message to say that I'd had to unscramble my plans at the last moment.

Why *me?* That's what taxed my brain. Why did a professional golfer like Donald Dukelow invite only one representative of a sport that had made him rich and famous? And why choose an Englishman with whom he had never been particularly close? Granted, we exchanged Christmas cards without fail and we were always delighted to see each other, but that was it. Similarities between us were only superficial. We were forty-something veterans, old enough to have acquired sizeable reputations yet still young enough to pose an occasional threat in a tournament where the conditions suited us.

Beyond that, there was nothing. Donald Dukelow came from a wealthy family in Boston who encouraged his ambitions to be a champion golfer. I grew up in the back streets of Leicester, tyrannized by a father who loathed the game and did all he could to stop me playing it. While I left school at sixteen, Donald went on to college to gain a law degree and prove that he could do much more than swing a golf club. I came up the hard way yet he seemed to soar effortlessly to the heights. I didn't resent him for that. I envied him.

One thing was certain. If—God forbid!—I was ever mad or desperate enough to get married again, I would never invite Donald Dukelow to the ceremony as the lone golfer. So why had he picked me? There had to be a good reason. My name hadn't come out of a hat. I recalled what he said about his first wife. Alan Saxon used to be one of her idols. Had I been included merely as a distraction for her? It was an unsettling thought. Or was I there to keep his mother in check, to lend some control to the proceedings? I had to have a function. What was it?

I was still asking the question when we touched down in Honolulu.

◇◇◇

After retrieving my things from the baggage hall, I pushed my trolley through a doorway and into the main concourse. A small crowd of people was waiting to welcome friends or relatives. Chauffeurs were holding up cards bearing the names of their passengers.

"Hi, Al!" he called out. "Over here!"

Even though he was semaphoring wildly with both arms, it took me a moment to pick out Donald Dukelow. He was not called the Invisible Man for nothing. The nickname originated on the golf course, where his habit of gliding unseen past his rivals was legendary. One minute, he didn't even register on the leader board; the next, he was sitting quietly at the top of it. In real life, he was also something of an invisible man, a person of middle height, medium build and a face so utterly nondescript that it was almost impossible to remember what he looked like unless he was standing directly in front of you. If I'd had those features, I'd have taken up a life of crime, secure in the knowledge that no victim would ever be able to describe me accurately enough for the police to issue a photofit.

Pushing through the crowd, he came over to embrace me warmly. There was a buzz of interest from the onlookers as some of them realized who I was. Being over six feet and having prematurely gray hair has always got me noticed. And there was a time when my picture appeared regularly on the sports pages. The irony was that people only recognized Donald Dukelow when they saw him talking to me.

"What kept you?" he asked. "When you didn't come out with the other passengers, I was afraid you might have changed your mind."

"And disobey a royal summons? I'd never do that, Donald. No," I explained, indicating my trolley. "My golf bag was the last thing to appear on the carousel and I couldn't leave without that."

"Oh, sure. You'll certainly need those clubs."

"Why? Are you and your good lady planning to walk out of church and under an archway of putters?"

"Hell, no! Nothing like that, Al."

"Good. That would be too corny for words."

"What we've gone for is even cornier, believe me." He laughed, slapped me on the back then guided me towards the exit. "Let's go and find the taxi. The others are dying to meet you."

"Is Zann here as well?"

"No, just Mom and Heidi."

As soon as we emerged into daylight, a uniformed chauffeur stepped forward to take my trolley from me. Our taxi turned out to be a stretch limo as long as a Greyhound bus but with much sleeker lines. Donald let me get in first and I sat opposite the two women. My host plopped down beside me. The seats were so far apart that I had to perch on the very edge of mine and stretch my arm to breaking point in order to exchange handshakes when I was formally introduced to the two Mrs. Dukelows.

Heidi, it transpired, had kept her married name. She was an attractive blonde who looked absurdly young even though she had to be at least forty. She had the kind of dazzling smile and healthy glow that are the hallmarks of cheerleaders but I also got a sense of keen intelligence. My first impression was that Donald must have been insane to part with such a striking woman. It was flattering to think that she had once been a fan of mine. In a matter of seconds, she acquired a devoted fan of her own.

Unfortunately, my gaze was not allowed to dwell on Heidi Dukelow. Her erstwhile mother-in-law compelled attention. Cora Dukelow was a formidable lady of generous dimensions, accentuated by her flowered dress, and with a handsome face that was anchored by a square jaw. She looked like a cross between a Daughter of the Revolution and a nose tackle for the Denver Broncos, dignified but fearsome, undeniably feminine yet built of solid teak. After sizing me up, she gave me a nod of approval. I was grateful that she seemed to like me. Cora Dukelow was not the kind of person that anyone in his right mind would want as an enemy. She would not take prisoners.

"Thank heaven you're here, Mr. Saxon," she said, closing one eye and peering at me through the other. "Perhaps you can talk some sense into Donald."

"Go easy on him, Mother," said Heidi, softly. "Let him get his bearings. Alan has only just got off a plane."

"So have we."

"Did you have a good flight?" I wondered.

"No," replied the old woman. "I wish I'd stayed in Rochester."

"Even though it's under six inches of snow?"

"If it was under six feet of snow, I'd still prefer to be there."

"Oh?"

"I hate the notion of coming to Honolulu. Shall I tell you why?"

"Another time, Mom," said Donald, raising a hand to stop her. "Please. We're here now. Why not make the most of it?"

"That's sensible advice," added Heidi.

The old woman was defiant. "Not from where I'm sitting."

Having stowed my luggage in the trunk, the chauffeur got into the driving seat and set the car in motion. It purred away from the kerb. Out of the corner of my eye, I could see Heidi smiling at me. I wanted to respond but somehow I could not turn my head away from Donald's mother. I had the feeling that she might box my ears if I did so. My admiration for my friend increased tenfold. It took real courage to hold out against the tangible displeasure of Cora Dukelow. I wondered if his new wife would share that courage.

"Are you married, Mr. Saxon?" asked the old woman.

"I was," I said.

"How many times?"

"Just the once."

"Once is enough for any man," she said, pointedly.

"I couldn't agree with you more."

"I was married to the same man for twenty-seven years. In those days, commitment meant exactly what it's supposed to mean. You make your choice and you stand by it."

"Even if there are problems between man and wife?"

"They should be solved together."

"I wish it had been that easy, Mrs. Dukelow."

"Do you have any children?"

"One daughter."

"How often do you see her?"

"Not nearly enough," I admitted, sadly. "If you play golf for a living, you have to be a rolling stone."

"Heidi soon learned that, didn't you?" she said, turning to her companion. "You spent all your time packing and unpacking suitcases."

"There were compensations," Heidi reminded her. "Lots of them."

Donald gave her a grateful smile. "Thanks, honey."

"It was great fun at first."

"Yeah," he conceded. "It was. Great fun."

"So why did you run off with that other woman?" demanded his mother. "Marriage should be built on a stronger foundation than a desire for 'fun.' There are such things as love, trust, understanding, tolerance."

I could feel her son wincing beside me. Cora Dukelow went on to read him a lecture on the purpose of holy matrimony and, although he had clearly heard it many times, he bore it with Stoic patience. The stretch limo suddenly felt much smaller. The old woman had a way of shrinking space so that she seemed to be right in your face. Even in an aeroplane hangar, a conversation with Mrs. Dukelow would be fraught with danger. She would instantly reduce any distance between you.

The longer she went on, the more I pitied Donald. He had been wise not to ask his beloved to meet us at the airport. The back of a car, however large, was not the place for a first encounter with a future mother-in-law. Zann would have been completely overwhelmed. When she hit her stride, Cora Dukelow was a woman of high voltage. If she'd turned her attack on me in such a confined area, I would have felt as if I was strapped in the electric chair. Yet Donald seemed impervious to her withering assault. He listened politely and nodded soulfully but there was no hint of repentance.

The maternal tirade carried us all the way to our five-star hotel overlooking Waikiki Beach. A porter wheeled out a trolley to collect our luggage. We got out of the car and went into the lobby to check in. When she was standing up, Donald's mother was much shorter than I had envisaged. It was her bulk that gave her such a commanding presence. Heidi, by contrast, was tall, slim, and elegant. Even in flat shoes, she was a good three inches taller than her former husband. I was surprised to learn that the two women were sharing a room. Heidi Dukelow was clearly going above and beyond the call of duty.

While I checked in, Donald escorted them to the elevator and sent them on their way. He returned quickly to the reception desk.

"Thanks, Al," he said.

"For what? I did nothing."

"With you in the limo, Mom was much more subdued."

I was amazed. "That was *subdued?* Then I'd hate to see her when she really lets herself go." He laughed mirthlessly. "Your mother has a strong personality."

"Overbearing is the word that most people use."

"Heidi seemed to cope with her."

"Heidi is an angel."

"I noticed."

"Look," he went on. "You go up to your room and settle in. I'm going to sneak off to see Zann alone. I need to prepare her for her first meeting with Mom. We're all dining tonight at her house, by the way. Meet in the lobby at seven-thirty. That okay with you?"

"Fine."

"And thanks again. I needed you."

"What as?"

"My bodyguard, of course."

◇◇◇

Honolulu is the most exotic city in the world. To begin with, there's the racial mix. Walk along a main street and, before you know it, you've passed fifty different nationalities. There's plenty of ethnic variation in Leicester but it comes with all the usual tensions and prejudices. These undoubtedly exist in Honolulu but they're kept below the surface most of the time. Everyone appears to be so pleased to see you on the island and not simply because tourism is their major source of income. The Koolau Mountains form a dramatic backdrop to the city and, even though it's sullied by high rise buildings and ugly industrial units, Honolulu has somehow preserved its charm and its Hawaiian character.

It's a giant chameleon, changing form and color to suit your individual needs. A modern city, rooted in an ancient culture, with something for everyone. When I'd found my room, I stepped out on to the balcony to get my first view of the incomparable Waikiki beach, covered, as it always is at that time of day, with surfers, sun-bathers, and a cosmopolitan collection of drifters who came in search of Shangri-la. Bronzed bodies of lotus-eaters gleamed up at me. Daredevils rode the waves on their prancing boards. The immaculate expanse of sand was splashed with sunshades and loungers that added myriad colors to an already iridescent scene.

Although there was a pleasant breeze coming off the sea, heat enveloped me in a tight embrace. I had a sudden urge to take a dip in the hotel pool. Before I could unpack my suitcase, however, there was a tap on my door. I opened it to find Heidi Dukelow standing outside.

"I'm sorry to disturb you," she said. "I just wanted to apologize."

I was baffled. "For what?"

"What happened on the drive here."

"No apology needed."

"I think there is, Alan."

"In that case, at least step inside for a moment." I moved aside so that she could come into the room, then closed the door behind her. "I must say that I thought it was very noble of you to share with Mrs. Dukelow."

"Cora is not as bad as she seems. Her manner is a little unfortunate at times, that's all. Well, you saw an example of it on the way here. That's what I wanted to apologize about."

"You're not responsible for Mrs. Dukelow's behavior."

"Maybe not," she said. "I just felt that you should know that she does have a nicer side to her. Believe it or not, Cora can be friendly, charming, and very kind-hearted. She was wonderful to me when my marriage to Donald hit the rocks. We've stayed close ever since."

"Did she ask you to speak to me?"

"No, Alan. She didn't need to do that. She knew that I would." Heidi spread her hands in a gesture of apology. "It was wrong of her to sound off at Donald in front of you and she's angry with herself for doing so. It won't happen again."

"That's a relief."

"Cora's done her tough old broad act for you. This evening, I fancy, you'll see a gracious lady instead."

"Two of them."

I ventured a grin and she accepted the compliment with a smile. Heidi Dukelow had looked pretty stunning when reclining in the back of the stretch limo. Alone with her in my room, and in close proximity, I was able to take a more detailed inventory of her and she quickly went up in my estimation. What interested me was that she was now wearing an expensive perfume. I'd caught a delightful whiff of it as she'd brushed past me. There had been no hint of it in the car. Why had she put it on when she was simply delivering an apology?

"How much has Donald told you?" she asked.

"Very little."

She clicked her tongue. "That's him all over, I'm afraid."

"He was always rather laconic."

"Oh, Donald has plenty to say for himself when he wants to, but he does have a habit of keeping his cards close to his chest."

"If I had a mother like that, I'd keep them hidden behind my back." She stifled a laugh. "Sorry. I didn't mean to be rude about her."

"It was fair comment."

"So what exactly is going on?" I said, hunching my shoulders. "I get this sudden phone call from Donald, telling me that I have to be on a plane to Honolulu next day. I'm still trying to work out why."

"Donald can be very impulsive at times."

"He's the complete opposite on a golf course. In total control."

"That's what struck me about him when we first met," she recalled. "That sense of iron control. He was so focused. It set him apart from all the other guys I dated. Donald seemed to know exactly what he wanted and precisely how to get it. Luckily, I turned out to be one of the things he wanted."

"I don't blame him, Heidi," I said, offering another grin. "Though I bet he had lots of competition. He says you met on a golf course."

"True. During our time at law school. We were in the same year."

"He looks so much older than you."

"An optical illusion. Actually, I was born ten days before Donald. He used to tease me unmercifully about that." She was aware of my scrutiny. "And, no, this is not cosmetic surgery. What you see is the real thing. I'm far too squeamish to let anyone near me with a scalpel. I wouldn't even consider a Botox injection."

"Mother Nature needs no artificial help."

"Thank you," she said. "To come back to Donald, he has a habit of making sudden decisions. He proposed to me, of all places, in a bowling alley when I was about to take my turn. How's that for romance? A month later, we were getting soaked to the skin in the middle of a golf course while the minister tried to marry us. I didn't know whether to make my vows or shout 'Fore!' It was such a crazy thing to do."

"How did Mrs. Dukelow take it?"

"Surprisingly well. When the skies opened, she let out a peal of laughter and told the minister to get a move on. Of course, her husband was alive then. He was a lovely man. Gentle, understanding, civilized. And so, so proud of his son," she added. "Donald was the pro golfer that Herb Dukelow wanted to be. Cora misses her husband badly." She heaved a sigh. "So do I."

"When did he die?"

"Shortly after his fiftieth birthday. Lung cancer. He liked cigars."

"Fifty is no age."

"It shocked all of us. Herb had always been so full of life. Cora was devastated. She just hadn't seen it coming." Pursing her lips, she shook her head slowly. "Three months after the funeral, Donald rang me at my office to say that he was leaving me. You probably met the reason why."

"Esmeralda."

"The only explanation I could get out of my husband was that she was *different* from me. Esmeralda was different enough to split us up."

"Yet they never married."

"No, he could never commit. Esmeralda did all she could to make him come through but he held her off with false promises. Then along came Janine."

"Yes, I met her as well."

"Nice lady. She was not as temperamental as Esmeralda. Not so much hot Spanish blood bubbling through her veins. In short—different. And every so often, as I learned to my cost, Donald has this strange hunger for difference."

"Is that why he's marrying for the third time?"

"Why else?"

"Where do you fit into all this, Heidi?"

"Me?" she replied with a curious smile. "I often wonder. I suppose that I've become a kind of alternative mother to Donald, one that he can actually confide in. When he first walked out on me, I was mad as hell but that wore off in time. Especially when I realized that I was at fault as well. In any marriage, it takes two to tango. I guess I forgot some of the steps. Anyway," she went on, "we discovered there was still a strong bond between us and we drifted into this lovely friendship. He unloads his problems on me and I unload mine on him. We offer mutual sympathy but not a word of criticism. And we do each other special favors." She glanced towards the wall. "I was the one who broke the news to Cora that he was getting married again."

"That must have been a memorable event."

"I've had quieter days. However," she continued, moving towards the door. "I didn't mean to give you a family history. Suffice it to say that you won't see Cora bare her fangs again. On her behalf, accept my apology. I'll get out of here and let you unpack."

"One last thing," I said, crossing to her. "You still haven't solved the mystery for me. I can see why you and Mrs. Dukelow are here, but why on earth was I invited?"

"Are you complaining?"

"Not in the least. I'm treating it as an adventure."

"Best thing to do."

"Donald said that he wanted me here as a bodyguard."

"What he always liked about you was your air of independence and your quirky sense of humor. Oh yes, and your discretion. Donald is a very private man. He puts a high price on discretion."

"Is that why he singled me out?"

"No, Alan. It was my idea to include you."

I was taken aback. "You?"

"I insisted on some kind of bait," she said, beaming. "Aloha!"

Heidi Dukelow opened the door and flitted out. Her brief visit had been an education. She left a memento behind. I could smell that exquisite perfume of hers for the next hour.

Chapter Three

Though the occasion was supposed to be informal, the ladies seized on it as an excuse to dress up. Wearing a full-length black evening gown, Cora Dukelow was covered in so many diamonds that I felt I was looking in the window of a jewelry store. A white chiffon stole was draped around her bare shoulders but it did not conceal the beautiful diamond necklace that sparkled near the upper reaches of the massive bosom. Large pendant earrings glittered and both hands had acquired a battery of rings that were like state-of-the-art knuckledusters. The bracelet on her right wrist was a thing of wonder in itself. I was grateful that she had drawn the line at a tiara. That would have been gilding the lily.

Heidi's attire was more restrained but no less arresting. She wore a sleeveless turquoise dress of shot silk that hugged her body like a wetsuit and advertised every enticing curve. Only one item of jewelry was needed—a gold clasp that encircled her left arm and that was etched with the design of a scorpion. I noticed that she now had a wedding ring on but I could not decide if it was out of nostalgia or bravado. As I complimented both of them on their appearance, I made sure that I got close enough to Heidi to inhale her intoxicating perfume again.

Donald soon joined us in the hotel lobby. He was wearing a red open-necked shirt beneath a white jacket. His blue slacks had creases in them that were almost razor-sharp. Since I had opted for my crumpled linen suit over a white T-shirt, I felt slightly unkempt. In the wake of his reunion with his fiancée, Donald was happy and confident. He kissed both his mother and Heidi before pumping my hand. Minutes later, we were clambering into the back of the same stretch limo. Donald elected to sit beside his mother, allowing me the pleasure of being next to Heidi. She seemed as content as I was with the arrangement.

As predicted, Cora Dukelow was on her best behavior. Poised and regal, she was clearly making an effort on her son's behalf and he was duly grateful. While the car picked its way through the traffic, he shot me a hopeful smile.

"Have you forgiven me yet, Al?"

"There's nothing to forgive," I said.

"Well, I did rather mess up your plans."

"You re-routed me, that's all. My partner was a little disturbed when I had to leave him alone in San Diego but Peter lives in a state of permanent agitation so he'll cope. Much as I love him," I went on, "there's a limit to how much leisure time I care to spend with Peter Fullard. He has no idea how to relax. I traded an over-anxious golf architect for a thrilling new experience in Hawaii."

He chuckled. "I'm certainly thrilled, I know that."

"We all are," said Heidi with evident sincerity. "Good luck, Donald! We're so happy for you."

He turned to his mother for corroboration and she squeezed his arm affectionately. There would be no more homilies to endure. Cora Dukelow now had an air of benign resignation about her.

Donald sat back. "This is going to be a fantastic evening," he said.

It was not long before we left the frenzy of Honolulu behind us and gathered speed as we made for Diamond Head. The Kaheiki family lived near Waimanalo in the southeast of Oahu and the journey took us past Koko Crater, one of the many tourist attractions. It encouraged Donald to show off his local knowledge.

"The Hawaiian name is *Kohelepelepe,*" he declared. "I bet none of you can guess what it means."

"I can see that you're dying to tell us," said Heidi.

"The literal meaning is Fringed Vagina."

"Really, Donald!" scolded his mother with a half-laugh of surprise.

"It's an interesting story, Mom. Since I met Zann, I've really gotten into Hawaiian folklore. They're a very superstitious people. Their legends matter to them. What happened was this, you see."

"Save it for later," she advised. "After I've had a drink or two."

"That goes for me as well," said Heidi.

"But it's a terrific tale," argued Donald. "At least, it is the way that Zann tells it. Maybe I should leave it to her."

"I think we'd much rather have some idea who we're going to meet this evening," said his mother, trying to deflect him. "How many people will be there? Apart from Suzanne and her parents, that is."

"Oh, it's a very select gathering. The only other guests are Zann's brother, Nick, and her sister, Melissa. That will make nine of us in all. At least, that's the hope."

"Why?" I asked. "Is someone doubtful?"

"Afraid so. Melissa. She's been invited but we're not sure if she'll show up. Apparently, she's the family rebel. Nick followed his father into the business but Melissa struck out on her own."

"What does she do?"

"Runs a small theater company with a feminist agenda."

I saw a flicker of disgust in his mother's eyes. Melissa Kaheiki was clearly not the sort of person she would have chosen as her son's future sister-in-law. Having forced herself to accept the fact that Donald was getting married against her will, she had exhausted her limited tolerance. To her credit, Heidi took a more liberal view of the young woman.

"Sounds like an interesting lady," she said. "I hope she turns up."

"So do I," I added. "If Melissa is a theater director, she may be able to give us some useful tips. There's a fair bit of acting involved in tournament golf. Pretending you can still win when you're fifteen shots off the pace, for instance. That takes nerve."

The coastal road took us past Hawaii Kai Executive Golf Course, an endless series of beaches, each with its individual charm, and Sea Life Park, a remarkable display of marine animals that swim freely in the ocean nearby. After driving for ten miles or so from the city, we turned off the road and went through a pair of wrought-iron gates that opened magically as we approached. The Kaheiki residence was in the middle of an estate of over sixty acres. Since land is at such a premium on Oahu, we had visual proof that we were the guests of a very wealthy family.

On either side of the winding track, bananas, papayas and anthuriums were grown in neat plots. Palm trees proliferated. When it finally came into view, the house itself was notable for its size rather than for any architectural excellence. Two stories high, it seemed to stretch in all directions, as if additional wings had been built from time to time as an afterthought. It was constructed of a light-colored stone but all of the verandahs were made of bamboo. When we pulled up on the gravel forecourt in front of the main entrance, Suzanne Kaheiki came out with her parents and her brother to give us waves of welcome.

Donald peered through the window. "No sign of Melissa," he noted with regret. "Pity. From what I hear, she's a real live wire."

◇◇◇

Eight of us eventually sat down in the large and decorative dining room, positioned carefully around a table that could have accommodated another half-a-dozen guests with ease. Jimmy Kaheiki presided over the meal with a smile that broadened into a grin at the least provocation. He was a big, brawny man in his sixties with a chubby face and a glistening bald pate that might have been polished for the occasion. He wore a pair of white trousers and the most extraordinary Hawaiian shirt that I had ever seen, a work of art that consisted of a series of rectangular panels, each with a different set of motifs. Made of the finest silk, it was vastly superior to the shirts that were on offer to tourists. Joseph would have exchanged it in a flash for his coat of many colors.

Nick Kaheiki also sported a superb Hawaiian shirt. Now in his thirties, he was a younger and shorter version of his father with the same facial features and a similar bull neck. If I'd not been told that he managed the factory where the shirts had been produced, I'd have put him down as wrestler or a nightclub bouncer. While he beamed at us as much as his father, there was a sense of suppressed power and anger about him. I had the feeling that he was not as overjoyed about the wedding as the rest of the family.

His mother was a woman who, in her day, must have been a vision of loveliness. Now in her late fifties and trembling on the edge of obesity, she still retained an eye-catching prettiness. Grace Kaheiki was a genial character whose happiness lay in making those around her happy. She could not have been a more obliging hostess. Having no real connection with either family, I was the true outsider in the room yet she went out of her way to make me feel at home, and there was an instant rapport between her and Heidi. She did not find it at all odd that Donald should have brought his first wife along.

It was Zann—Suzanne Piilani Kaheiki—who was the center of attention and who reveled in the fact. Contrast was evidently Donald's watchword. Zann was so emphatically different from the three other partners in his adult life. Heidi was an all-American girl with impeccable credentials, Esmeralda had been a Hispanic powder keg who exploded at regular intervals and Janine, his second wife, was an ice maiden with a Teutonic aloofness. Each had represented a distinct stage in his development.

In Zann, he had gone for youth, vitality, and Polynesian beauty. She was short but shapely, with long black hair that trailed artlessly around her naked shoulders and skin of the most gorgeous hue and smoothness. There was a natural effervescence about her that none of her predecessors could match, and an appealing directness of manner. I put her in her late twenties, at least fifteen years younger than Donald, but she was someone who must obviously have her own sexual history. Most men would have wanted to be part of it.

While she enjoyed being the focal point, Zann spent a lot of time talking to Cora Dukelow beside her, finding out as much as she could about her future mother-in-law and doing her utmost to win her over. Before long, there were clear signs that she was succeeding. Warming to Zann, the older woman was eager to quiz her.

"Is it true that you work in the tourist industry?" she said.

"Yes, Mrs. Dukelow. In senior management."

"Do you intend to give your job up?"

"Of course not."

"Good. That was the mistake that Heidi made."

"I put my career on hold for a few years, that's all," said Heidi.

"You let Donald make all the decisions."

"I got no quarrel with that," he said, winking at the other men.

"A wife should have an equal say in a marriage," asserted his mother. "Don't you forget that, Donald."

"I won't let him," warned Zann with a giggle. "Will I, Donald?"

"Hey!" said Jimmy Kaheiki, slapping the table with the flat of his hand. "Why are we still calling you Donald? My name is James but I've been Jimmy to everyone since the day I was born. Don't you think it's time you became Don or even Donny?"

"We prefer the name Donald," said Cora Dukelow, quietly. "I always think that Don sounds rather common."

"Donny is even worse," said her son, grimacing. "I'm not a member of the Osmonds. If you don't mind, Jimmy, I'd rather stick with my baptismal name. What's wrong with Donald?"

Nick Kaheiki leaned forward. "Reminds me of Donald Duck," he said with a snigger. "Quack, quack!"

"That's not funny," said Zann, shooting her brother a look of reproach. "I think that Donald is a lovely name. I don't want to be Mrs. Donny Dukelow. It's cheapening. Donald has class."

A discordant note had been struck and a long silence ensued. Cora Dukelow gave a nod of agreement, Donald leaned over to give Zann a kiss on the cheek and Heidi obviously sided with their choice of name. The gregarious Jimmy Kaheiki, however, was hurt by the rebuff and his wife shared his disappointment. Their son hid his hostility behind a smile. It was as if Donald had been set a first important test and he had failed it. In taking his part, Zann had driven a tiny wedge between the two families. It did not bode well. I searched for some witty and emollient words to break the silence. Before I could get them out, however, we heard the roar of a motorbike and, through the window, we saw someone racing towards the house before bringing the vehicle to a skidding halt in a shower of gravel.

Zann jumped up from the table with a whoop of joy.

"It's Melissa!" she shouted. "She came, after all."

Whatever their private reservations about the youngest member of the family, the others did not show them. They must have been very annoyed that she had not confirmed she was joining the party, and irritated that she had not had the courtesy to arrive on time, but they all hugged her warmly without a word of reproof. Jimmy Kaheiki did everything but kill the fatted calf for his prodigal daughter. When the effusive welcomes were over, Melissa was introduced to us and took a seat between Heidi and myself. She was soon wolfing down the first course as if she'd not eaten for days. Her parents looked fondly on.

Even in my crumpled suit, I felt like a picture of elegance beside Melissa. Short, fat, and with close-cropped hair that had been dyed a patchy blond, she was wearing a grubby yellow T-shirt with a pineapple print across the chest, knee-length shorts that were long overdue for a wash and a pair of trainers that were falling to pieces. Instead of making the best of herself, she did the opposite.

One of her ears was adorned by a dozen small rings and there was another outcrop along her left eyebrow. It was the titanium rings through her lips that mesmerized me. They jingled to and fro as she chewed merrily away and must surely have caused pain. Many young people feel the need to make a statement with their appearance. Melissa seemed to be making several simultaneously.

Donald and his mother were still absorbing the shock of her arrival but Heidi chatted to her with complete ease. I waited for my turn to engage her in conversation.

"I hear that you run a theater company," I said.

"That's right," she replied. "The Halikahiki."

It was one of the few words that I recognized. "The Pineapple," I observed. "That explains the T-shirt. Why did you choose that name?"

"Is it because some women are like a pineapple?" suggested Donald with a friendly smile. "Spiky on the outside but warm and succulent when you get through the hard exterior?"

"No," said Melissa, firmly. "We called it the Halakahiki Theatre because the pineapple is closely associated with these islands. Some of us prefer to remember our heritage."

"We all do, Melissa," said her father, indulgently. "We just express it in different ways." He flashed her a grin. "Thanks for coming, baby."

"I was curious." She pushed her empty plate aside and looked over at Donald. "I never thought that Zann would marry a *haole*."

"Donald is an American citizen," corrected Zann. "Just like us."

"He's still a *haole*."

It was another word in my diminutive Hawaiian vocabulary. *Haole* simply meant foreigner at one time but it was now used to refer to any white person or Caucasian. On Melissa's ring-pierced lips, the word was relatively polite. For some on the island, Howlie—as we were called—was a term of abuse. We were aliens, intruders, trespassers. We were the wrong color. We were not wanted.

"That may be," agreed Zann, trying to make light of the comment, "but he's the nicest *haole* in the world." She giggled. "And he's *mine.*"

"Thanks, honey," said Donald, blowing her a kiss.

"So where is the wedding going to be?" I asked.

"I told you, Al. That's a secret."

"Even *I* don't know," said Cora. "You'd think he'd tell his mother."

Or get his first wife to tell her, I thought.

"All in good time, Mom," said Donald. "It would spoil the surprise."

"I'm not too fond of surprises."

"This one is real nice, I promise you."

"Well," she said, tolerantly, "if it's what the two of you want."

"Oh, it is," affirmed Zann.

"They wanted privacy," explained her father, "and this is the only way to get it. I realize that our name might mean nothing to you but it counts for a lot on Oahu. We got celebrity status. If word got out that Jimmy Kaheiki's daughter was about to get married to a famous golfer, the media would be here in their hundreds. I'd hate that—so would Zann. That's why the whole thing is low-key."

It would suit Donald Dukelow. The Invisible Man had arranged an invisible wedding. What puzzled me is why he and Zann had not simply slipped away and got married in secret. It would have been much easier to confront Cora Dukelow with a *fait accompli.* She might have huffed and puffed but she wouldn't have been able to blow their union down. As I studied Zann, I realized that such a decision would have been impossible. She belonged with her family. Working on the mainland had only strengthened her bonds with them, and she would never have considered a wedding in their absence.

Paradoxically, Melissa had stayed on Oahu yet become isolated from the others. I suspected that their show of family solidarity had been more for their own benefit than for hers.

Zann looked completely at home while her sister might be eating in a restaurant.

The main course arrived—a seafood potpourri garnished with *limu*, an edible seaweed—and we all tucked in. Traditional Hawaiian cuisine was the order of the day, cooked to a high standard by the resident chef and served by two delightful young Korean waitresses. Zann was patently accustomed to being waited on. Melissa, on the other hand, was the sort of person who preferred junk food that she could carry around in her hand. By his lights, Donald had certainly picked the right sister.

Separate conversations had now broken out around the table. Zann was talking seriously to Cora Dukelow, Donald was doing his best to impress his future parents-in-law, and Nick Kaheiki was offering to show Heidi around the factory where the shirts were made and exported. I was left with Melissa.

"What are you working on at the moment?" I asked.

She turned to me. "Are you interested in theater?"

"I am, actually."

"What does that mean?"

I shrugged. "Exactly what it sounds like."

"In other words, you like cozy theater. Safe, soft, unthreatening drama that doesn't challenge you. Silly musicals or banal comedies or plays by Agatha Christie."

"I prefer something that stimulates me."

"Such as?"

"Brecht," I said, irked by her cynical tone. "My daughter was in a production of *The Caucasian Chalk Circle* at college last term. Though you'd probably call it *The Howlie Chalk Circle*." That made her sit up. "It was marvelous. I also saw her in *Anna Christie*—not Agatha Christie."

"Brecht is old hat," she countered, "and I've never had much time for O'Neill. He sold out." But at least her tone had changed. It was no longer close to a sneer. "Nevertheless, they did write real plays."

"What sort of stuff do you put on?"

"Experimental theater."

"Who do you experiment on—yourselves or the audience?"

"Both. We believe that a play should be a journey of discovery."

"I'd go along with that," I said, picking up a slice of king mackerel on my fork. "Do you have anything on at the Pineapple Theater? I'd be interested to see the kind of thing you do."

She was skeptical. "Would you?"

"Oh, yes. Give me live theater any day. It beats film or television."

"They're bastard arts."

"They have their place."

"Not in my life," she said, curtly. Her voice softened. "But if you really are interested, our next play opens in a fortnight."

"I'll be gone by then, Melissa," I said, popping the fish into my mouth. "I don't suppose there's any chance of me watching you rehearse, is there? What's the play called?"

"*Together.*"

"Who wrote it?"

"Nobody did," she replied. "Not in the sense that you mean. We don't work on finished texts. We develop our own material. *Together* has grown out of a series of improvisations we've been doing. No single author could ever come up with the range of ideas that we've used."

"Not even Agatha Christie?" I teased.

She smiled for the first time. "Especially not her." Melissa weighed me up for a few moments then reached a decision. "Okay. If you promise to keep quiet, you can come along and watch us in action."

"Thanks. I'd like that."

"You do realize that Halikahiki is a women's cooperative?"

"Of course, Melissa," I said with a grin. "There's nothing I admire more than a cooperative woman."

The longer the evening went on, the more blurred the dividing lines between the two families became. Much of the responsibility for this went to Jimmy and Grace Kaheiki, who worked tirelessly to persuade Cora Dukelow that her son had definitely not betrayed his heritage when he proposed to their daughter. I agreed with them. Zann would be a welcome addition to any family. She was alert, intelligent, and considerate towards others. More to the point, she was so obviously in love with Donald that his mother's opposition to the match weakened visibly. The age difference between the couple no longer seemed to matter.

For his part, Donald was in his element. Watched by his first wife and reconciled with his mother, he was able to let his true feelings for Zann show. It was touching. Even the most untutored eye could see that they had already tasted the forbidden fruit of pre-marital sexual passion but they played strictly by the rules. In the run-up to their wedding, Zann would sleep under the family roof while Donald spent nights of enforced celibacy in our hotel. Where they would go for their honeymoon was another closely guarded secret.

Such a pleasant atmosphere was created that even Melissa began to blend into the party. Apart from occasional moments when she and her brother exchanged remarks in Hawaiian that excluded us, she was quite sociable and let her affection for Zann show through. It was only too apparent that she had no sympathy at all with the notion of heterosexual marriage but that did not stop her from wishing her sister well. Donald Dukelow was her choice so Melissa was prepared to accept him, albeit grudgingly, in spite of the color of his skin.

By the time that we left, distinct progress had been made. As the onlookers, Heidi and I both witnessed it. In introducing his mother to the Kaheiki family, Donald had taken a gamble that seemed to have paid off. Zann's parents had liked her and, during the drive back to the hotel, Cora had nothing but compliments to pass about them. Notwithstanding her preference for Heidi, she had been very impressed with the next Mrs. Donald Dukelow. Indeed, she had planted an involuntary farewell kiss on Zann's cheek as we departed. She had also responded to Grace Kaheiki's warm embrace though she restricted Melissa to a brief handshake.

Heidi's comments were universally positive. Struck by the wealth and position of the Kaheiki family, she was genuinely fond of Zann, seeing her not as a rival but as a fit companion for the man with whom she had once shared her life. Because of her intimate knowledge of Donald, she knew exactly what to say to please him and she did so without dissembling. He spent most of the ride back basking in her observations. When we reached the hotel and sent the ladies up to their room, we adjourned to the bar for a final drink.

"Okay," said Donald as we sat down, "what's the verdict?"

"On what?"

"On Zann. On her family. On that amazing house of theirs. And on this cockamamie idea I have of marrying someone so much younger than me. In short, on the whole damn evening."

I sipped my drink. "How honest can I be?"

"Give it to me straight, Al."

"Then I will," I said. "Zann is gorgeous. Her family is delightful. Their house is crap. And you should call the wedding off so that I can marry her instead of you." He chortled happily. "Tell you what, Donald. We could settle this on a golf course. A play-off. The winner gets Zann."

"No deal. She's all mine."

"Spoilsport!"

He settled back in his chair. "How do you think Mom took it?"

"A lot better than I expected," I admitted. "By the time we reached the dessert, she was even able to talk to Melissa without flinching. No disrespect to your mother but I suspect she's not exactly used to having a meal with a gay woman."

"Mom is more broad-minded than she looks."

"Not when it comes to Fringed Vaginas."

He laughed again. "Maybe I shouldn't have brought that up. Still," he went on, "a word about tomorrow. I'm going to spend some time alone with Zann so I'll have to leave you to your own devices. Mom is lined up for a tour of the island with Jimmy and Grace. Not sure about Heidi's plans yet."

"We're playing a round in the morning," I told him.

"Great! She's no novice on a golf course."

"In the afternoon, Heidi's off to see the Kaheiki shirt factory while I'm watching a rehearsal at Melissa's theater."

"A rehearsal?"

"More of an improvisation, I think."

"Better you than me, Al. According to Zann, some of the stuff they put on at the Pineapple is pretty grim."

"In what way?"

"Oh, you know, lots of feminist propaganda and waving the Hawaiian flag. Melissa and her cohorts don't seem to have heard that their nation is just one more astral body on the star spangled banner."

"I like a bit of healthy protest, Donald."

"I hope you don't find it too healthy," he said. "That takes us on to tomorrow evening. Zann wants a ladies' night out so she's taking Mom and Heidi to her favorite restaurant. The main object of the exercise is to get Mom on her side, of course, but, if I know Zann, she won't pass up the chance to ask Heidi what I'm like as a husband."

"Isn't that dangerous?"

"I don't think so."

"Your first wife might put her off the whole idea."

"Heidi is very discreet. Like you."

"So what happens to us tomorrow night? A stag party?"

"Yes, Al. Just the three of us."

"Three of us?"

"You, me, and Andy Williams."

I banged the table. "Not on your bloody life!"

"Then it's you, me, and a lot of golden memories about golf," he said, drinking his whisky. "How does that sound?"

"Music to my ear," I said, "so I'll close with the offer. I might even get you pissed enough to tell me where the wedding is going to be."

"Not a chance!"

"At least, tell me when it is."

"Saturday."

"Only four more days of freedom."

"The wedding can't come soon enough. Tell me," he said, leaning in closer, "what did you really think of Zann?"

"I was bowled over."

"First time I saw her, I couldn't believe it. That face, that figure, that amazing skin. Oh, and that husky voice makes the hairs on the back of my neck stand up. Just fancy. You wake up in the morning and the first thing you see is that lovely smile of hers."

"I can fancy it only too easily."

"Zann is so *different*."

"You're a lucky man."

"She's the one, Al. Yes," he added, waving a hand, "I know that I said the same thing before but this time I really mean it. I want to spend the rest of my life with Zann. I think I'm even ready to start a family."

It was a huge step forward. Donald had always treated parenthood as something that was strictly for other people, and I knew that it had been a bone of contention with Esmeralda. He had seemed perfectly happy with her until she started agitating for motherhood. That would have obliged him both to marry her and to lose what he saw as his independence. Heidi and Janine, I suspected, had also had maternal urges that had been crushed by his refusal to take on the responsibility of fatherhood. Yet now he was actually looking forward to it. Zann had effected a transformation in him. It was a good omen.

"Know something?" he confided, finishing his drink. "I always envied the way you talked about your daughter."

"Really?" I said with surprise.

"She obviously means so much to you."

"Yes, Donald. She does. Lynette is my light and joy."

"I know. High time I let that kind of light and joy into *my* life," he announced, solemnly. "High time that I finally grew up."

Chapter Four

Heidi Dukelow was as good as her word. When I got down to the hotel lobby with my golf clubs early next morning, she was already waiting for me. She looked considerably brighter than I felt and was exuding an almost girlish enthusiasm. As we exchanged greetings, I remembered that it was Heidi who had invited me to play a round of golf, not in any spirit of challenge but as a means of keeping the pair of us out of the way so that we did not hamper Donald. I hoped that her suggestion—issued during the meal at the Kaheiki residence—was also prompted by the desire to get to know me better. Improving my acquaintance with her was the main reason that I willingly accepted her offer.

"I didn't see you in the restaurant," she said.

"No, I opted for room service instead. It's the one sure way to get me up at six thirty."

"That wasn't a possibility for me, I'm afraid. It was breakfast down here or nothing. I had to creep around the room so that I didn't wake Cora up. Fortunately, she's a heavy sleeper."

"No pun intended, I assume?"

"She does occupy a fair bit of a king-size bed," she conceded with a smile. "We've got two in the room as well as a three-piece suite, a coffee table, a writing desk, fitted wardrobes, a TV and a drink cabinet. Our view is magical. We must have one of the best rooms in the hotel."

"Jimmy Kaheiki is picking up the tab, apparently," I told her. "Donald and I had a drink after you'd gone to bed last night. According to him, Jimmy insisted on paying all our expenses while we're on the island." We headed for the exit. "How's that for generosity?"

"It's more like philanthropy," she said. "I mean, I can understand why he might want to pay Cora's bills. As the mother of the groom, she does have a special position. But you and I are just here to lend a spot of moral support."

"I fancy there's more to it than that, Heidi."

Taxis were waiting at the rank outside. The driver of the first one opened the trunk from inside his vehicle then leapt out to deprive us of our golf bags. We climbed into the rear and put on our safety belts. The driver, a chirpy young Filipino, soon got back into his seat.

"Which course?" he asked. "Koolau or Makaha?"

"Neither," I replied. "Ko Olina." As he started up the engine, I turned to Heidi. "It's the one course where I may be able to pull rank and get us squeezed in. I have friends there."

"Alan Saxon has friends at every golf club, surely."

"Don't you believe it! There are some places that have been glad to see the back of me. I've had too many rows with lazy tournament directors or green keepers who don't know how to prepare a course to the highest possible standard. However, I have no complaints with Ko Olina. You'll like it."

"Oh, I intend to," she said. "That's why I brought my clubs with me. It would be criminal to come to Hawaii and not play."

"I agree. This is one of the few places where you can get out on a golf course every single day of the year." I began to fish a little. "So what did Mrs. Dukelow really think of last night?"

"Exactly what she said. She enjoyed the evening."

"Give or take a few hairy moments."

She grinned. "Well, I don't think that she and Melissa would ever be sisters under the skin. But she got on surprisingly well with Zann. I was relieved to see that. Donald had obviously briefed Zann carefully."

"Did he brief you before you met your future mother-in-law?"

"Did he?" She rolled her eyes. "Oh, boy! He must have given me a hundred do's and don'ts. Trouble was, when I actually came face to face with Cora, I forgot every one of them. When you're only twenty years old, she can be very intimidating."

"I'm over twice that age and she still terrifies me."

"It soon wears off."

"I'll take your word for it."

"Is your own mother still alive, Alan?"

I heaved a sigh and shook my head. "She died years ago. But she was nothing like Mrs. Dukelow. She was a very shy, quiet, gentle sort of woman. I don't think she could have handled a situation like this—me, marrying a young Hawaiian beauty like Zann, I mean. It would have left her totally bewildered."

"Cora was a little bewildered at first."

"And very irate as well."

"She does have a temper."

"The person I take my hat off to is you, Heidi."

"Me?"

"Yes," I said. "I don't know any woman who would cheerfully turn up at the wedding of her former husband. My ex-wife wouldn't—unless it was to put her curse on the marriage, that is. Yet you've been a model of restraint throughout. How do you manage it?"

"Lawyers learn to manage with anything."

"But you're not here as a lawyer, are you?"

"That's right," she said, evasively. "I'm here to fulfil a life-long dream of playing a round of golf with my favorite British golfer."

"Is that the only reason you agreed to come to Honolulu?"

"Of course."

Her laughter gave nothing away.

The Ko Olina Golf Club is part of a resort on the leeward coast of the island. Driving west, we curved our way around Pearl Harbor, passing the industrial complex of Aiea and the old sugar town of Waipahu before following signs for Barbers Point Naval Air Station. Opened in 1990, Ko Olina is a haven of golf and other leisure activities at the southern end of the largely arid Waianae Coast. Given a flat dusty landscape to work with, the architect somehow managed to sculpt a wonderful golf course out of it, filled with gentle undulations, an abundance of water, and the kind of scenic beauty that no British course could offer.

Heidi took one look at the place and gave a gasp of delight. We were in luck. Someone had canceled at the last moment so we took over their tee time and got off to an early start. Even though she'd been married to a professional golfer, and must have played countless rounds with him, Heidi suddenly became very nervous. I could see her hands trembling as she checked her card for the distance of the first hole. But she expected no favors, spurning the forward tees and trying to keep pace with me. An excellent drive from the first tee gave her a surge of confidence. She had good technique. Donald had taught her well.

The par-4 second hole tested me severely and found Heidi out. At 412 yards, it's the most difficult hole on the course because it has a small green, set at an oblique angle, reached through a narrow neck. While I struggled to make par, Heidi dropped three shots but it did not rattle her. She'd developed a momentum now and was keen to press on. At the next two holes, she played her best golf of the morning. We were strolling down the fifth fairway when she spoke for the first time.

"This is such a lovely course," she said. "It manages to be functional and aesthetically pleasing at the same time."

"Wait until we reach the twelfth, Heidi. We have to go under a waterfall, then up to an elevated tee. On your left, you'll see two lakes connected by a series of step pools and, behind the green, the coconut palms will be waving to you in the breeze like hula dancers. Be warned. It's enough to distract anyone."

"Then I'll be distracted. After all, we're not only here to play golf."

I grinned. "That's what I was hoping."

"Apart from anything else, I wanted the chance to hear *your* opinion of what happened last night."

"My opinion?" I said. "That's easy. I think we had a delicious meal with a charming family."

"Did you find Nick Kaheiki all that charming?"

"Well, not really," I admitted. "I had a few reservations about him, especially after that Donald Duck remark. He was very hospitable but there were moments when the mask slipped a touch. I'm not sure that he likes Howlies."

"He insisted on showing me around their factory this afternoon."

"See if you can pinch one of those shirts for me."

"To be honest, Alan, I'm having second thoughts about going."

"Why?"

"Nick is rather intense," she said. "And I'm afraid that he wants to get me on my own so that he can quiz me about Donald. I'm just here as a wedding guest, not as a spy for the Kaheiki family."

"You can't blame him for wanting to know more about his future brother-in-law," I pointed out. "He's only being protective towards Zann. Let's face it, there's a lot more to Donald Dukelow than you can glean from the golf magazines—and who better to ask than his first wife?"

"I still have my doubts."

"It works both ways, remember."

"Does it?"

"Yes," I said. "Nick might gather some background information about Donald but you'll be in the perfect place to get the lowdown on the Kaheiki family. I'm sure that Mrs. Dukelow would want to learn as much about them as she can. By the way, the shirt factory is only a small part of their empire. From what I hear, Jimmy Kaheiki is involved in dozens of other enterprises as well."

She pondered. "You're right. I suppose I could do a spot of digging."

"See yourself as a daring counter-spy."

"Do counter-spies spend an afternoon looking at Hawaiian shirts?"

"If it serves their purpose. Besides," I said, remembering what Jimmy Kaheiki and his son wore on the previous evening, "it will be more like visiting an art gallery."

We turned our attention to golf. Ko Olina is a popular course and you're warned to spend no more than fifteen minutes at each hole in case you hold up the game behind you. Heidi and I kept up a reasonable pace. I thought that the baseball cap and the sunglasses might give me a degree of anonymity but I had reckoned without sharp-eyed golf fans. My height, distinctive swing, and telltale gait combined to give me away and I got cheerful waves from a number of people. They knew better than to interrupt our game by trying to speak to me.

Everything had gone well until we reached the eighth hole. The course was in good condition, I'd found my rhythm and I had the most delightful playing partner. Talking to Heidi in such a relaxed way, I came to appreciate in more detail why Donald had married her and it made me wish that Rosemary had been as interested in golf. A wife who actually enjoys the game that is her husband's source of income gives you far more peace of mind than one who bickers incessantly from the sidelines. But, then, I didn't marry Rosemary for her fascination with golf, only for her fascination with one particular golfer. How was I to know that my appeal would wear off so quickly?

"What's the trouble?" asked Heidi.

"Nothing."

"You keep looking over your shoulder."

"Do I? Sorry," I said, easily. "Force of habit."

"Habit?"

"I keep expecting Donald to do his Invisible Man routine and come up behind me. I never felt safe on the leader board when he was playing."

I was lying. What made me keep glancing over my shoulder was the feeling that we were being watched. It was not the casual interest of someone who might want to see a well-known British golfer in action but a serious scrutiny. Though I could not pick anyone out among the palm trees at our back, I was nevertheless certain that he or she was there.

Heidi was focused on the green ahead. The eighth hole was a par-3 that obliged us to drive from an elevated tee. Nestling behind a three-tiered waterfall 195 yards away was a split-level elevated green with a flag at the heart of it. The green was surrounded by so much lush vegetation that I wondered if I should have brought a trowel and a pair of secateurs rather than a set of clubs.

"It's like a well-tended garden," I observed.

Heidi was circumspect. "Outside my range. If I try to reach it with my tee shot, I'll either end up in the water or disappear forever in that bougainvillea." She made her decision. "Time to play safe."

To prevent me from having the honor at every single hole, we'd abandoned golf etiquette and agreed to take it in turns to drive first from the tee. It was the only concession she sought. Heidi had insisted that I play to win without holding back for her benefit. After selecting her 3-iron, she put her ball on the tee peg then stepped aside to take a couple of practice swings. She then addressed her ball, drew her club back in a graceful arc and unleashed its power. It was a good shot, putting her more or less where she was aiming. A pitching wedge would get her to the green with relative ease. With an accurate putt, Heidi might even make par.

I managed to find the green with my drive. Unfortunately, my ball rolled on to the very edge, in a spot that made a birdie well nigh impossible. Collecting our golf carts, we began a gentle stroll along the fairway. All that concerned Heidi was her next shot but I was still very much aware of a pair of eyes behind us. I gave no indication of this to her because there was no point in worrying her unnecessarily. When we reached her ball, Heidi abandoned her clubs and went up on to the green to take a closer look and to assess what was needed. I took the opportunity to spin round suddenly without warning.

This time, I did see him. Silhouetted against the blue sky, he was standing on the eighth tee, holding something that glinted in the sunshine. It was a pair of binoculars. We were being followed.

The Pineapple Theater was in a converted warehouse in one of the dingy parts of the city. Melissa Kaheiki's company clearly believed in minimalism. Wooden benches were arranged around a central space that contained nothing apart from a small table and two chairs. The only real sign of expenditure was on the battery of lights that hung overhead. Dark and chilly, the place smelled in equal proportions of rising damp, cannabis and the assorted leather ware that was once stored there. After a round of golf with Heidi and lunch at the hotel with her and Cora Dukelow, I was obviously in for a wholly different experience.

My arrival caused something of a stir. My age, my manner and my gaudy holiday attire set me apart from the kind of audience that the theater usually attracted, and there was some protest about my presence. Melissa had to go into a noisy huddle with the other six members of the cooperative in order to convince them that I was not an interloper. At length, she came across to me.

"Right," she said, crisply. "This is the deal. They've agreed that you can stay, provided that you sit at the back and shut up."

"Why did you need their permission?"

"We do everything by mutual consent."

"I thought that you ran the place."

"I'm technically in charge of this production, that's all. We have no overall director. We rotate the position with each play. It's more democratic that way."

"But some of you must be better at it than others."

"We don't compete, Mr. Saxon."

"Alan, please. Don't make me feel even older than I am."

"Okay—Alan."

"Why were the girls so hostile towards me?"

"They thought you'd come to sneer."

"No way," I promised her. "I don't sneer at anyone who does something they really believe in. And I can smell real commitment in the air—along with the pot, that is."

"Some of the girls need a little weed to keep them loose."

"That wasn't a criticism, Melissa."

"It had better not be," she said, bluntly.

She rejoined the others and I retreated into the shadows. It was not difficult. They were using only one working light for the rehearsal and it barely illumined their acting area. My interest in drama was not feigned. Ever since my daughter played Shylock in an all-female school production of *The Merchant of Venice*, I'd been hooked on live theater. What I now witnessed was also performed by a women-only cast but it was worlds away from what I'd seen in the sedate surroundings of an English boarding school. It was a revelation to me.

The seven of them formed a mixed bag. Including Heidi, there were three I took to be native Hawaiians, a Chinese girl with a shaven head, a stringy blonde with an Australian accent and two Japanese women. All of them were in their twenties and wore matching pineapple T-shirts of varying hues. What they were recreating in that small, ill-lit, uninspiring space was nothing less than the attack on Pearl Harbor by the Japanese Air Force in December, 1941. Their take on it was original. Instead of blaming the Japanese for the atrocity, they directed their fire at the Americans for using the island as a naval base, and thereby rendering it vulnerable to attack from the Far East.

Much was made of the way the American military had changed the tone and culture of Oahu. When army, navy and air force personnel were assigned to the island in such large numbers, it was inevitable that the major profession for women on Oahu swiftly became the oldest one. In the wake of the bombardment, it turned out, when the hospitals were suddenly deluged with casualties, blood supplies were quickly exhausted and the medical authorities appealed to the prostitutes to come forward as donors since there were so many of them. They duly responded.

All of this was acted out in sequence by seven talented young women, each playing several parts, male and female, and moving about their stage with great urgency. The air raid itself was done largely in mime with the two Japanese girls as the enemy, whirling around to inflict horrific damage on the fleet and its hapless crews, sending the furniture and the other members of the cast tumbling to the floor time and again. With clever lighting and sound effects it would be a very powerful scene but, even in its crude state, it was vivid and compelling. Melissa, who went down with the *USS Arizona*, made them repeat it four times before she was satisfied.

Lost in her work, she'd forgotten all about me. She was a versatile performer, able to shift at will between a whole variety of roles, yet still managing to keep a wary eye on what the others were doing. The Australian did not take criticism well and there was a fair bit of argument with her but Melissa's opinion always prevailed in the end. *Together* was really a plea for Hawaiian independence, underscored with some bitter hostility against the country that had first polluted it with military bases then co-opted it as the 50th state. *The Merchant of Venice* seemed hopelessly tame beside it.

It was almost two hours before they took their break. Three of them sloped off to the toilet, two lit cigarettes and the Australian started a quarrel with the Chinese girl. Melissa remembered that I was there.

"Well," she said, coming over to me, "what did you think, Alan?"

"I was held throughout."

"We've got a lot of rough edges to work on."

"But the main thrust of the piece comes through clearly."

Melissa was suspicious. "Do you mean that or are you just trying to be nice? No bullshit, please."

"I mean it. It's real, get-up-and-grab-you drama," I complimented. "I'd never have believed that seven women could create a piece that involved so many male characters. I wish the play well—but don't hold out any hopes of a transfer to Broadway," I cautioned with a grin. "You're up against American patriotism."

"We want to expose it for the sham that it is."

"Are you going to invite your family to see the production?"

"Mom and Dad will be here on the first night," she said. "They don't approve of what I do but they always support me. Nick won't turn up, though. He's far too restless. Couldn't sit still long enough."

"What about your sister?" I asked. "The play may still be running when she gets back from her honeymoon. Is Zann a theatergoer?"

"No. In any case, this is not her kind of thing."

"Too political?"

"Too honest. She's marrying a *haole*, after all. A mainlander. Her loyalties will change. Zann wouldn't like the way we deride the American psyche. She's bought into all that crap."

"I thought you liked Donald."

"What is there to like?" she said, hunching her shoulders. "He's a good-looking shadow, that's all. I prefer more substance in a person. I don't actually dislike Donald but I do despise what he represents. Still," she went on, scratching her head, "if my sister wants to marry a guy like that, I can't stop her. I just wish she'd picked someone else."

"A native Hawaiian?"

"There are still a few left, despite what you read in the guidebooks."

"Is that what your parents would have preferred?"

"Of course. They believe in tradition."

"Yet they haven't objected to Donald."

"They love Zann," she explained, "so they don't want to upset her by putting obstacles in her way. They did that once before and it caused a lot of bad blood."

"Oh?"

"It's all dead and buried now."

"Are you saying there was someone else before Donald?"

Melissa nodded. "She got involved with this jerk from L.A. He was the head honcho of a travel company she was working for at the time. Zann was all ready to get engaged to him until Dad spoke his mind. He loathed the guy on sight and said so."

"How did Zann take that?"

"She was livid," recalled Melissa. "Stormed out of the house and went back to L.A. in a huff. Month later, this guy dumps her for someone else. Took her ages to get over that."

"What was he like?"

"A complete dork. Yet he was so arrogant. Years older than Zann. She's always gone for mature men. Sign of insecurity, if you ask me," she said, curling a lip. "At least Donald looks as if he'll stand by her. I suppose that's in his favor. Who is he, anyway? I'd never heard of him."

"Donald Dukelow is a big name in the world of golf."

"That's what sold it to Dad. He's a bit of a trophy-hunter."

"You're not, obviously."

"This is my trophy," she asserted, looking around. "Right here. A theater. A social weapon. A place to open people's eyes to the truth of what's going on in the world." She studied me quizzically for a moment. "Thanks for coming, Alan," she said. "I wasn't sure if you'd make it."

"I keep my promises, Melissa."

"And you stuck it out. I thought you'd sneak out quietly after the first five minutes. But you stayed and you watched."

"Stayed, watched and *learned*."

"That means we're getting somewhere." She took my arm to help me up. "Come and meet the others," she said, warmly. "They're weird characters. Well, they'd have to be to work here. Oh, word of warning. Don't make any comments about what you saw."

"Why not? I liked the rehearsal."

"I believe you—they won't."

"Six of them, one of me. Will I be safe, Melissa?"

She brayed with laughter. "I think I can guarantee that," she said.

Having spent most of the day with his fiancée, Donald Dukelow was in a buoyant mood when we met up that evening. Zann had recommended a restaurant within easy walking distance of the hotel so we set off at a leisurely stroll. He was curious about how I'd spent my day.

"Heidi and I played a round of golf at Ko Olina," I said.

"Didn't you introduce her to the delights of Koolau?"

"I'm saving that for a game with you, Donald."

"It's never been my favorite course."

"Then I'm in with a chance."

There was a time when the Koolau Golf Course—a trial by ordeal that ran to almost 7000 yards—was rated by the USPGA as the toughest in America. I was inclined to agree. The spectacular mountainside course would put any golfer under the closest examination. I couldn't wait to tackle it in a head-to-head with Donald Dukelow.

"Where did you have lunch?" he asked.

"At the hotel—with Heidi and your mother."

"Is Mom still breathing fire through her nostrils?"

"Put it this way. I think that maternal affection is slowly getting the better of uncontrollable rage. You have Jimmy and Grace Kaheiki to thank for that," I said. "They gave your mother a grand tour of the island and that softened her up no end. I carried on where they'd left off."

"Thanks, Al. You're a real pal."

"Is that why I got invited? To soft soap your mother?"

"That's one of the reasons."

"I'm still waiting to hear what the others are."

Donald chuckled. "The night is young."

By the time we reached the restaurant, I'd told him all about my visit to Melissa's theater in the reclaimed warehouse. He was intrigued by the concept of dramatizing the raid on Pearl Harbor but he showed no interest in sampling the work at the

Pineapple Theatre for himself. Of the members of the Kaheiki family, Melissa was the one he would never manage to befriend. It would be a futile exercise. There was too much Hawaiian history dividing them.

Though it had a small frontage, the restaurant was quite cavernous inside. We were shown to a booth in a corner and studied our menus over an aperitif. At one time, Pacific Rim cuisine was a synonym for tourist food that was bland and unexciting but it's improved markedly over the years in taste, variety, and presentation. The fact that Zann ate there was a guarantee of its quality. So, I hoped, were the high prices.

"This is on me," insisted Donald. "Eat anything you like."

"At least, let me buy the booze."

"Forget it."

"You have to let me do *something.*"

"You're doing it, Al, believe me."

"I'd like to think I was more than decoration."

"You are. Zann is crazy about you and there's no need for me to tell you what Heidi thinks. Mom just loves that British reserve of yours."

"I didn't know I still had any."

"Just go with the flow. Enjoy."

The waiter arrived to take our order. Donald chose the wine. When we were alone again, I raised a subject that had been bothering me.

"Something rather odd happened at Ko Olina," I said.

He grinned amiably. "Heidi beat you?"

"No, she didn't. But it was not for want of trying. She has great concentration. That's why she didn't notice him."

"Him?"

"Somebody was stalking us."

I told him what had happened and he was puzzled. "Must have been another golfer who happened to recognize you."

"Golfers don't usually carry a pair of binoculars in their bag."

"Okay, he was a bird watcher who strayed on to the course."

"No, Donald," I stressed. "He was there to keep an eye on us. I felt it in my bones. When he realized that I'd spotted him, he disappeared. If he'd been a golfer or a bird watcher, he wouldn't have done that."

"Did you report this?"

"No point. He was long gone by the time we finished our round. And I didn't want to alarm Heidi. She still knows nothing about this."

"That was considerate. Did you get a good look at the guy?"

"He was too far away."

He gave a shrug. "Could be something or nothing."

"I'd plump for something," I said. "He made me feel uneasy."

"Why should he want to trail you—or Heidi, for that matter?"

"I wish I knew, Donald."

"Forget it. There's lots of crazies on this island."

"I can vouch for that," I said. "I'm sitting opposite one."

He chuckled. "I guess you're right at that, Al," he confessed. "I must look like a real fruitcake. I marry two beautiful women and live with a third one, and each time I cut and run. Moral? I'm just not able to sustain a loving relationship. So what do I do?"

"You take another shot at it."

"I'm like a guy who crashes every car he drives. Instead of taking taxis, I have this compulsion to order a new vehicle each time." His face hardened. "Except that, from now on, I'll be more careful on the road. Zann is my last chance to prove that I can hack it as a husband. And as a father, maybe. I swear I'll do it."

I raised my glass. "I'll drink to that."

"Thanks."

Donald clinked my glass with his own, then swallowed its contents in one gulp. He then began his interrogation. He wanted to know what I thought about Zann and about each individual member of her family, as if needing reassurance. It was no time to be negative. Subduing my doubts about Nick Kaheiki, I spoke well of everyone I had met, with, of course, particular praise for his chosen bride.

"Do you think Zann really loves me?"

"Of course, she does," I affirmed.

"How can you tell?"

"Only blind love would prompt a woman to marry a man who turns up at the altar with his first wife, his mother, and a random golfer from the other side of the world. It's more than love, Donald—it's obsession."

"That's what it is with me. I'm completely obsessed with her."

"It shows."

The meal was outstanding and the wine superb. My only concern was that Donald seemed to be drinking so much. Downing two glasses to every one that I had, he was soon calling for a second bottle.

"So where is the honeymoon going to be?" I asked.

"Every day with Zann will be like a honeymoon."

"In short, mind my own business."

"Wait until we send you a post card. Then you'll know."

"Will you be sending one to Heidi?"

"No, that would be unfair on her."

"I'm surprised you're not taking her along for the ride," I teased. "If you took Esmeralda and Janine with you as well, you could probably get a reduced rate."

Donald laughed. "No room for excess baggage on this trip."

We were enjoying each other's company so much that we didn't notice how the restaurant slowly filled up. A live band started playing Hawaiian music. The meal somehow tasted even better. Our thoughts soon turned to the game that had brought us together in the first place and Donald dipped freely into his memoirs. I could have talked golf forever with him in such a convivial atmosphere. We had so many shared memories. But someone was determined to interrupt them.

"Why don't you go back to your own country?" demanded a voice.

We looked up at a short, chunky Hawaiian in his fifties, who had risen from his seat and who was swaying uncertainly in front of us. His lips were pulled back to disclose a row of tobacco-stained teeth.

"We don't need any white trash on our island," he declared.

Donald bristled. "You're drunk, friend. Go home."

"This *is* my home. You two are the intruders. Get out of here."

The commotion was attracting a lot of attention. As I glanced around the room, I saw that Donald and I were the only people there with white faces. We were isolated. The man staggered forward and bumped against our table, making the china rattle.

"*Hele I loko, haole 'ino, aka ha'awi mai kala!*" he sneered.

There was a rough translation in his smoldering eyes. It made Donald rise angrily to his feet and I got up to restrain him. Before the man could abuse us any more, he was grabbed unceremoniously from behind by a much bigger individual and frog-marched to the door. They had a heated conversation in Hawaiian, then the troublemaker was forcibly ejected. Our savior came back to our table with an apologetic smile. I put him in his mid-thirties. Tall and strapping, he had the classic features of the native Hawaiian.

"I'm sorry about that, gentlemen," he said, softly. "Some guys just can't hold their drink. As far as I'm concerned, you're both very welcome here."

"Thanks," I replied. "What exactly did he say?"

"It doesn't matter. He was speaking out of turn."

"But it does matter," insisted Donald, conscious of the fact that he was just about to marry into a Hawaiian family. "We want to know what he said—don't we, Al?"

"Yes," I agreed, taking my cue. "I somehow had the feeling that he wasn't passing a compliment. Am I right?"

The newcomer paused for a moment, then he pulled out the empty chair from beneath our table and sat down. He looked from Donald to me, lowering his voice so that we were the only people able to hear him.

"Are you sure you want it word for word?" he asked.

"Especially the rude ones," I specified.

"It was only the booze talking."

"What did it say?"

"Go home, you Howlie scum—but leave your money behind."

"Who does he work for?" I joked. "The Tourist Board?"

Chapter Five

Looking back, I find it difficult to believe that it happened. The man was a complete stranger, who only came to our rescue to save us from an awkward confrontation, yet, within a minute, he seemed like an old friend. Whether it was the heady wine, or the atmosphere, or the feeling of gratitude we had towards him, I do not know, but his manner was so warm and reassuring that we both took to him instantly. Neither of us objected when he ordered another bottle of wine for us.

"Let me introduce myself," he said, offering his hand. "I'm Gabriel Mahalona—but you can call me Gabe." We shook his hand in turn. "No need to tell me who you guys are. I'm a pretty good golfer myself. Not in your league, of course, but I can dream dreams." He beamed at us. "Right now, one of them is coming true. Wow! I'm sitting down with Donald Dukelow *and* Alan Saxon."

"Keep your voice down," I said. "We're traveling incognito."

"Some chance!"

"What do you do, Gabe?" asked Donald, fearful that the man might be a journalist, sniffing a story. "You're not with the press, I hope."

"Me?" said Mahalona. "Hell, no! The only bits of the papers I read are the sports pages and the ads. I run my own business," he went on, taking out his billfold and extracting a card. He passed it to me. "We manufacture top quality swimming pools—no rust, no rot, no leaks, no liner, that's our boast."

"You must be doing well if you can afford to eat here," I said, glancing at the business card before handing it to Donald. "Is it a lucrative game?"

"It brings in the bucks. Hey," he said, slipping his billfold into the pocket of his silk shirt. "I don't suppose that either of you is in the market for a new pool. We do export and I could offer a tempting discount on the retail price."

"Not for me, thanks," said Donald, putting the card down on the table. "My house came with its own pool."

"Pity. What about you, Mr. Saxon? We make a terrific product."

"You're wasting your sales talk on me, Gabe," I told him. "When I'm in the U.K., I spend most of my time living in a motor caravan. There's not much call for a swimming pool when you keep on the move."

"I guess not." He sat back and spread his hands. "So what brings the pair of you to Honolulu?"

"We're just passing through."

"Seeing the sights, eh?"

"Yes," I said with feeling. "It's something you never have the chance to do when you play in a tournament here. All you get to look at is the hotel where you stay, the course itself and the road between them. And as soon as it's all over, you're off to the airport to fly to the next venue. It's like being on a treadmill," I complained. "I'm thinking of giving it up and selling swimming pools instead."

Mahalona shook with mirth. "Great idea!" he said. "I'll take you on as my overseas director. Within a year, you could make partner."

The waiter brought the wine and poured it into our glasses. After a meal like that, I would have preferred a coffee but Donald was ready for more alcohol. He lifted his glass.

"Thanks for helping us, Gabe," he said.

"My pleasure, Mr. Dukelow."

"I've never come up against that kind of thing before."

"I'm sorry you had to get a taste of it now," said Mahalona. "I hate it when guys play the nationalist card like that. We're all Americans now, for God's sake, and I'm proud of the fact. Only a tiny percentage of us are genuine descendants of the original Polynesian settlers. Look at me," he invited, tapping his chest. "I was born in Honolulu but I've got Samoan, Indonesian, Chinese, Fijian, even a little Irish blood in me. Most of us are like that. Why deny it?"

"Nice to meet someone who actually likes Howlies," I said.

"Like them? I *love* them. They're my best customers."

Gabriel Mahalona was good company. He was pleasant, easy-going and highly articulate without being glib. We were lucky that he was still in the restaurant when we came under verbal attack. Having dined with a prospective client, Mahalona had stayed behind to pay the bill and was therefore on hand to come to our assistance. Had he not done so, I would have ended up having to drag Donald away before he got involved in a fight. Though he was mild-mannered and innocuous as a rule, my friend evidently had a temper when roused. It was a side of him that I'd never seen before.

Time passed and the conversation flowed. Mahalona was soon showing us a photograph of his wife and two children. While I had difficulty finishing my glass of wine, he and Donald made short work of the rest of the bottle. To my alarm, Donald was even talking about a round of liqueurs. I thought that he'd already had enough alcohol and was about to suggest that we call it a day, but it was, in effect, his stag party so it seemed churlish to stint him. Mahalona took charge.

"Listen," he said, "if you want a *real* Hawaiian drink—the kind you can taste for days—I know just the place. It's an exclusive club that I can get you into as my guests. It would be an honor to buy you guys a drink that you'll remember forever."

"Then let's go," said Donald, cheerfully.

"We have to pay the bill here first," I reminded him, "and it's getting late. I'm not sure that a club is such a good idea."

"One drink, that's all," said Mahalona. "How long will that take?"

"Is the club nearby?"

"Five minutes in a taxi."

"Sounds great," decided Donald, indicating to a passing waiter that he wanted the check. He grinned. "Do they have girls there?"

"Some of the best hula dancers on the island," replied Mahalona. "They put on an amazing show. Real class—nothing sleazy." His brow furrowed. "I hope that's what you meant, Mr. Dukelow. You want the other kind of girl, count me out. I'm a family man. There are dozens of places in Waikiki where you can have big tits and cute ass wiggled in your face all night. That what you guys are after?"

"No, no," I said, quickly. "Not our scene at all."

Mahalona looked relieved. I was disappointed in Donald. For a fleeting moment, he'd had the urge to visit exactly the kind of girlie bar that lusty male tourists tend to flock to at night. I was seeing another new side to his character. Donald seemed to have forgotten that he was about to marry someone who was far more desirable and infinitely more wholesome than any of the so-called exotic dancers who inhabited the tacky nightclubs. Who needed to buy his sexual thrills when he had Suzanne Kaheiki waiting for him?

When the bill was paid—Mahalona insisted that the last bottle was on him—we tumbled out into the night. Hailing a cruising taxi, Mahalona gave the driver instructions before piling into the back seat with us. Donald was showing all the signs of someone who had already reached his alcohol limit. His speech was slurred, his movements were unsteady and he kept laughing at inappropriate moments.

"One drink and that's it," I decreed.

"You've been holding back all evening, Al," said Donald, wagging a finger. "You turn teetotal on me all of a sudden?"

"Somebody has to get you back safely to the hotel, Donald."

"I'll give you a hand," volunteered Mahalona.

"No, I'll manage, Gabe—after that one last drink."

"One, it is, then. I'll make sure it hits the spot."

The taxi took twice as long as he'd predicted to get us to our destination. It turned out to be a discreet nightclub down a narrow street. When Mahalona rang the bell, someone peered at us through the grill in the door. There was a brief conversation in Hawaiian then the door opened to admit us. I noticed that Mahalona slipped the doorman a tip. A second man also needed to be sweetened with a twenty-dollar bill before he let us through the next door.

We stepped into a large, low room with subdued lighting. A small band was playing at the far end of the room. Most of the space was taken up by a series of tables, arranged in horseshoe pattern around the dance floor. Running the full length of the wall to our right was a well-stocked bar that was being kept very busy. The décor was tasteful, the atmosphere welcoming. An attractive young Hawaiian waitress showed us to our table, but that was all she was permitted to do apart from fetching our drinks. The women at some of the other tables were patently there as guests rather than employees of the club. I relaxed.

Donald reached for the drink menu but Mahalona stopped him.

"Trust me," he said, getting up. "I know exactly what you want."

"Make mine a soft drink," I said.

"In a place like this?" He pulled a face. "That would be an insult. Won't be a minute, gentlemen. I want to have a word with the owner."

He crossed to the bar and started talking to a short, skinny man in a white tuxedo. It gave me the chance to speak to Donald alone. Eyes glazed, he was staring at the band and moving his head in time to the twang of the Hawaiian guitar.

"When are the hula dancers coming on?" he asked.

"Don't worry about them. One drink and we're off out of here. You've got to get your beauty sleep, Donald. I'm expecting a round of golf out of you tomorrow afternoon."

"You'll get it. Book a time and I'll be there."

Putting his elbows on the table, he leaned forward but one of his arms slipped and he almost keeled over. I caught him just in time. Instead of thanking me, he just giggled.

"Go easy," I warned. "You've had a skinfull tonight."

"Shelebrating my freedom before I give it up."

"Yes, but think what you get in return—Zann."

He grabbed my arm. "Isn't she gorgeous, Al? I can't believe that she'd go for someone like me. Zann is the best thing that's ever happened to me. The very best."

"And there was I, thinking that it was me."

"You're a friend, a good friend."

"You've got lots of friends, Donald. What's special about me?"

"The coinsheedience," he said, introducing two extra vowels into the word. "When I needed someone in Hawaii, you were right there in San Diego. That's fate. We had to go for you."

"We?"

"I consulted with Heidi. She agreed. You'd be ideal."

"As what?"

"A kind of best man. Someone from outside my circle. Someone who didn't come with any baggage. Someone who wouldn't spill the beans to the press. A neutral, if you like. Someone who wouldn't make judgements."

Donald was wrong about that. I'd been making judgements ever since he insisted on that second bottle of wine. The third one had been too much for him and, in my judgement, he should quit now while he was still able to stand up, albeit uncertainly, on his own two legs.

"What did you tell Zann about me?" I asked.

"The truth. You're a wonderful pal."

"I didn't feel very pally when you beat me in that last play-off."

He laughed. "You can get your revenge tomorrow, Al."

"Only if you're in a fit state to play."

"We timed it just right," said Mahelona, returning with a tray of drinks in his hand. "The dancers are due back on in a few minutes. Isn't this music fantastic?" he went on, setting a tall glass in front of each of us before handing the tray to a waitress and sitting down. "This comes from the Hawaiian soul. This band doesn't play those standard numbers that have been done to death. This is Hawaiian music for Hawaiians."

"I thought you were proud to be an American," I said.

"I still got some drops of Polynesian blood in my veins."

All that Donald was interested in was the drink. Served on a bed of crushed ice, it had to be sipped through a colored straw. When he took a first long taste, Donald was almost delirious with pleasure.

"This is really something, Gabe," he exclaimed. "Try it, Al."

"Don't rush me."

"Come on," encouraged Mahalona. "Just taste it."

Against my will, I obliged. It was deliciously cold and tangy. I could pick out the rum and the lime but the other ingredients were a mystery. It coursed through me and left a most delectable aftertaste. I gave our host a nod of approval.

"I told you it would do the trick," he said, chuckling. He looked around. "What do you think of the club?"

"I like it, Gabe," I replied. "Nice feel to it. Full of character."

"It's the kind of place a man can bring his wife to and you can't say that about every nightclub in Honolulu. Actually, I try to bring clients here. After a couple of glasses of this," he said, holding up his drink with a broad grin, "they tend to buy much bigger and better pools than they'd planned. That's a trade secret, by the way. Keep it under your hat."

"I'm not wearing a hat," said Donald, confused. "Or am I?"

Mahalona laughed and slapped him familiarly on the arm. I'd hoped to have a quick drink and then get my friend out of there but the arrival of the dancers ruined that idea. They were hypnotic. Bursting on to the floor to the beat of the drums, the six Hawaiian girls spread out into two parallel lines and went into their first routine. They were true artists. For most tourists, hula means little more than a group of dusky maidens in grass skirts, shaking their bodies in a controlled frenzy. In fact, hula has deep roots in the history of the islands. It's far more than simply an ethnic dance. It's an expression of the Hawaiian spirit.

Beginning as part of a religious ritual, it was only danced by highly trained men at first. When girls were allowed to join in, only the most beautiful, graceful, and talented were selected for tuition. Each dance tells a separate story and they were taught to use every part of their body to enhance the narrative. The troupe on show at the club had mastered all the aspects of hula. Their hands were amazingly expressive and I knew how important it was to interpret their gestures. A glance at Donald told me that he was more interested in other parts of their anatomy. Sipping his drink, he watched with widening eyes.

There was an excitement in the hectic pace of the dance and, while I admired the sheer athleticism of the girls, I also noted the contribution of the band. Providing the rhythm in the background was the *pahu*, a large bass drum made from hollowed coconut and covered with a shark-skin membrane. The lead instrument was the *ipu*, fashioned out of two gourds joined together, and either thumped on a mat or slapped with the hand. In a supporting role were the *punui*, a small drum made from a coconut shell and beaten in counterpoint to the *puni*, the *uli uli*, a gourd filled with shells or pebbles and used like a rattle, and the *ili ili,* stones that are clicked together like castanets. The volume that was generated was extraordinary. It reached out to surround us and sweep us away.

After the frantic speed of the first dance came a much slower and more eloquent hula. I was intrigued to see how the facial expressions were used to complement the body movements, clarifying the story as it unfolded. In the warm room, I was glad of the cooling drink but I took only small sips. To my dismay, Donald, having drained his first glass, was already accepting the offer of a second from Mahalona. I declined but I could not reason with my friend. Exhilarated by the dancers, he was in no mood to be balked.

"Lighten up, Al," he urged. "Let yourself go."

"Yes," added Mahalona as the waitress brought their drinks. "Are you sure you won't join us?"

"No, thanks."

"I thought you liked it."

"I do, Gabe. Far too much."

I also loved the hula dancing. There was no way that I'd leave while those girls were still evoking the very essence of Hawaii with their sequence of dances. There was something so powerful and elemental about the scene, and yet, at the same time, there was great subtlety. I nursed my drink until the very end of their performance then joined in the burst of well-deserved applause. Donald, too, wanted to show his appreciation but his hands simply refused to clap together. His coordination had gone. He swayed wildly in his seat and then, losing his balance, he collapsed against me.

"Time to go," I announced, pushing him upright.

Mahalona was concerned. "Is he okay?"

"He will be when I get him back to the hotel."

"Let me help you."

"No, no," I said, feeling that it was my responsibility. "You stay here and finish your drink. I'm afraid that Donald has had too much."

"Who says so?" demanded Donald, rallying slightly.

"I do. Come on." I stood up and heaved him to his feet. "Thanks, Gabe. It was kind of you to bring us here. The dancing was a real treat."

"Glad you enjoyed it. Here," he said, getting up to take one of Donald's arms. "At least, let me help you out to a taxi."

I was grateful for his help. Donald could barely stand. It took two of us to get him across the room and out through the door. When he felt the night air on his face, he came alive again and began to struggle.

"I want to see some more hula," he protested. "Bring on the girls."

"Another time," I told him.

"I'm fine, Al. There's nothing wrong with me."

Donald tried to break away from us but lost his footing. We propped him against a wall and waited for a taxi. As I held him tight, he seemed to go off to sleep. Mahalona was penitent.

"Gee!" he said. "This is my fault. I had no idea this would happen."

"He was hitting the bottle at the restaurant, Gabe."

"Sure you can manage on your own?"

"Yes," I said.

"At least, let me pay for the taxi."

"No, you've been too generous as it is."

"I feel guilty, Mr. Saxon."

"So do I. He should never have been allowed to get into this state."

Donald's eyes had opened again and he was trying to speak but no words came out. Fortunately, a taxi turned into the street, bringing some other guests to the club. When they got out, Mahalona helped me to ease Donald into the rear seat.

"That offer about the swimming pool stays open," said Mahalona with a friendly grin. "I'd cut you a great deal. Tell him that when he wakes up."

"I will, Gabe. Goodbye—and thanks."

I gave the driver the name of the hotel and we set off. The last I saw of Gabriel Mahalona was the cheery wave he was giving us. I concentrated on trying to keep Donald awake, patting his cheek with the flat of my hand and talking to him constantly. He was in a complete daze. From time to time, he would recover enough to burble something and even thresh about a little but I held him fast. I felt ashamed that I'd let him get into such a condition. When we set out for the evening, I'd expected nothing more than shared reminiscences over a leisurely meal. Donald Dukelow had behaved out of character. At a moment in his life when he was entitled to be supremely happy, he seemed to have been driven by some inner demons.

The important thing was to keep him away from the public gaze. I wanted to spare him that embarrassment. What really worried me was the fear that we might bump into Heidi and

Cora Dukelow at the hotel. After their night out with Zann, they might well be awaiting our return. I could imagine what his mother would say if she saw me lugging her drunken son across the lobby. She'd be furious with Donald and none too pleased with me. My credit with Heidi would also be adversely affected and I didn't want that to happen. When the hotel came into sight, therefore, I asked the driver to drop us off at the side entrance. He gave me a hand to get Donald out of the vehicle and earned himself a good tip from me.

Holding his arm around my neck, I practically carried my friend into the hotel, choosing the service elevator in order to avoid meeting any of the other guests. It took us up to the third floor. By the time we got there, I'd managed to find his billfold and take out his card key. As I slipped the billfold back into his pocket, he went limp and sagged to the floor. I had to haul him up and throw him over my shoulder like a sack of potatoes. He was much heavier than I'd thought. I prayed that he was not about to vomit all over me.

Staggering along the corridor, I got to Donald's room and tried to open it with the card key. It proved impossible. I had to shed my load before I could concentrate on what I was doing. With Donald sitting against the wall in a stupor, I inserted the card again. An elderly Asian man came down the corridor and walked slowly past. He said nothing but shot us a look of disgust. Donald was oblivious to it. Getting him into the safety of his room was paramount. There was no time for niceties. I simply took him by the shoulders and dragged him through the door. Only when it closed behind us did I feel secure.

I, too, was now suffering the effects of alcohol and I was panting from the strain of getting my friend back to his room. I switched on the light. Leaving him on the floor, I went into the bathroom to splash some cold water on my face, then I drank a glass of it in the hope that it might sober me slightly. When I got back to him, I saw that Donald was clearly beyond the reach of sobriety. Flat on his back, he was snoring away with a contented smile on his face. All that I could do was to put him to bed and make him comfortable. It was no easy manoeuvre.

With a concerted effort, I lifted him upright but he began to resist. I could not understand it. He seemed to be unconscious yet his arms were flailing about madly. As I tried to manhandle him towards the bed, his elbow caught me hard enough on the nose to produce a sharp pain. I felt a slow trickle of blood on my upper lip but dared not let go of Donald to wipe it off. Holding him in a bear hug, I more or less bounced him across the room and pushed him on to the bed, picking up his feet and swinging them round so that he lay in a straight line. He began to snore again.

The softness of the mattress deprived him of any urge to fight back. When I slipped the pillow under his head and removed his shoes, he did not move a muscle. He was wearing an open-necked shirt and a pair of fawn trousers. They would be his pajamas for the night. I saw that some of my blood had gotten on to the collar of his shirt. It made me return to the bathroom to stem the flow with a tissue. My nose was still smarting. In the mirror, I could see how flushed and disheveled I was. Thank heaven his mother had not spotted us!

When the bleeding had stopped, I checked on Donald again and found him sleeping peacefully. There was nothing more that I could do. I suspected that he would have the most dreadful hangover and decided to look in on him first thing in the morning. To that end, I kept his card key in my pocket and retreated to the door.

"Goodbye, Donald," I said, switching off the light. "Sleep tight."

Too much alcohol always gives me bad dreams and I had a whole series of them that night. The one I remembered most clearly involved—who else?—Rosemary. I was about to marry a gorgeous young Hawaiian girl in a sort of futuristic cathedral in Honolulu when my ex-wife came running down the aisle to denounce me in loud voice and to scatter the congregation by throwing golf balls at them. She saved the sand wedge for me. Having sent everyone else packing, she tossed the club aside and showered me with kisses. I woke up with a start and found that I was running with sweat.

I didn't need a psychiatrist to interpret the dream. Over the years, I've had endless variations of it. Rosemary always takes the role of the destroyer. At heart, she's a bitch in a manger. Not wanting me for herself, she nevertheless reserves the right to prevent me from getting too close to any other woman. By the same token, I have to confess, I'd hate to see her getting hooked up with another man. Why deny it? I miss her. The good times with her really were phenomenal.

Donald Dukelow's situation was so different. While I was still being haunted by the woman I divorced several years ago, he was not only dreaming of his new bride, he was actually getting married with the visible approval of his first wife. He might wake up with a headache but I suspected that he'd had a better night's sleep than I enjoyed. It was well after eight, far too late to try to get another hour's sleep. Besides, I was feeling parental. My duty was to look in on Donald.

A shower and a shave made me feel human again. I was also hungry and took that as a healthy sign. After I'd dressed, I studied myself in the full-length mirror and was relieved to see that I looked something like my old self. The bags under my eyes no longer had lead weights in them. My gray hair, as always, gave me a touch of distinction. I was ready to meet the world. First, however, I had to get my friend into the same condition and that might take a lot longer.

It was almost nine o'clock by the time I reached his room. Opening the door with the card key was vastly easier now that I was sober and unencumbered by a body over my shoulder. The first thing I noticed when I went inside was that the light was on. I was sure that I'd switched it off when I left. Was it conceivable that Donald had got up in the night to relieve himself, switching on the light so that he could see his way to the bathroom and forgetting to put it off again? It was unlikely.

Crossing to the bed, I saw that he was in exactly the position that I had left him, on his back with his eyes closed. But there were some crucial differences in his appearance. The pillow I had slipped under his head was now stained with blood and it had not come from my nose. Sticking out of one ear was the end of a meat skewer that had been drilled through his brain. Death had robbed him of all dignity. It had emptied his bladder posthumously and soaked his trousers with urine. Vomit had surged up through his mouth. The smell was sickening. I was horrified. Instead of waking a friend, I was staring at a murder victim.

I stumbled back as if from some invisible blow. My eyes misted over and my stomach began to heave. I had to turn away for a couple of minutes before I felt able to look at him again. Donald was beyond my help. Remorse swelled up inside me like a tidal wave. I was partially to blame. When a friend was in such a vulnerable state, I should have taken more care of him. Everybody else would say the same. I'd left him alone in his room, utterly defenseless. It was almost as if I was an accessory to the crime. My temples began to pound unbearably.

I made a supreme effort to pull myself together. Practicalities had to be considered. Who should I ring first? The police? Hotel security? Cora Dukelow? Zann Kaheiki? The thought of breaking the news to either woman made me shiver. One had lost an only son, the other had had a husband snatched away from her on the very eve of the marriage. I was not sure that either of them could cope with the tragedy. I was certainly not the person to inform them. Others were trained to do such things. The police would probably offer trauma counseling. I could never do that. It was something I needed myself.

After dithering hopelessly, I eventually opted for a phone call to the duty manager. He took the news with surprising equanimity and asked me to remain where I was. A few minutes later, he and the security officer let themselves into the room and confirmed that what I'd reported was true. Richard Meeker, the duty manager, was a short, slim, neat Floridian in his thirties with a Clark Gable mustache. His stocky companion was a native Hawaiian. I couldn't imagine that finding a dead body in such circumstances was a daily event at the hotel but they behaved as if they knew exactly what to do. While the security officer took a closer look at Donald—making sure to touch nothing—Meeker rang the police and spoke with commendable calm. When he'd reported the crime, he turned to me.

"They're on their way, Mr. Saxon," he said, putting the receiver down. "You are requested to stay here with us."

"I had no intention of going anywhere," I told him.

"Mr. Dukelow is a friend of yours, you say?"

"He's staying here with his mother and with…" I hesitated. I did not want to get into an explanation of Heidi's unusual status. "And with a close friend of the family. This will devastate them."

"I'm sure. I am deeply sorry this had to happen."

"So am I. It's lousy publicity for your hotel."

"That's why we want the crime solved as quickly as possible."

While I chatted with Meeker, the security officer made a series of calls on his cell phone, alerting other members of the hotel staff to the emergency. Downstairs, most probably, Heidi and Cora Dukelow were having breakfast in the restaurant. I hoped that the police would not arrive at the hotel with blaring sirens. I did not want the women to be aware that anything was amiss just yet. They would not connect it with Donald at first but his continued absence was bound to worry them.

"I wonder if I should go downstairs and stall them," I suggested.

"Who, sir?" asked Meeker.

"The ladies. If Donald doesn't show up for breakfast, they're bound to start wondering. Sooner or later, they'll ring this room."

"I'll speak to them, if that happens."

"But I can play for time. Put them off the scent, so to speak."

"No, sir. Your face would give the game away."

I glanced in a mirror. He was right. My cheeks were ashen and my eyes were bulging. I looked as if I'd just witnessed the end of the world from a front-row seat. Trying to account for Donald's absence to his mother and his first wife would be a foolish thing to do. The security officer let me know that it was not even a faint possibility. His hand closed firmly around my arm.

"I can't allow you to leave this room," he said, quietly.

"No," added the other man. "We have our orders."

Chapter Six

Being in a state of shock makes you lose all track of time. It seemed only minutes before the police arrived but it must have been substantially longer. All I had done in the interim was to avert my eyes from the bed at the other end of the room and brood on the consequences of what had occurred. They were frightening to contemplate. It was a relief when I was finally interrupted. First through the door of the hotel room was Captain Clay Rapoza of the Honolulu Police Department, a tall, angular, cadaverous man in his forties with a pock-marked face and a world-weary air. He introduced himself and Sergeant Emily Tenno, a stout yet attractive woman in her thirties with the close-cropped hair favored by Melissa Kaheiki, but with an attention to smart clothing and personal hygiene that the latter would consider far too bourgeois.

Once they had taken a look at the corpse, they turned over the murder scene to the forensic team. The room was large but there were far too many of us in it. Richard Meeker, the duty manager, conducted us along the corridor to an empty room that he had assigned for police use. Having let us in with a master card key, he vanished with the security officer. In the wake of the murder, they had more than enough to do. I was left alone with the two detectives. Rapoza studied me.

"Take a seat, Mr. Saxon," he said. "You look pretty rough."

"I feel it," I said, lowering myself onto the sofa.

"Are you sure you didn't touch anything in that room?"

"I was too scared to, Captain."

"How did you get in there in the first place?"

"I had Donald's card key."

"He gave it to you?"

"No, I took it from him when he was out cold."

"Ah."

He raised an eyebrow, then sat in the armchair opposite me. Emily Tenno perched on an upright chair, pen in hand and pad on the knee of her crossed leg. Her skin had the most beautiful light brown color. She gave me a pitying smile.

"Feel ready to tell us what happened?" asked Rapoza.

"I think so."

"Take it from the top, Mr. Saxon."

"How far back do you want me to go?"

"As far as necessary."

"Right."

"And don't hurry."

I sat back to compose my thoughts. I didn't believe that Donald's original phone call to me in San Diego was at all relevant so I began with my arrival in Honolulu and gave them as coherent an account as I could manage. The name of Jimmy Kaheiki registered with both of them and they exchanged a knowing glance. Omitting all mention of my round of golf with Heidi and my visit to the Pineapple Theater, I went straight into the fatal evening spent with Donald, throwing in as much detail as my addled brain could manage. Rapoza listened carefully. Tenno wrote swiftly. I think that she recorded every one of my pauses and nervous coughs as well.

The name of Gabriel Mahalona produced another joint response. Rapoza gave her a quizzical look and Tenno nodded her head. I had the uncomfortable feeling that they did not believe what I was telling them. When I got to the end of my statement, Rapoza ran a tongue over his lips.

"That it?" he queried.

"More or less."

"Oh, there'll be a lot more to come, I'm sure. When your memory's been jogged a little, that is. You're still rather stunned by it all. Only to be expected. Right, Emily?"

"Too right, Captain," she said, referring to her notes before looking back at me. "You told us that a Gabriel Mahalona joined your table at the restaurant."

"Yes, Sergeant," I replied.

"Are you quite certain that was his name?"

"Of course. He gave us his business card."

"Do you happen to have it with you, by any chance?"

"No, I gave it to Donald."

"So we should find it in Mr. Dukelow's effects?"

"Yes," I said, confidently. "No—no, wait," I added. "I think that it may have been left on the table at the restaurant. Yes, it was. I'm sure of it. Check with them. They may still have it." They stared at me blankly. I became defensive. "Listen, his name was definitely Gabriel—or Gabe—Mahalona. He manufactures swimming pools here in the city. His name must be in the Yellow Pages. Look him up. Gabe was a nice man. He even showed us a picture of his children."

"Then he took you off to this club?" resumed Rapoza.

"That's right."

"But you don't know its name."

"He didn't tell us the name."

"And you can't remember exactly where it was."

"About ten minutes from the restaurant."

"Terrific!" he said with mild sarcasm. "That narrows it down to a mere fifty or sixty places that have a live band and hula dancers. Can't you be more specific than that, Mr. Saxon?"

"The taxi driver," I suggested. "All you have to do is to find the man who took us from the restaurant to the club."

He winced slightly. "You know how many taxis we got here in Honolulu? They breed like flies. Ask for a driver who picked up three guys from that restaurant last night and dozens will come forward. And they're not all golf fans, sir," he pointed out. "Many of them wouldn't have recognized who you were."

"What about the driver who took us back to the hotel?"

"Did you get his name and cab number?"

"Of course not."

"Then finding him could also be tricky. I daresay that you and Mr. Dukelow were not the only people he drove last night. In an evening shift, the guy will have had no end of fares. You can't expect him to remember every passenger and every destination." He gave a pained smile. "Help us, Mr. Saxon. We need more guidance."

"Yes," said Tenno, looking at her notes again. "So far, all we've got is this mystery man, buddying up with you at the restaurant, giving you a business card you didn't keep, taking you off to an anonymous club in a part of the city you can't identify, and buying you a drink that apparently has no name." She raised her eyes. "Are you always so hazy about your movements, sir?"

"No, Sergeant."

"How much alcohol did you consume last night?"

"A lot less than Donald."

"Was that deliberate?"

"Yes."

"Why?"

"I was trying to keep a clear head."

"But you were happy enough for your friend to get drunk?"

"I couldn't stop him. And it was, after all, a kind of celebration."

"Jimmy Kaheiki won't see it that way," noted Rapoza. "Before you tell it to him, I'd advise you to get your story straight. If he's bankrolling your stay on the island, he'll expect something in return."

I became edgy. "It wasn't my fault that Donald got himself killed."

"We've still to determine that, sir."

"What do you mean?" I said, hoarse with indignation. "Surely, you don't think I'm involved in this crime, do you? Donald was my friend. We've known each other for years."

"Yet you didn't realize that the guy couldn't hold his liquor."

"That did come as a shock, I must admit."

He narrowed his lids. "What else came as a shock to you?"

"The way he behaved."

Before I could explain what I meant, there was a tap on the door. A uniformed officer stepped into the room. His manner was deferential.

"They're almost finished in there, Captain," he said. "The M.E. wants to know if he can have the body moved to the lab."

"Sure," answered Rapoza. "I'll speak to him myself."

After signaling to Emily Tenno, he went out with the officer and closed the door behind them. She walked across to the drink cabinet.

"Anything I can get you, Mr. Saxon? Orange juice, maybe?"

"No, thanks."

"What about a coffee? They got quite a choice here." She checked the items on the tray set out on the cabinet. "Can't see any tea, I'm afraid. Being English, you'd prefer that, I guess."

"I'm fine, Sergeant."

"You don't look it, sir. How about a glass of water?"

"Forget me. Think about the others."

"Others?"

"Donald's mother," I explained. "And Heidi, his first wife. They're both here in the hotel. Shouldn't somebody be telling them what's happened?"

"That's one of the things Captain Rapoza went off to organize. He wanted a clearer idea of what happened first." She saw my anxiety. "Don't worry, Mr. Saxon. The news will be broken to the ladies as gently as possible. We're very sensitive to people's feelings when they suffer a blow like this. It's something we pride ourselves on in the M.C.U."

"M.C.U.?"

"Major Crime Unit."

"Yes," I realized, "I suppose that's what this is—a major crime. Donald was an international figure. This story is bound to be picked up by papers all over the world."

"That's why we must make sure they get the details right."

"What about the Kaheiki family? They deserve to be told."

"Captain Rapoza will ring Jimmy Kaheiki personally."

"Why? Does he know him?"

"Very well."

"I'd hate to make that phone call myself."

"You'll have to face Jimmy Kaheiki sooner or later," she cautioned. "He'll want a first-hand account of what took place. He's that kind of man. If his daughter was about to get married, he'll have invested a great deal in the event—and I don't just mean financially. He'll want answers."

"So do I, Sergeant."

"Understandably."

"It's incredible," I said, gesticulating. "I mean, who, in God's name, could possibly want to kill Donald Dukelow? He was such a likeable man. He didn't have a single enemy."

"You may be wrong about that, sir." She checked her notes. "You dined at the Kaheiki estate, then?"

"Yes, we had a delicious meal there."

"What did you think of the house itself?"

"I expected the architect to be nailed to the nearest palm tree."

Her grin revealed twin dimples. "It's a plantation house," she said. "It was designed for practical purposes, not to win any architectural prizes. I'm told it's very comfortable inside."

"Comfortable and well-decorated."

"Money is no object to Jimmy Kaheiki."

"I get the impression that he's a big wheel in Honolulu."

"He has interests throughout the islands. Next time you pick up a copy of one of our local papers, you're bound to find his name among the advertisements. The family owns all kinds of things." She sat down again. "Including a funeral service."

"I'll take your word for it," I said. "I certainly won't be looking at any of your papers, I can promise you. I prefer to see my name in the sports section—not on the front pages."

"Unavoidable. You're a crucial witness."

"I'm glad to hear it, Sergeant."

"Why is that?"

"I was getting the impression I might be a suspect."

"We have to consider every possibility, Mr. Saxon."

"Except the possibility that what I told you might be true."

She smiled. "Oh, we haven't ruled that out entirely."

I warmed to her slightly. Emily Tenno was not at all like my notion of a Honolulu detective. I'm old enough to remember the endless repeats of *Hawaii Five-O* that I saw on television in my youth, breathless adventures that always ended with the arrest of the villain and the curt command from Steve McGarrett—"Book him, Danno." It had given me an entirely false picture of how policing operated in this part of the world. Emily Tenno was no high-powered TV detective who could solve any crime in the course of a single episode. She was a plump, engaging, businesslike woman with a cool professionalism. I observed her wedding ring. Off duty, I suspected, she'd have two lovely children and a doting husband. The family would be regular in their church attendance on Sundays. If she hadn't worked for the police, I could have liked her.

After a lengthy pause, she checked her watch, wrote something on her pad then looked across at me again. Her tone was pleasant.

"What was your schedule for today?" she asked me.

"I was hoping for a round of golf with Donald. That's obviously gone by the board, and I can't say I'm in the mood for a game any more. Besides," I went on, "I daresay that you'll rearrange my plans."

"Captain Rapoza will want you to come down to headquarters."

I blanched. "Why? I'm not under arrest or anything, am I?"

"Of course not, sir. But you have to make a formal statement."

"I thought I'd already done that."

"We'll want your voice on tape," she said. "When the interview is over, we'll have it typed up and you can read through it to make any changes you wish before you sign it. Also, you'll need to look at some photographs for us."

"Why?"

"Captain Rapoza will explain."

"How long will all this take?"

"Who knows?"

"I'd like to see Donald's mother fairly soon," I said. "I feel that I owe her an explanation. Heidi, too. She'll be shattered by the news as well. They may want a shoulder to cry on."

"All in good time, sir."

"You can't hold me against my will."

"That's not what we'll be doing."

"Then why take me to headquarters when we can talk here?"

"Captain Rapoza will explain."

"Aren't *you* allowed to give any explanations?"

"That depends."

"On what?"

"A number of things."

"Such as?"

But she was not given time to answer. At that moment, the door opened and Rapoza swept into the room. His expression was grim.

"Jimmy Kaheiki didn't take the news at all well," he said to me, resuming his seat. "When I rang him, he insisted on coming down to headquarters to speak to you when we're through."

"Is he in a position to insist?" I wondered.

"In the circumstances, I believe that he is." He shrugged an apology. "Sorry to leave you like that, Mr. Saxon, but I wanted a medical opinion on the likely cause of death."

"I would have thought that was obvious."

"Oh?"

"Someone pushed a meat skewer into Donald's brain."

"Before or after death?"

"Before, of course," I asserted. "It's what killed him."

"Were you able to determine that just by looking at him?" he asked, dryly. "I wasn't and neither was the M.E.—and we've seen dozens of murder victims. Could be that Mr. Dukelow was killed by other means. The skewer might've been inserted afterwards to make sure that he was actually dead. I'm keeping an open mind till we get the autopsy report."

"Oh, I see."

"You should do the same."

"I will," I said, chastened. I thought of Cora Dukelow. "Has anyone spoken to Donald's mother yet?"

"It's all in hand, Mr. Saxon. We don't keep information like this from close relatives for any longer than we need. Putting that aside," he said, briskly, "let me come back to what you told me before I left. You said that you were shocked by Mr. Dukelow's behavior last night."

"Yes," I agreed, "and it wasn't just the way he was drinking."

"Go on."

"He was unsettled. Donald should have been overjoyed at the prospect of the marriage yet I sensed eleventh hour doubts. Not about his bride," I emphasized. "He loved her. He spent ages extolling Zann's virtues. No, these doubts were about himself. Something was definitely bugging him."

"Any idea what it was?"

"No, Captain."

"Money worries? Health fears? Another woman, maybe?"

"He didn't say. Perhaps that's why he drank so much," I speculated. "To keep his demons at bay."

"Could be."

He stared at me with a mixture of curiosity and distrust. I began to feel distinctly like a suspect again. Emily Tenno was also gazing intently at me. I shifted in my seat.

"Why are you both looking at me like that?" I said.

"It's this other guy you mentioned," said Rapoza. "Gabe Mahalona."

"What about him?"

"Can you remember him clearly?"

"Very clearly. I gave you a detailed description of him."

"Anything to add to it?"

"No, I don't think so."

"And you reckon he has a business making pools?"

"No rust, no rot, no leaks, no linings—that was his boast."

"Then he must have one heck of a strong voice, Mr. Saxon. You heard it through six feet of solid earth." He turned to the Sergeant. "Tell him, Emily."

"Gabriel Mahalona was murdered months ago," she announced. "His body was found at the bottom of his own swimming pool. Weighted down with a concrete block so that it would not float to the surface. The crime is still unsolved."

"On behalf of the Department," said Rapoza, "I attended the funeral so I saw with my own eyes who was lowered into that grave. It was Gabriel Mahalona. Can you hear what I'm saying?"

I shuddered. "We had a drink with a ghost last night."

"There was an unusual feature to the homicide," he continued. "At first glance, we thought he'd been drowned to death. It was only when we hauled him out of the water that we noticed he had a meat skewer sticking out of one ear." He gave me a crooked smile. "That ring any bells with you, Mr. Saxon?"

To leave the hotel with the two detectives and a uniformed police officer, I had to cross a lobby that was filled with nosy guests and inquisitive staff. Having caught wind of the crime, they assumed that I'd been taken into custody in relation to it and subjected me to ghoulish scrutiny. Though I was not actually wearing handcuffs, I felt that I ought to be. Someone had tipped off the press and the first photographer was on the scene, flashing away at me and pursuing us all the way to the car. I wished I'd had a blanket over my head. There was worse to come.

When we reached police headquarters, the media were converging on it at speed. TV cameras were being lifted onto shoulders, microphones were being checked and photographers were adjusting their equipment. It was like running the gauntlet. Questions were fired at me and microphones thrust in my face. Warned by Captain Rapoza, I said nothing. Emily Tenno hustled me into the building while her superior remained outside to issue a brief statement to the media. There was no point in hoping that my name was not mentioned. I'd already been recognized by many of those besieging the place. Fame is a treacherous attribute. When you most need anonymity, it always betrays you.

The feeling that I was under arrest was intensified when I was asked to give my fingerprints—"In order to distinguish them from others in Mr. Dukelow's room, sir"—and, even more alarming, a blood sample. It was only when the latter was being taken that I recalled that I'd made no reference earlier to the nose bleed that Donald had inadvertently given me. If I mentioned it now, I'd have to explain why I suppressed the information, yet, if I said nothing, the sample could be matched with the stain on the collar of Donald's shirt. I was in a quandary.

The interview room into which I was eventually escorted was small and featureless. A table and four chairs stood against one wall. On the table was a tape recorder. I looked for hidden cameras or double-sided mirrors but saw none. There was the faintest tang of disinfectant in the air. It added a clinical air to the proceedings. Sergeant Emily Tenno had certainly become more clinical. Stone-faced and watchful, she sat opposite me, her notepad open on the table so that she could check details and prompt me. I tensed immediately.

Seated beside her, Captain Clay Rapoza had a large manila file in front of him. His manner bordered on polite hostility. Now that he was on home ground, he seemed to have come fully awake and peppered me with a barrage of new questions before we even switched on the machine. Tenno joined in the interrogation. I was being systematically softened up. Any moment, I feared, they were going to search me for meat skewers. My throat was dry. I was grateful for the glass of water that had been provided. It was their one concession.

"Ready?" asked the captain.

"I think so."

"Tell it like it happened. Nice and slow."

"Do my best," I said.

He depressed the switch on the machine. "Interview with Mr. Alan Saxon on Thursday, December 11, 2004 at 11:52 a.m.

For the benefit of the tape, also present in the room—Captain Clay Rapoza and Sergeant Emily Tenno." He pointed a finger at me. "Well, sir?"

I began haltingly, nervous in such surroundings and afraid that I might unwittingly say something that contradicted my earlier statement. There was a marked change in my recital. At the hotel, I'd been trying to piece together the sequence of events so that they had a sense of logical continuity. At police headquarters, I felt as if I was making a confession. There were few interruptions. Giving me free rein, they faded into the background. The only time that Emily Tenno spoke was when I admitted that some of my blood would be found on Donald's collar.

"Why didn't you tell us this before, sir?" she asked.

"It slipped my mind."

"Don't you think it's a very important detail to overlook?"

"I suppose that it is, Sergeant."

"Are you sure you didn't deliberately conceal it from us?"

"No, no," I replied. "Why should I do that?"

"I might ask you the same thing."

"Go on with your statement, Mr. Saxon," ordered Rapoza.

Having ceded one new detail, I found a few others that aroused their interest as well but they did not press me on any of them. As I came to the end of my statement, I heard myself repeating phrases that I'd used during the interview at the hotel. It made the closing minutes sound as if they'd been carefully rehearsed.

Rapoza's finger hovered over the switch. "Interview terminated at 12:19 p.m." He cut off the power. "Thanks, Mr. Saxon. Very revealing."

"In what way?"

"We learned much more about you this time."

"Was it a pleasant experience?"

"Not really. You don't like cops, do you?"

"No, Captain," I replied, honestly.

"Any particular reason?"

"My father was a policeman."

"Ah."

"Unfortunately, he could never forget that he was involved in law enforcement. When he got home, he was still on duty. As a result," I said, opening an old wound, "I had a miserable childhood. Other kids had nice fathers, who played football with them and took them on holiday. I had this hulking bully in a blue uniform who never showed any paternal feelings for me."

"Does that mean all cops are lousy fathers?"

"Not at all," I replied. "Some of them make very good parents, I daresay. Mine wasn't one of them. His mission in life was to keep me on a very tight rein. It turned me against all authority figures."

"I can see that you're a rebel."

"I just try to steer clear of any policemen, that's all."

"And how do you do that, Mr. Saxon?"

I contrived a smile. "By being exquisitely law-abiding."

"I'll need convincing of that," he said, stroking his chin. "As it happens, my father was a cop as well. He was a great guy. I looked up to him. It's one of the reasons I joined the Police Department. It was a job where I could make a difference." He watched me closely. "Your father still alive?"

"Yes, he retired from the force years ago. Reluctantly."

"Mine was forcibly retired," said Rapoza, bitterly. "He was shot dead in a bar in Waimanalo by some punk who had a phobia about cops. Just like you."

"I haven't killed any yet, Captain."

It was the wrong thing to say, especially in such a jocular way. Rapoza glowered at me and Tenno was equally unimpressed. There was an awkward pause. I was grateful that the tape recorder had been switched off. In the hope of smoothing things over, I asked a question of my own.

"How did the killer get into Donald's room?"

"That hasn't been established yet," said Rapoza.

"Were there any signs of forced entry?"

"No, sir."

"I made sure that the door was locked when I left."

"Did you search the room before you did so?"

"Why should I?"

"Because the perpetrator might already have been inside it when you and Mr. Dukelow arrived. Plenty of places to hide—in the wardrobe, behind the curtains, under one of those huge beds."

"But how would he have got in?"

"A pro will always find ways."

I felt another tremor. The idea that someone was lying in wait for Donald was deeply troubling. It made me feel as if I'd delivered him up to his killer. Rapoza anticipated my next question.

"How did the guy *know* that Mr. Dukelow would arrive in that condition?" he asked. "Haven't you worked that out yet?"

"No," I admitted.

"Then you should have paid more attention to your father. You might have picked up a few pointers." He opened the manila file and took out a photograph. "Recognize anyone here?"

I studied a picture of four people, beaming at the camera as they stood beside a swimming pool in blazing sunshine. It was an archetypal happy family. The man was short and stringy. The woman, clearly his wife, was more compact and she had long black hair trailing down to her shoulders. Though the parents were complete strangers to me, I'd seen the two children before.

"Gabe Mahalona's kids," I decided.

"With their mother and father. That," he said, pointing to the man, "is their father, the real Mr. Mahalona. Behind them is the pool in which we found him."

"I see. So the man we met at the restaurant—the one who told us that *he* was Mahalona—might well have been the killer?"

"Possibly. Him or one of his accomplices."

"Accomplices?"

"Those two guys at the restaurant."

It slowly dawned on me. "Of course," I said, annoyed that I hadn't spotted the ruse before. "That man who abused us wasn't drunk at all. He was set up so that Mahalona—or whatever his name really is—could win our confidence by coming to our rescue."

"Don't forget the guy he was dining with—the one he said was a prospective client. Another accomplice. They chose a table nearby and watched you and Mr. Dukelow until they thought the time was ripe."

"That drink we had at the club," I went on, thinking it through. "No wonder he went to the bar to get it himself. He spiked Donald's glass with something. That's what knocked him out."

"Now you're talking like the son of a cop."

"Donald and I walked straight into a trap."

Rapoza nodded. "What we have to decide is who set it—and why?" He put the photograph back into the file. "Think you can put your prejudices about us aside and actually help?"

"Just tell me what to do, Captain."

"First of all, you'd better eat something. You had no breakfast this morning. We don't want you keeling over on us then suing the Police Department for negligence. Tell him what's on the menu, Emily."

"Yes, Captain."

"Mr. Saxon can choose whatever he wants."

"What is this?" I quipped. "The condemned man's last meal before execution?"

He eyed me coldly. "We aim to keep you alive a little longer than that."

◇◇◇

Having asked for a Caesar salad and a glass of orange juice, I was allowed to eat my lunch alone in the interview room. Rapoza went off to report to his superiors and Tenno disappeared with the tape recorder so that my statement could be transcribed into print. It was not the ideal place to consume food. I kept thinking of the hundreds of crooks who must have been questioned there, subjected to all the techniques that police can use to worm information out of suspects. I wondered if physical brutality was ever used. My father certainly employed it in his early years on the beat. In what he called the "good old days," the dedicated policeman had much more license to threaten, hassle, or extract evidence by force. He reveled in his work.

Emily Tenno eventually returned and took me off to an office that was manned by a dozen detectives and positively buzzing with activity. I gazed at a screen for almost an hour, trying to identify the man we'd met at the restaurant the previous night. I must have seen a thousand mug shots of known criminals. Some had a vague resemblance to the fake Gabe Mahalona but that was all. I couldn't remember any salient details about the man who had feigned drunkenness in order to taunt us and I hadn't even seen the accomplice who'd had a meal with our rescuer so that the latter was in exactly the right position to come to our aid.

"No dice?" asked Tenno.

"He's not here," I said. "If he was, I'd certainly pick him out."

"That's bad news. He may have no criminal record."

"I'll go through them again, if you like."

"No, sir. You've done you're best. In any case, you have to see Mr. Kaheiki now. He's been waiting a long time."

"What sort of a mood is he in?"

"How would you feel if your prospective son-in-law was murdered?"

"Hopping mad."

"Then you got some idea what to expect."

Prepared to meet an angry Jimmy Kaheiki on his own, I was taken aback to find that his son, Nick, was also in the interview room. The father was able to contain his rage, even rise to a token smile, but the son simply glowered at me. To him, I was obviously responsible for what had happened. When I was left alone with them, I felt extremely uneasy. Jimmy Kaheiki came across to shake my hand.

"This is a terrible crime, Alan," he said. "Terrible. And what a shock for you! When you found the body, you must have been knocked back on your heels."

"I was, Mr. Kaheiki."

"Feeling any better now?"

"Not much."

"Sit down and tell me exactly what happened."

I took a seat. "Hasn't Captain Rapoza spoken to you?"

"Yes," he replied, sitting opposite me. "I had a long chat with Clay. He's a good cop. But I wanted to hear it from your own lips."

"How is Zann?" I inquired, softly.

"Poor kid is really cut up."

"I can imagine. It's a dreadful tragedy."

"Zann doesn't know what hit her. It's so *unfair*."

"And cruel. I do sympathize with your daughter."

"We need to catch this guy," said Nick, still on his feet. "We need to catch him and his sidekicks right away."

"So let's hear it in your own words, Alan," encouraged his father. "Take us through it. Step by step."

I did my best to oblige but it was not easy with Nick Kaheiki standing just behind me. He was a menacing presence. I could feel his eyes boring into the back of my head, disliking me, distrusting, assigning blame. The old man was far more controlled. Fixing his gaze on me, he listened with rapt attention, his face expressionless. Only when I got to the end of my tale did he speak.

"What did you do during the rest of the day?" he asked.

"I played a round of golf with Heidi in the morning, had lunch with her and Mrs. Dukelow, then paid a visit to the Pineapple Theater."

He was startled. "Melissa's place?"

"Yes, your daughter invited me to go."

"How long did you last?"

"A couple of very enjoyable hours."

"Really? You must have peculiar tastes."

"Those girls have talent."

"Misused talent," he said. "They're spitting in the wind. They want to be actors, they should go where the money is, not work in that derelict warehouse with its stink of leather." He pulled a face. "Melissa thinks that money only corrupts."

"I have some sympathy with that point of view, Mr. Kaheiki."

"Discuss it with her, then. Don't waste my time."

"Have you any idea who this guy was?" asked Nick, coming round to confront me. "The one who conned you at the restaurant. Were you able to pick him out from photographs?"

"No," I said. "I'm afraid I wasn't. He may not have been convicted."

"He soon will be."

"We don't even know if he's still on the island."

"Oh, I think he is, Alan," said the old man. "In fact, I'd bet on it."

"How can you be so sure?"

"Never mind."

"We got reasons," said his son. "Our big worry now is you."

"Me?" I said.

"Yes, he may not stop at Donald Dukelow."

"What do you mean?"

"Be quiet, Nick," warned his father. "You've said enough."

"We don't want it to happen again, Dad."

"It won't—if Alan takes our advice."

"What advice, Mr. Kaheiki?" I wondered.

"Just this," said Nick, ignoring his father. "Watch your back."

"My back?"

"As long as you're on the island, keep looking over your shoulder."

I thought of the man who had trailed us on the golf course with a pair of binoculars. I recalled the photograph of the real Gabriel Mahalona, standing with his family in front of the swimming pool in which his corpse was later found. And I remembered, most vividly of all, the sight of the meat skewer protruding from Donald's ear.

"I'll keep my eyes well and truly peeled," I vowed.

Chapter Seven

I loathe police stations. Having spent my formative years in what was, in effect, a miniature version of one, I find them highly uncongenial. No matter how large they may be, I always have a profound sense of claustrophobia inside them. It's an eerie sensation, as if four blank walls are slowly and inexorably moving inwards to crush my body. Yes, I know that law enforcement is a necessity—"Somebody has to do it" was my father's favorite mantra—but the physical embodiment of it in bricks and mortar somehow overwhelms me. Police stations make me feel guilty. I may walk in as a completely innocent man yet I soon start believing that I must have committed the crime of the century.

When I was finally allowed to leave police headquarters in Honolulu, it was like being released from prison. I couldn't wait to breathe the clean, clear air of freedom. As it was, I only managed to fill my lungs once before I was helped into the rear of Jimmy Kaheiki's stretch limo. While I'd read through my statement before signing it, Nick Kaheiki disappeared but his father waited until Captain Rapoza had finished with me. The old man insisted on taking me back to the hotel in his chauffeur-driven car. He was not simply offering me a degree of protection from the prying eyes of the media, he wanted to see for himself where the murder had occurred.

Jimmy Kaheiki and I sat side by side on the plush leather seat.

"Your son seemed rather touchy," I remarked.

"Nick? Yes, he has a short fuse sometimes."

"I noticed."

"He loves his sister dearly," explained the old man, "and feels Zann's loss as if it was his own. Nick and Zann have always been close. Melissa? Well," he added with a sigh, "you've met her. She's one of us and that will never change, but she prefers to go her own way."

"Yet she stayed in Oahu," I noted. "Unlike her sister."

"Zann wanted to spread her wings. I encouraged that. She has an independent streak that I admire. It's not the same as Melissa's. Zann doesn't reject her family and its values." He looked at me. "You have a daughter of your own, don't you? Would you hold her back if she wanted to make her way in the world?"

"No," I said. "Whatever Lynette decides, I'd back her to the hilt."

"I'm the same. That's fatherhood."

"Yet you don't back Melissa to the hilt."

He stiffened. "Why do you say that?"

"You're not at all happy about what she's doing."

"That's not true."

"Isn't it? From what I could judge—"

"It's not your place to judge," he said, interrupting me with sudden vehemence. "You know nothing about us. With respect, you've only been on the island for five minutes. Don't presume to make comments about the Kaheiki family. Especially as—may I remind you—you're on this island as our guest."

"I meant no criticism of you, Mr. Kaheiki."

"I hope not."

"If you want to know the truth," I said, trying to calm him down, "I was very struck by the warm familial atmosphere at your house when we dined there. You all seemed so happy to be with each other."

"We were. That's our way."

"I envied you, having all your children around you."

"It was a very special evening."

"You're a lucky man."

"That's what I used to think—until now."

"How well did you know Donald?" I asked.

"Hardly at all," he replied. "I knew his reputation as a golfer, of course, but that was about it. Seemed like a pretty straight guy when we actually met. And he was head over heels in love with my daughter, no question about that." He searched for the right words. "We tried to see him through Zann's eyes," he went on at length. "Donald was her choice and we accepted that."

"With some reservations, I think."

"No, none at all."

"That's not what Melissa says."

"Then Melissa's got it wrong."

"According to her—"

"Stop it!" he barked, rounding on me again. "I'm not going to sit here and be contradicted by you—or anyone else—about what goes on inside my family. And I certainly won't let you throw the words of my younger daughter back at me."

"I'm sorry, Mr. Kaheiki. I meant no offence."

"Then stop goading me."

"That's not what I was doing," I said. "The last thing in the world I want to do now is to tread on any toes. Please—accept my apology."

"As long as you back off."

"I will, I will."

Cursing myself for provoking him like that, I spent the rest of the journey trying to mollify him. By the time we reached the hotel, I think that I'd been forgiven. He even produced his trademark smile.

If I'd not had a specific request from Jimmy Kaheiki, I'd never have dreamed of retracing the steps I took on the previous night. Though it was put very quietly to me, it was more of an order than a request and I knew that I couldn't refuse. There were two obvious benefits. The exercise might dislodge a few more details from my tired memory and, by sneaking into the hotel again through the side entrance, I'd avoid any reporters who might still be lingering in the lobby. We stepped into the service elevator.

"This how you went up?" he asked.

"Not exactly, Mr. Kaheiki," I said, recalling the struggle I'd had. "You're standing on your own feet. Donald had collapsed on me."

"The best rooms are on the third floor. That's why I put you all up there. I like to do things properly."

"Oh, you certainly did that. Though the third floor might not be so popular after this. The duty manager was braced for people demanding a change of room. I fancy that number 315 may be out of commission for some time."

"Was that Donald's room?"

"Yes." We reached the third floor and the steel doors parted. "Turn right. Three fifteen is halfway along on the left."

He didn't need directions because a uniformed officer had been posted outside the room in case anyone tried to defy the strips of police tape that had been stuck across the door to bar entry. We strode towards him. My companion was upset that he was not allowed to view the murder scene and he tried to argue with the guard but—even though he clearly knew who Jimmy Kaheiki was and spoke to him with respect—he stood his ground. I had no wish to re-enter the room myself.

While the argument went on, I was mentally rehearsing what had happened on the previous night. Having relieved Donald of his card key, I'd dumped him on the carpet so that I could open the door of the room before dragging him in. With a start, I realized that there was something that I'd forgotten, or dismissed as irrelevant, something that was not in my statement to the police at all and which now came burrowing into my brain like another meat skewer. Donald and I had not been alone in the corridor. There was a witness. An elderly Asian man had walked past and shown his disapproval with a fleeting glance at us.

Who was he and what was he doing there at that time of night?

◇◇◇

Unable to gain access to the murder scene, Jimmy Kaheiki abandoned me and went off to talk to the duty manager. I was able to walk back down the corridor to my own room. Mindful of the warning that he and his son had given me, I entered the room gingerly and searched it with great care. Captain Rapoza had floated the possibility that Donald's killer might have been in the room when we got back there. That disturbed me. Before I looked under the beds, I armed myself with a putter from my golf bag. In the event, it wasn't needed, but until I was absolutely certain that I was alone, I couldn't begin to relax.

A light was flashing on my telephone to indicate that I had voice messages. Three were from crime reporters on different newspapers, looking for an interview, a fourth from a TV station, asking me to contact them. Since the police had advised me to make no public statements until my story had been checked out, I ignored all four calls. It was the fifth that interested me. Heidi Dukelow's voice was tearful.

"Alan," she said. "Ring me as soon as you can. Room 303."

I didn't hesitate. As soon as I dialed the number, the receiver was snatched up at the other end. Heidi spoke in an urgent whisper.

"Alan? Is that you?"

"Yes," I said. "I just picked up your message."

"Are you alone?"

"At long last."

"I can't talk over the phone," she explained. "Cora's asleep at the moment and I don't want to wake her up. I must see you."

"Fine. Come straight away."

I put down the receiver and crossed to a gilt-framed mirror to check my appearance. I still looked shaken up, and a bloodhound would have been proud of the bags under my eyes, but I was no longer quite so horror-stricken. Using both hands, I smoothed my hair down. Seconds later there was a tap on the door and, after peering through the spyhole, I opened up to admit Heidi. Words were redundant. She simply flung herself into my arms. We hugged each other for comfort and shared our grief. I fought back tears. Eventually, I led her across to the sofa and we sat down together.

"How is Mrs. Dukelow?" I wondered.

"She was shattered by the news. So was I."

"Who told you what had happened?"

"One of the detectives," she replied. "I didn't catch her name. As soon as she explained that Donald had been killed, my mind went blank. I've been in a daze ever since. Cora was beside herself. She held up well in front of the detective but, when the woman left, she was inconsolable. We must have cried for the best part of an hour."

"Yet you say that she's asleep now?"

"She began to have severe palpitations. I called for the hotel doctor and he prescribed a mild sedative. Cora should sleep for a while but," she said, resignedly, "the pain will still be there when she wakes up."

"Afraid so." I took her hand. "How are *you* coping, Heidi?"

"The tears have stopped—I've no more left to cry—but the anguish seems to get more intense. Donald is dead. We'll never see him again." She was close to despair. "I just can't take it in, Alan. While we were fast asleep last night, someone was creeping into his room to murder him in cold blood." She shivered. "I've just gone to pieces."

I squeezed her hand. "Bear up. Mrs. Dukelow is going to need a lot of support and you're the only person who can offer it. Hang in there."

"I keep thinking about Zann."

"Poor woman!"

"She's the person I worry about. Does she know yet?"

"Oh, yes," I said, releasing her hand. "Zann has been told. Captain Rapoza rang her father from the hotel. The whole family knows. Jimmy Kaheiki came straight over in that stretch limo of his so that he could speak to me at police headquarters. In its own way, talking to him and his son was more grueling than giving a statement to the police. He's *involved.* His reactions were wholly emotional. Captain Rapoza was much more detached."

She was tentative. "Do you feel up to telling me what happened?"

"Only if you feel up to hearing it."

"The detective didn't go into details." Heidi gritted her teeth. "She didn't need to. The mere knowledge that Donald had been killed was enough to knock the stuffing out of us. It must have been even worse for you, Alan—actually stumbling on the crime like that."

"It was pretty gruesome," I confessed.

Having been through it all with the police, in exhaustive detail, and with Jimmy Kaheiki and his son, in a more edited version, I wasn't thrilled at the prospect of telling my tale yet again. But there was an advantage. Heidi was on my side. Captain Rapoza had listened with a degree of professional suspicion and Nick Kaheiki had been openly resentful. It was a relief to have a friendly audience. There was another bonus. By confiding in Heidi, I'd save myself the trouble of having to do it all over again for Donald's mother. It was a task that my companion would take from me.

Beginning with our visit to the restaurant, I took her swiftly through the main events, sacrificing many details in the interest of letting the narrative flow. There was no point in hiding the uglier aspects of what I saw in Donald's room that morning. It would all be on TV and in the local papers. I wanted Heidi to hear it from me rather than find out by a more impersonal means. She squirmed at the mention of the meat skewer inserted in the ear of her former husband. For a long time, when they had lived together, she had whispered intimacies into that same ear and enjoyed the surging passion that she'd released in a man who was now lying on a slab in a laboratory as the autopsy was carried out. Heidi's face was an open book. She still loved him.

"Thank you," she murmured when it was all over.

"Ask me anything else you want."

"No, no. I think I've heard enough, Alan."

"You've been very brave to listen to it."

"Cora will be the same when I tell her," she predicted. "Now that the initial shock is over, she'll hold up well. She has inner strength."

"She's going to need it," I said. "But enough from me. I want to hear what happened to you yesterday. You weren't looking forward to being taken around the factory by Nick Kaheiki. How was it?"

"Fascinating. I'd never been in a garment factory before. I found the whole thing riveting. Although the shirts are all for men, one of their main designers is a woman. She showed me her design for a new line they were about to start—it was amazing."

"Did you get a free sample for me?"

"I'm afraid not," she said with a smile, "but I learned a lot about the Kaheiki empire. Nick felt the need to brag about it. I think he was trying to get the message across that Donald wasn't marrying into a family of country hicks from some Hawaiian backwater."

"Did he quiz you about the Dukelow family?"

"Non-stop. He was particularly interested in why I got divorced."

"What did you tell him?"

"The truth," she replied. "That Donald and I came to a fork in the road and chose to go different ways. Nick did his best to squeeze details of Donald's second divorce out of me as well but I played dumb. I wasn't going to rake over that marriage. And then—would you believe—as I was leaving the factory, he came very close to making a pass at me."

"I can't blame him for that, Heidi. You're a very attractive woman."

"But we hardly know each other."

"Why do you think he invited you to see his factory?"

"It never crossed my mind that he was setting me up."

"Yes," I said, "on reflection, it was a bit indelicate."

"Indelicate?"

"Hitting on you when you're the first wife of the man his sister is about to marry. There are boundary lines here. Nick overstepped them."

"He never even knew they were there, Alan."

"I take it that you didn't encourage his interest?"

"Quite the opposite. He's just not my type."

"That doesn't surprise me."

"Too young, too macho, too full of himself," she said. "He kept telling me that he'd run the Kaheiki empire one day, as if that alone would make me go weak at the knees. Also...." She broke off and bit her lip. "Also—if I'm honest—I find him a bit creepy."

"I think he's dangerous," I told her. "The first time we met him, I saw what I thought was latent anger. At police headquarters, some of that anger came bursting out. It was a bit unnerving."

"He wasn't too pleased when I gave him a polite brush-off."

"Yet he fancied you. I thought he disliked Howlies."

"Oh, Nick didn't have a permanent relationship in mind."

"Just as well," I said, chuckling. "You'd have ended up as Heidi Kaheiki—what a mouthful that would have been—and imagine the family get-togethers you'd have had with Donald and Zann." I chided myself for the thoughtless comment. "Sorry. For a moment, I forgot."

"Don't apologize. Maybe it did us both good to forget. We can't brood about Donald all the time. He'd have hated that."

"How would he have got on with his brother-in-law?"

"You know Donald. He'd make allowances for anybody. Nick was part of a family he was marrying into," she said. "If his brother-in-law had had two heads and a three-foot tail, Donald would have accepted him gladly. It was one of the things that Zann loved about him—his readiness to embrace her entire family."

"Even Melissa?"

"Even her. With all her drawbacks."

"I'm not sure they're drawbacks, Heidi. I liked her a lot."

"She obviously liked you. Zann noticed it. She told us how unusual it was for Melissa to show interest in any man. Especially a *haole*."

"My scintillating conversation won her over," I boasted.

"How was that rehearsal of hers?"

"Eye-opening."

"You sound impressed."

"I was—though I was disappointed she didn't make a pass at me."

Heidi laughed for the first time since she'd come into the room. Her face lit up so brightly that I had an urge to reach out and hug her again. Then she remembered why she had come and lapsed back into a more solemn mode. Getting up from the sofa, she crossed to the windows to look out at the beach, then turned back to me.

"This changes everything," she sighed. "I so enjoyed yesterday morning at Ko Olina. I had hopes of fitting in another round of golf with you before we left Oahu."

"Same thought crossed my mind," I said, getting to my feet. "It was such fun. But, while we're on the subject of Ko Olina, there's something you ought to know. I kept it from you at the time because I didn't want it to interfere with your game. In view of what's happened to Donald, I feel that you have a right to be told."

"Told what?"

"Somebody was watching us, Heidi."

"Watching us?"

"Shadowing us with a pair of binoculars. I saw him clearly. When he realized that he'd been spotted, he beat a hasty retreat." She was clearly troubled by the news. "I didn't mean to spring it on you like this but it's only fair that you should know."

"I'm grateful you mentioned it, Alan. It helps to explain something."

"Oh?"

"A strange feeling I had when we left the factory yesterday," she recalled. "As Nick Kaheiki drove me back to the hotel, I was certain that we were being followed. He obviously thought so, too."

"How do you know?"

"Because he kept making sudden turns down side-streets, as if trying to shake someone off. And he kept one eye on the rear-view mirror. We came back to the hotel by the most circuitous route."

"Maybe he just wanted to prolong the amount of time with you."

"No, it was more than that."

"Did you say anything?"

"I was too eager to get rid of him," she said. "After he tried to flirt with me, the atmosphere in the car was rather tense. I sat in silence all the way back to the hotel."

"How did he take that?"

"None too well," she said. "Of course, I thanked him as I got out of the car, and I took the opportunity to glance back down the street. There was no sign of anybody tailing us. Maybe I was wrong about that."

"I don't think so, Heidi."

"And you say it happened at Ko Olina as well?"

"Definitely."

"Oh." She shivered again. "That's rather alarming. Why should anyone want to stalk us like that? Do you have any theories, Alan?"

"One or two," I said. "None of them are very comforting. That being the case, I wouldn't mention any of this to Mrs. Dukelow. She's had enough upset already."

Heidi checked her watch. "I'd better be getting back to her."

"Before you go...."

"Yes?"

I hesitated. "It's rather personal, I'm afraid."

"We're friends, aren't we? Ask anything you like."

"It's about Donald," I explained. "I told you how much he was drinking last night. I can't believe that was normal behavior."

"It wasn't. He's usually quite abstemious. In all the years I've known him, I never once saw him drunk."

"Nor me—until last night. That raises the question of why he reached for the bottle like that. Something was on his mind, Heidi. Something to do with the wedding. It was almost as if he was trying to convince himself that he was doing the right thing." I saw her eyelids flicker. "Have you any idea what was troubling him?"

"No—why should I?"

"Because you know Donald as well as anyone."

"I used to think that—until he walked out on me."

"Did you see any telltale signs in him?"

"Of what?"

"Fears. Worries. Last minute doubts. Did you sense any problem?"

"No," she said, levelly. "I didn't."

When her eyelids flickered again, I knew that she was lying.

After letting Heidi out of my room, I opened the windows and stepped out on to the balcony, moving from the pleasant chill of the air conditioning into a hot afternoon. Unaware of the brutal murder that had taken place, the hordes indulged in the usual rituals on Waikiki Beach. I envied their sense of freedom. In the cafés and bars, people would be writing post cards to their friends, telling them what a wonderful holiday they were having in the idyllic surroundings. It wasn't something I could jot on the back of a picture of Oahu. When I sent my daughter the promised photograph of Waikiki, my comments would be short, sweet and—apart from the love I sent—wholly dishonest. At least, she would know that I was thinking of her. There was rarely a day when I didn't.

My attention shifted back to the hideous crime that had reshaped the lives of everyone close to Donald Dukelow. The image of the Asian man came back into my mind. I wanted to know who he was. When I rang the duty manager, I was told that he was busy but that he would ring me back. That gave me time to make myself a black coffee and sample some of the biscuits provided. The telephone rang as I was about to sink my teeth into my third custard cream.

"Yes?" I said, speaking into the mouthpiece.

"Mr. Saxon? It's Richard Meeker here."

"Thanks for ringing back."

"I'm sorry it took a little while," he said. "I've only just got rid of Mr. Kaheiki. He's been berating me about our lax security."

"You can't have patrols twenty-four hours a day."

"He seemed to think that we should."

"This is a hotel—not Fort Knox."

"I tried to make that point, sir. It fell on deaf ears," he admitted. "Still, enough of that. What can I do for you, Mr. Saxon?"

"I wanted the room number of another guest."

"Reception could have told you that."

"Only if I supplied his name, and I don't happen to have it."

"Then how can I help you?"

"It's quite simple. There can't be many elderly Pakistanis staying on the third floor. Identify the one who is, please."

"It's not our policy to disclose information about our guests, sir."

"Even if it's relevant to a police investigation?"

I explained what had happened outside Donald's room and his manner changed. As we talked, I could hear him tapping on a keyboard to get the hotel guest list up on his monitor.

"Are you sure that the gentleman was a Pakistani, sir?"

"That would be my guess."

"Is it only a guess?"

"I went to school in Leicester, England," I explained. "It's a city with a large Asian population. A lot of my friends were second-generation Indians or Pakistanis. I used to break up fights between them in the playground. Take my word for it, Mr. Meeker," I said. "I only got a glimpse of him, but I'm sure that this man was a Pathan. That makes him either a Pakistani or an Afghan."

"Well, he did not have a room on the third floor, sir. I can see no Asian names here. I suppose that he could have changed it."

"Highly unlikely. Muslims take great pride in their names. I've never met one who'd insult his family by Anglicizing his given name. This man must have been staying on another floor."

"Give me a moment and I'll check."

The moment turned into the best part of five minutes but I was patient. Meeker was extremely thorough. When he came back on the line, he'd been through the complete list of guests, hundreds of names in all. His eyesight was keen.

"We have very few Asian guests," he told me. "The vast majority of people staying here are from the mainland, Europe or Japan. The only Pakistani visitors I can pick out are a Mr. Bhatti, a Mr. Khan, and a Mr. Dhaliwal."

"I can see that you weren't brought up in Leicester."

"What do you mean?"

"Bhatti and Dhaliwal are Hindu names."

"Oh, I apologize. I didn't realize."

"Tell me about Mr. Khan. What's his first name?"

"Mohibullah."

"Muslim without doubt. I used to sit next to a Mohibullah Khan at school," I recalled. "Any idea of his age?"

"Mr. Khan is staying here with his wife and two small children."

"That rules out my man, then," I decided. "Unless he has a way with the ladies and a secret source of Viagra. Thank you, Mr. Meeker. You've been very helpful."

"This gentleman could have been visiting a guest," he suggested.

I agreed that he could though I somehow had grave doubts. After thanking him again, I rang off and made a mental note that, if I ever quit the world of professional golf, I'd never go into hotel management. In the course of one day, Richard Meeker had had to endure a murder, an invasion by the Honolulu Police Department, a media frenzy in the lobby, an irate Jimmy Kaheiki, and a string of requests from the third floor about an immediate change of room. He'd also had me badgering him for a favor. It was a dog's life. Meeker spent his whole day trying to put out fires. On balance, I think I'd rather sell swimming pools.

That thought put the face of the bogus Gabe Mahalona back in front of my eyes. Since he'd shown us a photograph of the children of the deceased man—not to mention his business card—he had to be involved in the earlier crime. Before being tossed into the water with a concrete block attached to his ankle, the real Gabriel Mahalona must have been deprived of his billfold. It had yielded the items needed to mislead Donald and me. I hoped that Mahalona's widow never got to hear about the deception. She'd be mortified to learn that her children were unwitting accomplices of a criminal.

What was the connection between a manufacturer of swimming pools and a professional golfer? Why had both their murders involved the use of a meat skewer? Who had followed us around the golf course, and was it the same person who had tried to stay on the tail of Nick Kaheiki when he drove Heidi back to the hotel? How far had the police got? Had they tracked down the nightclub yet? Why had I been warned to watch my back? Had I really seen a man in the corridor last night or was he a figment of my imagination? Why had Heidi Dukelow lied to me?

The last question was the one to which I fancied I might get an answer. Heidi knew something that she was, as yet, not prepared to tell me. To draw it out of her, I'd have to win her confidence. That would involve no hardship on my part. Circumstances had brought us together and adversity had pushed us closer. I could still feel her warm body in my arms. Even though she had to chaperone Cora Dukelow, there might still be times when Heidi and I were alone together. I looked forward to them. There was definitely something between us.

The phone rang. Thinking it might be her, I rushed over to grab it.

"Yes?"

"Hi, Alan. This is Melissa."

"Oh, hello there," I said, trying to conceal my surprise. Melissa Kaheiki was the last person I'd expected. "How are you?"

"I'm fine," she replied, "but how are *you*?"

"Surviving."

"Dad rang to tell me what happened. I was pole-axed."

"That's a pretty good description of how I feel."

"I tried to talk to Zann on the phone but she's not up to it. Mom is with her. She asked me to give Zann a little time before I went home to see her. All she wants to do is to lie on her bed and cry."

"So your father told me."

"You've spoken to him?"

"He came to police headquarters to see me. Nick was with him. Your brother was in a vengeful mood, Melissa."

"Yeah, he gets like that sometimes."

"Why, has this kind of thing happened before?" She fell silent. "Did you hear what I said?" I prompted.

"I heard, Alan."

"So why did you go all quiet on me?"

There was another pause. "I think we should meet."

"Now?"

"That possible?"

"Yes. Why don't you come here? Room 324."

"No," she said, firmly. "Not at the hotel. I know a place. Get a piece of paper to jot the name down. Meet you there in twenty minutes."

◇◇◇

When Melissa suggested a café on Waikiki Beach, my first instinct was to object to the venue. I was afraid of going anywhere in public lest I attract too much attention. Then I saw that she had picked the ideal place. In the confines of the hotel, I might be watched and pointed at as the man who had discovered a murder victim. Amid the crowds on the beach, however, I'd be just another anonymous figure. To get there without attracting too much attention, I changed into a T-shirt and shorts, put on my floppy hat with the wide brim, and reached for my sunglasses. The mirror confirmed that only my friends could recognize me at a glance.

It worked. The disguise got me out of the rear of the hotel, past the swimming pool and on to the beach without arousing more than a casual look. A steady stroll brought me to the café that Melissa had nominated. She, too, was camouflaged by the sheer size of the crowd. In the lobby of a five-star hotel, she would have turned a lot of heads. At the café, she blended in as easily as I did. Her bulging body and ring-covered lips went unnoticed. She was wearing a pair of frayed denim shorts and the grubby T-shirt with the pineapple on the front.

I ordered drinks then thanked her for agreeing to meet me.

"You're the one member of the family I can actually talk to," I said. "Your father was not at his most forthcoming and your brother was quite rude. I got the feeling he'd gone off me."

"Nick takes time to get to know people."

I could have pointed out that he tried to speed up his acquaintance with Heidi in the most direct manner but I didn't want to betray a confidence. In any case, although she'd spurned the comforts of family life, Melissa would still have a vestigial loyalty to her siblings. I didn't wish to alienate her.

"How did the rehearsal go today?" I asked.

"It was a shambles. I lost my temper with them."

"When did your father ring you?"

"About an hour ago. I was still at the theater."

"As late as that? He knew about the murder this morning," I said. "Why did he take so long to pass on the news to you?"

"I'm always at the bottom of the list."

"But Donald was going to be your brother-in-law."

"I won't pretend that I was excited by the idea."

"He was a lovely man, Melissa. Don't speak ill of the dead."

"I wasn't going to say anything," she countered. "I didn't know him well enough to make any comment. Or to mourn for him. My sympathy goes to Zann—and to you."

"Thanks."

"You're the first straight guy who didn't snigger at what we do."

"What was there to snigger about? It was dynamic theater."

"You wouldn't have thought that if you'd seen today's fiasco. Anyway," she said, drinking straight from her bottle of iced beer, "that's not what I came to talk about. I want to know what happened."

"Mind if I give you the shortened version?"

"Sure."

"If I have to go through the whole thing again, I'll get dizzy."

"Just tell me about how you stumbled on the body."

"I can do that in a couple of sentences."

In fact, I stretched it out to a few paragraphs. They were explicit. Melissa didn't turn a hair when I told her about the meat skewer in Donald's ear. Her face was inscrutable throughout.

"How did the cops treat you?" she asked.

"There wasn't much tea and sympathy."

"Were they rough on you?"

"They were doing their job," I said, easily. "I'm used to that routine hassle. My father was a policeman. I had years of it."

"Who's in charge of the case?"

"Captain Rapoza."

She was interested. "Clay Rapoza?"

"You know him?"

"Oh, yes. Our paths have crossed once or twice."

"He seemed to be very friendly with your father."

"Most people on this island are friendly with my father," she told me. "Or, at least, they make the effort to appear as if they are. Dad's approach is simple. You're either for him or against him."

"No room for anyone in between those extremes?"

"Not in Dad's world. Or Nick's, come to that."

"What about you?"

"I'm hang-loose. I try not to make value judgements about people."

"That wasn't what I meant, Melissa," I explained. "I still haven't worked out where you fit into the family. You've cut your ties to some extent yet you're still a Kaheiki at heart. How does your father see it? Are you viewed as a friend or an enemy?"

"A bit of both. I'm in a unique position."

"Does that trouble you?"

"Wouldn't have it any other way, Alan."

"Have you always been out of step with the others?"

She grinned proudly. "Had my teenage rebellion when I was eight."

"Why wait so long?" I joked. "I first defied my father when I was only five. I think I still have the marks of his leather belt to prove it. His attitude to the rest of the human race was warped. He didn't even divide them into friend and foes. They were all enemies and it was his mission to keep them in line. The only people he really liked were other policemen. He loved talking in that private language of theirs. I've never seen anyone who put on his uniform with more alacrity."

"We all wear uniforms of one kind or another."

"True. Maybe I'm too hard on him."

"You did what I did—escaped from your father."

"I had good reason, Melissa," I said, looking her in the eye. "My father tried to grind me down. What about you?"

She gave a shrug. "Daddy and I don't always get along."

"I've got a feeling that's an understatement."

"He was never happy about my sexuality. What father would be? If it were left to him, I'd be just like my sister—beautiful, gracious and infinitely marriageable. Ending up as a wife and mother. That scenario makes me want to throw up. It's just not me."

"Is that the only reason you don't see eye to eye with your father?"

"No, Alan."

"What about your brother? How does he cope with your lifestyle?"

"Not very well," she said. "In fact, Nick gave me more of a hard time than my parents. He could only see it from *his* point of view—didn't I realize how it embarrassed him to have a gay sister and so on. As if I'd made my choice deliberately to upset him."

"Over the phone, you told me that he could be vengeful."

"Did I?"

"I saw a hint of that earlier on. There's a lot of aggression swirling around inside your brother, isn't there?"

"I'm afraid there is."

"Why, Melissa? What's going on?"

She drank some more beer and pondered. Torn between family loyalty and a desire to help me, she took a long time to reach her decision. In the end, she got up slowly from the table.

"Let's go for a walk," she said.

Chapter Eight

Walking beside Melissa Kaheiki was a curious experience. Instead of feeling conspicuous and out of place, I was relaxed for the first time that day. It was inexplicable. Alone in a hotel room with Heidi, I'd shuttled between sadness and excitement, grieving for the loss of a dear friend yet stirred by the presence of his first wife in a way that I was still trying to understand. When I strolled along Waikiki Beach with a gay woman, however, I felt all the tension go. It didn't trouble me that Melissa must have looked like a moving advertisement for body piercing or that she waddled along in her disintegrating trainers as if she were a hobo in search of a hand-out. I liked her. We were friends.

It was time to test the precise limits of that friendship.

"I wouldn't have thought this was your territory," I observed.

"Beach life?"

"All these tourists, occupying your island, getting away from it all, toasting themselves in winter sunshine. Doesn't it make you angry?"

"Depressed," she said, gazing around. "I hate sloth and that's what I see here—acres of sloth and self-indulgence. Have people got nothing better to do than to lie around like so many sides of bacon? Why are they so afraid to engage their minds? Look at them," she went on with distaste. "All they want are creature comforts—sand, sea, and sex."

"Don't forget the booze."

"That, too, of course. They switch off their brain and drink."

"I've been known to do that myself, Melissa," I confessed. "Well, we both enjoyed a beer just now. Mind you, I've never been one for sun bathing. I always end up like a mottled pipe cleaner." We turned down an alleyway between two hotels. "I was asking about your brother. There's a violent streak in him, isn't there?"

"He won't let anyone push him around."

"Would anyone dare to try?"

"Oh, yes," she replied, "and they lived to regret it."

"In what way?"

"Nick is Nick. You have to take him as you find him."

"What's this about someone living to regret it?"

She flicked a hand. "It's not important. Forget it."

"But I'd like to know."

"I spoke out of turn."

"*Please*, Melissa. Tell me."

She needed some time to think about it, not wanting to give too much away about her family yet feeling that she somehow owed me an explanation. In the end, our friendship tipped the balance.

"Six or seven months ago," she admitted. "There was an incident."

"Involving your brother?"

"He was in a bar one night and this man was goading him. Really provoking him—at least, that's the way Nick tells it. So he waited for the man in the car lot and had a fight with him."

"What happened?"

"The man finished up in hospital and Nick was arrested on a charge of assault. If my father hadn't used his influence with Captain Rapoza, then Nick could have been in deep trouble. As it was, the charge was dropped."

"Was that the only time he'd fallen foul of the law?"

"No, Alan. My brother was a bit of a hell-raiser in his day. He was very lucky that Dad was always there to bail him out."

"I had a feeling there was a history of aggro there."

"He put it all behind him," she insisted. "Nick is a new man now."

"Yet he still beats people up."

"That was unusual. He's really smartened up his act. Daddy wouldn't put him in charge of the garment factory if he didn't trust him. Nick is on the straight and narrow now."

"What changed him?"

"He got married, had a child, learned about responsibility."

I was astonished. "He has a wife and family?"

"Yes, they live on Kauai."

"You mean, they're separated?"

"No," she explained, "it's the way that they both wanted it. Puamana, his wife, comes from Kauai and prefers to live there. It's such a beautiful island."

"Doesn't he miss his family?"

"Nick sees a lot more of them than you'd imagine. He pilots his own helicopter. Kauai is his escape. My brother has his faults but he works extremely hard. He needs a getaway."

"But what about the wedding? Wasn't his wife invited to that?"

"You'll have to ask Zann."

I was more interested in passing on the information to Heidi Dukelow that he was married. The impression that Nick Kaheiki had given both of us was that of a roving bachelor who took his pleasures where he found them. He obviously didn't pine for his absent wife. I wondered if Melissa knew that.

We turned into the street and picked our way through the crowd.

"Nick said something that alarmed me," I confided.

"Oh? What was that?"

"He told me to watch my back. It was when I met him and your father at police headquarters. Nick said that I had to be careful. His exact words were, 'he may not stop at Donald Dukelow.' Have you any idea what he meant by that?"

"Didn't you ask Nick at the time?"

"Your father shut him up."

"I see."

"They both seemed to think that I was in danger."

"Then I'd heed their warning, Alan. It wasn't given lightly."

"Is that all you can tell me?"

"I opted out of the family," she said, evasively. "My work keeps me away from the house. I don't really know what's going on any more."

"Come on, Melissa," I pressed. "You can do better than that. If you were that detached from family affairs, you wouldn't have got in touch with me. I'm in jeopardy and I want to know why. Call me a coward, if you like, but I'd rather not expose myself to any undue peril." I put a hand on her shoulder to stop her. "Whatever you tell me is between the two of us. I swear it. Now, what gives?"

Our eyes locked and she breathed heavily through her nose. There was an air of defiance about her at first, and I feared that she was about to tell me—in ripe language—to mind my own business, but she gradually came round to an appreciation of my position.

"Okay," she said at length, "but you didn't hear this from me."

"Go on."

"I told you how Daddy divides people into friends and enemies. Well, one of those enemies decided to show how he felt about the Kaheiki family. One night, he trashed a convenience store that my father owns."

"Was the man caught?"

"No, Alan."

"Do they have any idea who he is?"

"Not really. There are too many people to choose from. If it had been an isolated crime, Daddy might have shrugged the whole thing off and let the insurance company take over. But it didn't end there," she went on, shaking her head. "A month later, there was a robbery at one of the Kaheiki warehouses. Goods to the value of hundreds of thousands of dollars were taken."

"This is serious stuff, Melissa."

"There's more to come."

"Why—what happened next?"

"One of the gas stations belonging to us was burned to the ground. That was scary. Somebody seemed to be conducting a vendetta against the family. My fear is that the same person is behind the murder."

"I see what you mean," I said, uneasily. "We're talking escalation here. Vandalism, robbery, arson, then murder. There's a definite pattern. On the other hand," I reasoned, as we started to walk again, "Donald Dukelow was not another piece of Kaheiki property."

"He would have been after the wedding."

"But that was being held in secret. How would anyone know that he and Zann were getting married? Only a handful of us had any idea what was afoot. No," I concluded, "I'm not sure that I accept this link to the other crimes. If someone wanted to strike at your father, they'd target someone in the family and not Donald."

"That's one way of looking at it, I suppose."

"But you don't agree."

"No, I don't," she said. "My father's a wealthy man, but he didn't have that wealth handed to him on a plate. He had to fight for every penny. When you build up an empire like his, you have to cut corners, take chances, be ruthless. People sometimes get hurt in the process."

"So they try to exact revenge."

"That's right. But not by killing Daddy or Nick or anyone else in the family. They'd rather keep them alive so that they can watch them *suffer*. That's all part of the fun. What they take out are things with the Kaheiki brand on them—and your buddy was about to have it stamped on his ass good and proper."

"Why didn't your sister warn Donald about all this?"

"I doubt if she knows all the details. She lives on the mainland."

"Zann must be aware that your family is not universally popular in Oahu. Couldn't she at least have mentioned it to her future husband?"

"She probably didn't think it was necessary. Let's face it. Nobody was supposed to know about the secret wedding. Jesus!" she exclaimed. "I was only told about it the day before you got here, and I'm her sister. How could anyone connect your friend to Zann?"

"I don't know, but someone did."

"So it seems."

"Zann should never have brought him to the island."

"I bet she realizes that now. Think of the guilt she must feel."

"Oh, we all have our share of that, Melissa," I said, soulfully. "Big time. I'll never forgive myself for helping to lead Donald into a trap."

"Don't blame yourself."

"I should have been there for Donald—and I wasn't."

"Your friend is dead, Alan. Think of yourself."

"What do you mean?"

"Take my brother's advice. Watch your back."

"But I'm nothing to do with the Kaheiki family."

Melissa looked at me with a mixture of pity and distant affection.

"You are now, I'm afraid—whether you like it or not."

Our walk had taken us in a complete circle. When we came back to the café, I saw Melissa's motorcycle parked outside. Before she kicked the vehicle into life, she kissed me on the cheek and told me to keep in touch. I thanked her for being so honest with me. I now had a vague idea of what was going on. It was odd. With her beside me, I'd felt completely safe, but the second she rode off, I had a sense of foreboding. Could I really be on someone's hit list? The notion was fanciful until I remembered what had happened to Donald Dukelow. He'd been cunningly set up before being murdered in his bed.

My only comfort came from the fact that my drink could have been spiked along with Donald's yet it was not. I'd been deliberately spared. I hoped it was because my life was not in danger but it could equally well have been the case that I was needed to get Donald back to the hotel. Having done that, I might now be at risk myself. Jimmy Kaheiki and Nick clearly thought so. Melissa agreed with them. I didn't simply have an unfortunate link with the family. I was the one person who could identify the man who had convinced us that he was Gabe Mahalona. All of a sudden, I felt as if someone was painting a target on my back.

I also became much more aware of how hot it was. The Hawaiian islands have never experienced a British winter. They don't know what driving snow and biting frost are. Even in December, the temperature was in the high seventies and it was difficult to believe that Christmas was just around the corner. What the islands did suffer, of course, was the occasional punitive hurricane to remind them that Mother Nature is not entirely beneficent. People are sometimes killed, buildings often destroyed when the weather turns bad. Today, however, it was behaving itself. We were in a giant microwave that was making us simmer. The only hurricane was the one inside my head.

Melissa's intervention was welcome yet hardly comforting. Most people in my position would simply pack up and catch the next plane but it was not an option for me. Quite apart from the fact that Captain Rapoza had asked me to stay in Honolulu, I had obligations to Heidi and to Cora Dukelow. I couldn't desert them. I also felt, obscurely, that I owed it to Suzanne Kaheiki to remain so that I could assist the investigation. But my biggest debt was to Donald, who had invited me there in the first place and who had been so pleased to have me beside him. For his sake, I wanted to do what I could to track down the man with a sadistic penchant for meat skewers.

When I retraced my steps to the hotel, I was much more furtive but nobody looked at me. They were too busy oiling their bodies, or quaffing their iced drinks or riding the next foam-capped wave as it lunged towards the shore. On Waikiki Beach, it was my turn to be the Invisible Man and that suited me. As I passed the long line of cafés, bars and hotel patios, I noticed a number of Asian faces. They usually belonged to catering staff though a few were there on holiday as well. None was over the age of fifty. Evidently, the elderly man I'd seen outside Donald's room was not a natural Waikiki denizen.

The longer I walked, the more confident I became. Nobody would be stupid enough to attack me with so many witnesses at hand. Besides, I was no torpid figure lying in bed as Donald Dukelow had been. I was a strong, fit, and alert man who'd fight tooth and nail against any adversary. Playing golf for a living may have its down side—back trouble, frustration, intense humiliation—but it does keep the muscles in trim. I rarely walk less than four miles around a typical course. I never hit fewer than three hundred balls in a golf range. While I wouldn't admit it to my rivals, I even work out regularly with weights to increase my upper body strength. It's put valuable extra yardage on my drives.

Reaching the hotel, I went up the steps at the rear, then swung round from my elevated position to see if anyone was following me. My fears were groundless. Nobody was even glancing in my direction. I continued on my way, avoiding the main staircase and the elevators and making for the emergency exit. When I trotted up the concrete steps to the third floor, it helped me to make an interesting discovery. As I left the staircase and pushed open the door, I still had a few yards to go before I turned into the corridor. What I was standing in was a perfect hiding place from which someone could keep an eye on the comings and goings on the third floor. The Asian man had walked towards us from this direction. Had he been lurking in the recess?

It was something I intended to raise with Captain Rapoza—or, preferably, with Sergeant Emily Tenno. She was far more approachable as a person and might not be so subject to the influence of Jimmy Kaheiki as her boss. It was possible, as the duty manager had suggested, that the man I saw had simply been visiting someone on the third floor but I could not take a chance. His appearance at that moment might not have been quite so coincidental. I had to report it.

The policeman was still outside Donald's room, looking bored and shifting his feet to ease the ache in his legs. When I came into view, he straightened up and hitched a thumb into his belt. He looked as if he knew how to use the gun in his holster and would welcome the opportunity to prove it. His uniform was enough to cow me. I gave him a desultory wave then let myself into my room.

Relief flooded through me. The sensation did not last. Something was wrong. All my instincts were telling me to be on guard. My muscles tightened at once. Yet when I looked around the room, everything seemed to be exactly in its place. Making for my golf bag, I grabbed the putter again to use as a weapon and conducted a swift search. There was nobody under the beds, behind the drapes or in the fitted wardrobe. That left the bathroom. Raising the putter to strike, I kicked open the door but the place was quite empty. No killer behind the shower curtains, no assassin crouched beside the bath. My instincts had misled me. I was about to return the putter to my bag when I saw something out of the corner of my eye. It made me jump back in alarm. My toothbrush had been removed from the glass in which I stood it.

In its place was a meat skewer.

◇◇◇

When the guard saw me coming, he moved a cautionary hand to his holster. Rushing out of my room with a putter in my hand, I must have looked as if I was about to launch an attack on him.

"Have you been on duty all afternoon, officer?" I asked.

"Yes, sir."

"My name is Alan Saxon. I'm staying in Room 324."

"I know who you are, sir," he said. "I was here when you went off with Captain Rapoza. What seems to be the problem?"

"Somebody got into my room."

"I didn't see anybody, Mr. Saxon."

"Are you sure?" I said, brandishing the putter. "It would have been within the last hour or so, while I was out."

"Stop waving that thing at me," he warned, holding the putter. "If you don't control yourself, I'll have to take it away from you."

"Sorry, officer." I put the club by my side.

"There's no need to get so excited."

"Oh, I think there is."

I told him what had given me the scare and he agreed that I had cause for anxiety. He also insisted that I contact Rapoza immediately to report the development. But he was adamant that nobody had crossed my threshold while I was out of my room.

"Not even someone from housekeeping?"

"No, Mr. Saxon."

"What if you'd been looking the other way at the time?"

The suggestion insulted him. "I saw everything," he asserted, fixing me with a stare. "If one or more persons had gone into Room 324, I'd have made a mental note of it. I'm not just watching over the scene of the crime. Captain Rapoza asked me to keep your room under surveillance. The only visitor you had was that lady earlier on."

"Heidi Dukelow?"

"I can tell you exactly how long she was in your room."

I was at once reassured and disturbed, relieved to know that I had police protection but worried that it had somehow been eluded. If the person who left the meat skewer in my bathroom had not gone in through the door, how had he gained entry into the room? It was baffling. Thanking the officer for his help, I walked back down the corridor with the putter over my shoulder. The first thing I did when I let myself back into my room was to ring the police. Rapoza was unavailable so I was put through to Sergeant Tenno. I told her about my discovery.

"Whatever you do," she said, "don't touch it."

"I'm afraid even to go in the bathroom."

"Somebody will be with you in due course."

"Thank you, Sergeant."

"We can update you on the investigation then."

"You've made progress?" I said, hopefully.

She was non-committal. "You'll be informed."

Before I could press for detail, she rang off. I decided to play at being a detective myself. How had the intruder got in? The only other means of entry was through the windows and I reproached myself for leaving them open while I was having my rendezvous with Melissa Kaheiki. I stepped out on to the balcony. At either end of it was a high wooden screen that shielded it from the adjacent balconies. I peered round the edge of one screen. If someone were agile enough, it would not have been difficult for him to balance on the rail, cock a leg around the screen and pull himself onto my balcony.

Glancing upwards, I saw that there was another possibility. A real gymnast could have swung down from the balcony above, though a rope would have been needed to get him back up there again. The timing was crucial. Since the meat skewer was left in my bathroom while I was some distance away, it raised the question of how the intruder knew that I had left the hotel. Was I watched? Had my disguise been penetrated? Or—a much more disquieting thought—had someone gained entry in order to thrust the skewer into my ear and, finding me absent, simply left it as his calling card? None of the explanations gave me any comfort. Stepping back into the room, I closed the windows and locked them securely.

The telephone rang. Expecting it to be the police, I picked it up.

"This is Cora Dukelow," she said in a brittle voice. "Are you alone?"

"Yes, Mrs. Dukelow."

"I don't suppose that you could spare me a few minutes?"

"Of course. Right now?"

"Please."

"I'll be there in a tick," I said.

It would take the police some time to reach the hotel and I didn't need to stay entombed in my room until they did so. As I went down the corridor, I told the guard where I was going so that I could be summoned if his colleagues arrived while I was still in the other room. Hoping that I'd have the chance of seeing Heidi again, I was disappointed when it was Cora Dukelow who opened the door and invited me in.

"Heidi popped out," she explained, waving me to a seat. "At my request. I wanted to speak to you alone. She told me how you found Donald this morning. I don't need to know any more details. What I have to come to terms with is the fact of my son's death, not the manner in which it occurred."

It was different for me. After the discovery in the bathroom, my preoccupation was with the precise manner of his demise but I was not going to mention the meat skewer to Cora Dukelow. I had no wish to upset her any further. She deserved my sympathy. Though she was still grieving inwardly, there was no indication of it in her face. As she sat in the armchair opposite me, she looked remarkably calm and self-possessed.

"Donald was very fond of you," she began.

"I'm not surprised, Mrs. Dukelow," I said. "I was his favorite loser. Did you know that he beat me in something like five successive play-offs? If any other golfer had done that, I'd have hated him but I only came to like Donald the more for it. He had genius."

"On a golf course, perhaps. Elsewhere, he had his weaknesses."

"Just like the rest of us."

"Most people don't let their private lives get into such a mess."

"Whenever I met him, Donald seemed happy with his private life."

"Oh, he was," she said. "For a time. The trouble was that his happiness always depended on novelty. As soon as he got something that he really wanted, his eye began to wander again. I'm not criticizing him for it," she went on, hands clasped in her lap. "Especially at a time like this. All I wish to remember are the good things about my son and there were so very many of those."

"He was one of the nicest people in the world, Mrs. Dukelow."

She gave a quiet smile. "He took after his father in that respect."

"Your husband must have been very proud of his son."

"Oh, he was, and rightly so. Herbert taught him how to play golf when Donald was barely able to hold a club. He was thrilled by Donald's success." Her lower lip trembled for an instant. "I'm just glad that he didn't live to see all this. It would have torn him apart." I thought she was on the brink of breaking down but she quickly recovered. "The reason I wanted to see you was to explain one or two things about Donald."

"I only knew him as a golfer, really."

"That might have distorted your judgement."

"In what way?"

She took a deep breath. "You know what my feelings were about this marriage, Alan. I don't need to repeat them. To be candid, I'm rather ashamed of the way I behaved on the drive to the hotel. That outburst of mine was inexcusable."

"Forget all about it, Mrs. Dukelow."

"It was really a cry of pain."

"Pain?"

"Yes," she said. "I felt as if Donald was doing it deliberately to hurt me. To inflict pain. I know that sounds silly, even paranoid. You probably think it's the mindless ranting of a thwarted old woman."

"I don't think that at all."

"What you don't understand is the background to all this."

"Heidi did give me some insight into it."

"Heidi could only tell you what she knew. There was a period when she dropped out of Donald's life altogether." She stifled a sigh. "Heidi was the ideal wife for him. Beautiful, intelligent, loving—and so patient. Heidi always put him first. Instead of pursuing her own career, she kept Donald company on tour. She adores golf."

"I'm told that's how they met. Heidi caddied for him."

"It was a tournament held at their law college. Donald won it."

"And found a wife into the bargain."

"We couldn't have been more delighted, Alan," she told me. "Until then, he'd always been a bit of a rover. At last, he was ready to settle down. With Heidi behind him, his career really took off."

"Yes," I remarked. "I know. I was one of his many victims."

"Donald had it all—yet he still wanted more. You could see it in his eyes. Herbert was a restraining influence while he was alive. But as soon as my husband died—God rest his soul—Donald did the most appalling thing imaginable."

"Heidi told me."

"He took up with a Spanish lady," she said, harshly. "I could hardly bear to have her in the house. Esmeralda, that was her name. In her own way, I'm sure that she was a perfectly nice woman but I could never get beyond what she represented—the loss of a daughter-in-law I loved. Needless to say," she continued, "Donald tired of her in time and reached out for someone else. And at least, he had the decency to marry that one."

"I met Janine," I told her. "And Esmeralda, for that matter."

"Could either of them compare with a woman like Heidi?"

"Not in my book."

"This child bride of his is the same," she argued. "Zann Kaheiki. When I first heard of her existence, I fear that my prejudices got the better of me. Her passport may tell me that she's an American citizen but I still thought of her as foreign. You know, not really one of us. Also, I took against her because of her name. Why on earth call her Zann when Suzanne is so much nicer?"

"Whatever her name," I observed, "she's a delightful young woman."

"Utterly charming. Having met her, I can see exactly what attracted Donald to her but, for the life of me, I couldn't see it lasting. If only he hadn't been so determined to have me here," she said, wringing her hands. "Donald did everything he could to persuade me to come here, even to the extent of bringing Heidi along."

"He needed your approval, Mrs. Dukelow. Your ratification. Zann is part of a close-knit family," I pointed out. "He couldn't just turn up for his wedding with me in tow. I'm no blood relation. Donald had to have his mother. You were his credentials."

"I shouldn't have come, Alan. In my heart, I could never condone what he was doing and I'm sure that Heidi felt the same. But," she added with a faraway smile, "he was my only child. I felt obliged. I spoke my mind—well, you heard me doing so—but I did what he asked in the end. It was a fatal mistake."

"Why was that?"

"If I'd refused to come, Donald might still be alive."

"You've no proof of that, Mrs. Dukelow."

"I think I have."

"Oh?"

"A moment ago, you put your finger on the main reason he wanted me to be here. It was to legitimize the marriage. To make it a union of two families instead simply of two people. I was weak. I should have put my foot down."

"Donald would still have got married," I said.

"But not here, not in Hawaii, not in this secretive way."

"He relied so much on your permission."

"By agreeing to be here, I was effectively giving it."

Cora Dukelow looked wistful. Regardless of the many unpleasant surprises he'd given her over the years, she was still his mother and she talked about Donald as if he were an errant child rather than a man in his forties. It was as if she had never allowed him to grow up properly. Her face suddenly darkened.

"There was something else, Alan."

"Was there?"

"I've told nobody about this—not even Heidi. If I'm honest, it went right out of my head until...." There was another long intake of breath. "...until this happened. Before we left Rochester, I had a phone call. The man asked to speak to Donald. He wouldn't give his name."

"And?"

"I didn't hear what he said but I saw Donald's reaction. I've never known my son to get so worked up. There was real outrage in his voice. In the end, he just slammed down the telephone."

"Did you ask him what it was all about?"

"He refused to discuss it."

"Even though it upset him so much?"

"It was on his mind for days. I could tell."

"Did you have any idea of what was said to him over the phone?"

"Oh, yes," said Cora Dukelow. "That was why he was so livid." The memory drained all the color from her face. "I'm certain that the caller warned him to stay away from Hawaii."

I stayed with her for another twenty minutes, sharing fond memories of Donald with her and learning the kinds of details about a son that only a mother could give you. His death had transformed her, taking away the hard, crepuscular edge to expose a touching softness. Before I left, she kissed me on both cheeks, then hugged me with gratitude. When we finally parted, my mind was in turmoil. Given a warning to stay away from the island, why had Donald insisted on coming there and bringing us with him? Was it perversity or bravado? Why hadn't he told *me* about the potential risk involved? Who was the mystery caller and what made him issue the blunt advice to my friend?

The questions were still buzzing around my brain like so many angry bees when I saw Emily Tenno striding down the corridor towards me. I gave an involuntary gasp of relief. After she'd paused to exchange a few words with the officer guarding the scene of the crime, she came on to my room and I let her in. Taking a plastic bag from her purse, she went into the bathroom to retrieve the meat skewer. I felt embarrassed by the reversal of roles, standing outside like a timid girl who's afraid of spiders while the gallant man goes in to deal with the creature. When she reappeared, the skewer had been put away.

"It's a long shot," she admitted, "but we might get something."

"Fingerprints?"

"DNA. Don't bank on it. We're up against a pro."

"I found that out, Sergeant."

"Must have given you a nasty shock, seeing that in the bathroom."

"Someone was trying to give me a message."

"We'll get him, Mr. Saxon."

"But will I still be around to celebrate?"

"Oh, I think so."

I wished that I could share her confidence. We sat down and I gave her an account of how I discovered the skewer, and tried to work out how the intruder had got into the room without being seen by anyone. Jotting it all down in her pad, she also wanted to know my movements since we last met. I told her about my brush with Jimmy Kaheiki on the drive back to the hotel and how retracing the steps I'd taken the previous evening had reminded me of the Asian man who strolled past us. She was interested to learn of the call I'd made to Richard Meeker, the duty manager.

"That was good thinking," she said, admiringly. "We'll make a detective out of you yet, Mr. Saxon."

"What I'd really like to have done is to knock on all the doors between Donald's room and the emergency exit to see if any of the guests had had a Pakistani visitor that night. The thing is," I explained, "I was so busy trying to get into Donald's room that I wasn't sure where the man came from. He might have materialized out of thin air."

"You saw enough to decide that he was a Pakistani."

"A Muslim, anyway. They don't touch alcohol."

"Hence the look he gave you and Mr. Dukelow."

"Donald was obviously as drunk as a skunk."

"I'll follow up your suggestion," she said. "We've already spoken to everyone else on the third floor. None of them saw or heard anything last night. We'll go back and ask if any of them had an Asian guest."

"And if they didn't?"

"Then we have another little problem to solve."

"Just solve the big one, Sergeant—who killed Donald Dukelow?"

"That might take time, sir."

"How far have you got?"

"We're advancing on a number of fronts," she said, evenly, "though we've made no significant breakthrough as yet. What I can tell you is that, so far, your story has checked out."

I was angered. "Did you think I was telling a pack of lies?"

"Standard procedure. We have to be sure."

"I bet that Captain Rapoza was disappointed."

"Why do you say that?"

"Because he didn't trust me for a second."

"We have to be objective, Mr. Saxon," she told me. "The restaurant confirms that you and Mr. Dukelow ate there last night. The manager also remembers the confrontation you had with the man who told you both to get out."

"Mahalona's accomplice."

"He couldn't give a clear description of either of them. However, the manager does recall that the three of you left together. That was our first piece of luck."

"Luck?"

"Yes," she replied. "It seems that there's a handful of taxis that use that particular restaurant as an unofficial cab rank. The manager knows all the drivers. We checked them out and soon found the one who drove you to Reuben's."

"Was that the name of the nightclub?"

"Nothing to do with Rubens, the painter. It's run by a guy called Reuben—the one you saw behind the bar. He remembered you all."

"Was he able to give you a lead on the man who took us there?"

"Unfortunately, no."

"But we were told it's an exclusive club. With a membership list."

"Your companion was not on it. He got you in by slipping a bribe to the doorman. Reuben says that he's been in there once or twice before but he has no idea of the man's name."

I was crestfallen. "In other words, you drew a blank."

"Not at all, sir. We confirmed your story."

"But *he's* the criminal—not me."

"Reuben's description of him tallied with your own."

"That's a big consolation," I said, sarcastically. "The man is still out there and he, or his accomplice, is still posing a threat to me. I know that Captain Rapoza asked that officer outside to watch my door but that didn't stop someone getting into my bathroom."

"I'll talk to Liam about that."

"Liam?"

"Liam Broderick. He's the officer on duty. I'll ask him if he saw anyone going into the rooms either side of you while you were out."

"Almost any of the rooms on the rear of the hotel," I suggested. "The man could have worked his way along from balcony to balcony. Or dropped down from the one above like Batman in Gotham City."

"Leave it to me, Mr. Saxon. We'll explore every avenue."

"I'd like to explore one of my own, Sergeant."

"Go on."

I plunged straight in. "Let's not beat about the bush," I said, bluntly. "What exactly is the relationship between Captain Rapoza and Jimmy Kaheiki?"

"I'm not sure that I understand the question, sir."

"Come off it, Sergeant. My father was a police inspector and he was involved in a number of murder investigations. There's no way that he'd allow a key witness to be interviewed on police property by a local businessman."

"Jimmy Kaheiki is more than a local businessman."

"You're beginning to understand my question."

"Be careful, Mr. Saxon."

"Is Captain Rapoza a close friend of his?"

"I'm not at liberty to discuss this with you."

"From what I hear, he does a lot of favors for Mr. Kaheiki."

"That's a private matter."

"Not if it affects me," I responded. "It was bad enough being grilled by the two of you in there. Then I was turned over to Jimmy Kaheiki and his son. What's so special about them? They had no right to be there."

"I think you've said enough, sir," she warned, getting to her feet.

"Let me finish, Sergeant. I'm the pig in the middle here and it's not a role I'm enjoying. Alright," I went on, standing up, "I know that I have a jaundiced view of policemen but, if I do have to deal with one, I'd rather it wasn't a man who seems to be in the pocket of Jimmy Kaheiki."

"That's a very serious allegation," she retorted.

"Then deny it."

"I'd rather pretend that you didn't say that, Mr. Saxon."

"Is it too near the truth?"

"I won't listen to any more of this," she said, asserting herself. "Captain Rapoza is a fine officer with an excellent record. You should be grateful that he's in charge of this investigation. He'll do all he can to bring it to a swift conclusion."

"For whose benefit—mine or Jimmy Kaheiki's?"

"For *everyone's* benefit, sir—and in the interests of justice."

Her voice was icily calm. She stared me in the eye, daring me to go on, challenging me to produce evidence to back up what I'd alleged. There was no point in pursuing the matter. For all her human qualities, Emily Tenno was one of them. She'd hear no criticism of her superior. It was a lesson I'd been taught by my father time and again. In the face of any hostility, the police always close ranks. Though I thought I had a genuine grievance, I was made to feel guilty for even voicing it.

"There's something else I need to tell you," she said, opening her purse to take out a billfold in a small plastic bag. "This was taken from the shirt pocket of the deceased."

"At least, they didn't try to steal his identity as they did in the case of Gabriel Mahalona. Don't give it to me, Sergeant," I said as she offered it. "By rights, it should go to his mother."

"I know that but I wanted you to see it first. There's a photograph that may interest you. I'm not sure that Mrs. Dukelow should have it."

"Why not?"

"Look at it."

I took the billfold from her and removed it from the plastic bag. Opening the billfold, I extracted the one photograph inside it. I gaped in astonishment. Since he was so deeply in love with the woman he was about to marry, I thought it would be a snapshot of Suzanne Kaheiki, but it was not.

"You see our dilemma, sir. We'd hate to upset his mother."

"Then don't give it to her," I decided.

I stared at the photograph. Donald had surprised me yet again. On the eve of his wedding, he was carrying a photograph of his first wife, and it was a very striking one. Standing beside a bed, Heidi Dukelow was stark naked.

Chapter Nine

I studied the photograph with a mixture of dismay and fascination, concerned, for her sake, that Heidi's nude body had probably been pored over by lecherous male eyes at police headquarters, yet struck by the classical beauty of her figure. Because she had retained her youthful appearance, it was impossible to put a date on the picture but I assumed it must have been taken during her marriage to Donald.

"I'm told that it's his first wife," said Emily Tenno.

"That's right, Sergeant. Heidi Dukelow."

"Detective Wilson identified the lady. She was responsible for breaking the news of the murder to them. And no," she stressed, reading my mind, "it was not passed around among the men. We protected the lady from that embarrassment."

"Thank you. She'll be very grateful."

"The question is—what do we do with it?"

"I don't think that Donald's mother should see this," I said, looking up at her. "It would cause her a lot of pain. Technically, it's Heidi's property. As a lawyer, she'd insist on having it returned to her."

"Perhaps I could leave that task to you, Mr. Saxon."

"If you wish."

I wasn't sure whether to be pleased or troubled by the assignment, but it would give me the chance to ask Heidi how the photograph came to be in Donald's billfold long after the two of them had been divorced. I sensed that its presence in his pocket might help to explain why he had behaved so uncharacteristically at the restaurant. Crossing to the desk, I slipped the photograph into one of the envelopes with the hotel crest embossed on it. After carefully sealing the flap, I put the envelope in the drawer. Tenno watched me with amusement.

"Why not lock the drawer as well, sir?"

"I didn't want to leave it lying around for anyone to see."

"Nobody will come in. Officer Broderick will make sure of that."

"He can't stop all intruders—as we found out."

"I'd like to give the billfold to Mrs. Dukelow," she said, holding out a hand. "Then I'd have the opportunity to introduce myself." I passed her the billfold. "According to Detective Wilson, she's a strong woman who coped amazingly well with the shock. Does that surprise you?"

"Not at all," I replied. "Cora Dukelow is tough and resourceful. I was talking to her myself just before you arrived. She's not the sort of lady who'd ever need smelling salts."

"Good. I'll spend a moment with her before we leave."

"We?"

"Yes, Mr. Saxon," she explained. "I'm afraid that I have to ask you to come with me to headquarters again. The media have been hounding us for a look at you. Captain Rapoza wants you to make a statement in front of the cameras. Afterwards, there'll be a press conference."

"Do I *have* to come?" I complained.

"Would you prefer to have the media hammering on your door?"

"I suppose not."

"Captain Rapoza may have some more news for you."

"An arrest?"

"Maybe nothing as dramatic as that," she conceded. "But the preliminary report from the M.E. will have come through. We'll have a clearer idea of how the victim died."

With a nude photograph of his first wife in his pocket, I thought.

There was a message in that as well.

◇◇◇

So much had happened in the course of the day that I was surprised to learn that it was still only early evening. Primed by Captain Rapoza, I stood in front of the cameras and said my piece, wondering if Heidi and Cora Dukelow would be watching the live broadcast on TV. Afterwards, I underwent a full interrogation by the local press, keeping to the script and taking care not to be pushed into speculation about the motive behind the crime. At the end of it all, I felt as if I'd just donated at least three pints of blood. What I needed was a lie down and a cup of tea. Instead of that, alas, I had an abrasive exchange in his office with Captain Clay Rapoza.

"Why didn't you tell us about this Asian man before?"

"I forgot."

"Deliberately?"

"Of course not."

"Then why do I get the feeling that you're holding something back?"

"Professional skepticism."

"Ah, I see," he sneered. "We're back to your father again."

"He always believed that I was guilty until proven innocent."

"I'm beginning to see why."

"Everything I told you in my statement was confirmed."

"What about the things you *didn't* tell us?"

"There weren't any, Captain."

"Apart from that bloody nose Mr. Dukelow gave you," he reminded me. "That was omitted from your first statement. And now you come up with this tale about a man who walked past you in the corridor."

"It may not have been a coincidence."

"All the more reason not to withhold the information from us."

"I didn't do it on purpose, you know."

"Oh, I think you did," he said, eyeing me shrewdly. "All that practice you must have had with your father has left its imprint. Resenting him, avoiding him, finding excuses, concealing things, telling downright lies. Know what *manao* means?"

"No, Captain."

"It's the Hawaiian word for intuition, for having a hunch. Shall I tell you what? I got this strong *manao* about you, Mr. Saxon."

"You think that *I* murdered Donald Dukelow?" I taunted.

"I think you like obstructing cops in the exercise of their duties. You're the kind of guy who does everything on purpose. What you claim was a bad memory is really willful perversity."

"Why should I obstruct you?"

"Because I'm a cop. Same breed as your father."

"I want the murderer caught as much as anyone," I contended. "And not just for Donald's sake. I'm in the line of fire, remember. That wasn't a large toothpick I found in my bathroom, you know. It was a meat skewer with my name on it."

"No, sir," he said. "It was a symbol."

"Of what?"

"People who don't listen. They need to have their ears syringed. Gabriel Mahalona refused to listen so he ended up dead in his swimming pool with a skewer in his ear. It's on the cards that Donald Dukelow didn't listen either." He took a step towards me. "Is that true?"

I thought of the warning he'd been given before he left Rochester but I said nothing. It was too late. If I told Rapoza about it now, I'd be accused once more of hindering the police by keeping things from them. Besides, it was something that Cora Dukelow had passed on to me in confidence. If she wanted the police to know, she'd volunteer the information to them. What it confirmed in my mind was that, in coming to the island, Donald had been brave but foolhardy. He knew the risk. It might have been the reason that he drank so heavily at the restaurant.

"Well, sir?" pressed Rapoza. "Was it true of your friend?"

"Not as far as I know, Captain."

"It's obviously true of you."

"Since when?" I said, defensively.

"Since the day you stopped listening to your father. You're one of these guys who's into selective deafness—and it looks as if I'm not the only person who thinks that."

"You don't cure deafness by ramming a skewer into a man's brain."

"Yes, you do. Permanently."

He showed his teeth in a lopsided grin. I didn't rise to the bait this time. On his territory, he had all the advantages and my claustrophobia was already setting in. I lapsed into what my father always called dumb insolence. Rapoza leaned over his desk and picked up a sheet of paper.

"Early words from the lab," he explained. "More to come. As we speak, the M.E. is still cutting him up into small pieces, happy in his work." He glanced at the paper. "But this is the story so far."

"What does it tell us?"

"Exactly what you predicted about the cause of death. Massive brain hemorrhage."

"I finally got something right then."

"Part of it, anyway," he said, grudgingly. "But my guess was on the button as well. There were very faint traces in his blood of a substance called gamma hydroxybutyrate. Better known as GHB."

"The date rape drug?"

"Don't worry. The guy who took you to Reuben's didn't want to jump your buddy's bones. There was no sign of sexual interference. Taken with alcohol, GHB can be fatal on its own sometimes. In this case," he said, putting the paper back on his desk, "it was used to render the victim defenseless so that he could be murdered."

"At least, Donald would not have suffered."

"If he'd been allowed to sleep it off, he'd never have remembered what happened at Reuben's. The drug is colorless, odorless, and difficult to trace in the bloodstream. Knocks out your memory completely. Hey!" he decided. "Maybe that's what *you're* on, Mr. Saxon. It would explain why you keep forgetting things."

"Have you finished with me, Captain?"

"Not yet."

"This place depresses me."

"But we just love having you around," he said with mock pleasure. His voice became curt. "You'll go when he comes to collect you."

"Who?"

"Jimmy Kaheiki's chauffeur. You're going out to the house."

"Why?"

"You'll find out."

"Don't I have any choice in the matter?" I said in annoyance.

"Sure. Refuse to go, if you wish. But it will upset her."

"Her?"

"Suzanne. She's the one who wants to see you, Mr. Saxon. Have a heart," he advised. "When that meat skewer went home, you only lost a golfer who kept beating you in play-offs. Zann Kaheiki lost the next thirty or forty years of married life." He reached for the phone. "Like me to contact the house and say that you can't make it?" I shook my head and he replaced the receiver. "That's more like it."

Since I had to be there, I tried to make virtue of a necessity. As I recalled what Melissa had told me about her family, I went on the attack.

"Is it true that Jimmy Kaheiki has been having difficulties?"

"Difficulties?"

"Vandalism at a convenience store, robbery from a warehouse, arson at a gas station. Unsolved crimes that were aimed at the Kaheiki empire. Am I right?"

"Those things needn't concern you, sir," he snapped.

"But they do, Captain. Can't you see a pattern there? What if the murder was committed by the same hands?"

"Believe it or not, that thought did occur to us."

"What did you decide?"

"Too early to tell."

"And what about Gabriel Mahalona? Where does he fit in?"

"You just worry about your friend," he cautioned.

"That's what I am doing, Captain," I said, letting my anger show. "I worry that he was killed solely because of his connection with the Kaheiki family. But for that, he'd still be alive today. Now, is that an unreasonable anxiety?"

"Frankly, yes."

"I don't think so."

"You're not a cop."

"Oh, I see. You're speaking as a policeman. I thought you might be speaking as a friend of Jimmy Kaheiki."

"What's that supposed to mean?" he demanded.

"Can you deny you've done favors for him?"

He squared up to me. "You'd better watch that mouth of yours."

"All I'm repeating is what I heard. A little bird told me that when Nick Kaheiki was brought in here on an assault charge, his father used his influence with a certain person to get the charge dropped."

"That's what a little bird told you, is it?"

"Yes, Captain."

"Then let me tell you something about ornithology," he said, his face inches away from mine. "Know what happens to little birds on this island? They get gobbled up by much bigger ones."

Thinking that he was on the point of hitting me, I got ready to defend myself but the blow never came. Instead, the telephone rang. He snatched it up, listened to a short message then put it down again.

"Scram!" he told me. "The chauffeur's arrived."

I moved to the door. "Goodbye, Captain."

"Just get your ass out of here!"

The jibe was irresistible. "Shall I give your regards to Jimmy Kaheiki?" I asked. He went puce with rage. "Perhaps not, then."

◇◇◇

The stretch limo was ridiculously large for one person. I had the same chauffeur as before. His name was Tony, a short, beefy man in a neat black uniform and cap. He looked like a native Hawaiian. As we purred along, I talked to the back of his neck.

"Doesn't Mr. Kaheiki possess any smaller cars?"

"Yes, sir."

"Then why not come in one of those?"

"I got my orders, sir."

"Your employer likes to impress people, doesn't he?"

"I wouldn't know about that, sir."

His tone of voice told me that I was up against a loyalty barrier that I was not going to breach in the course of a single car journey so I settled back in my seat to make use of some valuable thinking time. What was I going to say to Donald's fiancée? Zann would be in a fragile state and one wrong word from me could cause her unnecessary pain. I could hardly tell her about the photograph of Heidi Dukelow. It still shocked me that Donald should be carrying it around in his billfold at such a time. Had he intended to take it on his honeymoon? Its existence cast a real shadow over the prospects of a happy third marriage.

It brought home to me once more that I didn't really know Donald all that well. Heidi had given me a verbal portrait of him, and his mother had added some brush strokes of her own, but his essential character was still not entirely clear to me. Why bring one wife to the wedding of another? Was it merely to placate his mother or was there another reason? While one woman was panting to share her life with him, another was secreted in his billfold. Heidi claimed that she and Donald were best friends. Where did that leave Zann Kaheiki? I began to wonder if the Prince of Play-offs was living up to his reputation.

He was playing one wife off against another.

Grace Kaheiki was waiting for me as I got out of the limo. Giving me a warm hug of welcome, she ushered me into the hallway.

"Thank you so much for coming," she said, squeezing my hand. "Zann is over the worst now. At least, I hope so. She just wanted to speak to you in person. I think it might help."

"Then I'm happy to be here. How is she now?"

"Much quieter. The tears are over. Zann is brooding."

"Where is she?"

"In her room. I'll take you up."

As I followed her up the stairs, I realized what a privileged position I was in. Melissa, a member of the family, had actually been kept away from the house. She was not needed, whereas I was. Seeing the upstairs of the building did not endear me to the architect. Though it was beautifully decorated and furnished, there was the same air of improvisation about the layout of rooms. Grace took me to the end of a long corridor and knocked on a door before opening it. We both went in.

Suzanne Kaheiki was curled up on the bed like a child who'd been reading a book. Wearing a bathrobe with a flowered pattern, she looked smaller and younger than I remembered her. The vitality seemed to have been drained out of her, leaving her subdued and listless. Her only form of greeting was a pale smile. Grace studied her.

"Is this a good time, darling?" she inquired.

"Yes, Mom," whispered Zann. "Hello, Alan."

"Hello," I replied.

"Take a seat."

"Please do," said Grace, grabbing an upright chair and moving it close to the bed. "Can I get you anything, Zann? A drink, maybe?" Zann shook her head. Grace turned to me. "What about you, Alan?"

"No, thank you," I said, sitting down.

"Not even a glass of wine?"

"Later, perhaps."

There was nothing I could have enjoyed more at that moment than a glass of wine but I'd have felt uncomfortable drinking it with Zann there. My job was to offer sympathy to her, not to slake my thirst. Grace stayed long enough to make sure that her daughter was able to cope, then she slipped out. We were left alone in the bedroom. Like everything else that the Kaheiki family owned, it was distinguished by its size. I could have parked the stretch limo in there and still had plenty of space for the king-size bed, the dressing table and the cane furniture. A padded door gave access to the en suite bathroom. My guess was that the bath would be the size of a small swimming pool.

Mahalona-style. No rust, no rot, no leaks, no lining.

"It was good of you to come, Alan," said Zann, quietly.

"I'm pleased that you're up to seeing me."

"I couldn't have done so this morning. I just blanked out."

"That's understandable."

"I felt as if I'd been hit between the eyes by a baseball bat. I just couldn't think straight. And the *pain*—it was excruciating." She tried to pull herself together. "But I mustn't think only of myself. How is Donald's mother taking it? And Heidi? They must be in despair as well."

"They are, Zann. Old Mrs. Dukelow had to be given a sedative."

"Oh dear!"

"She's much better now. She felt able to talk to me earlier."

"But how do *you* feel? I mean, you were the one who found him."

"I'm still rather shell-shocked," I admitted.

"Then I won't keep you too long. I just wanted to know what happened. Not this morning," she added, quickly. "I don't think I could bear to hear the details of what you actually saw in his room. Last night. That's what I want you to tell me about. Donald was so looking forward to having a meal and spending some quality time with you."

"Any time with Donald was quality time," I said, honestly.

Her eyes moistened. "That's so true, Alan."

"And everything started off so well last night."

Speaking slowly, I kept it simple. I told her about the meal, the rude interruption from the apparently drunken man, and our rescue. Without mentioning the hula dancers, I talked about the nightclub and the difficulty I later had putting Donald to bed. Zann hung on every word that I uttered. When I finished the questions came thick and fast.

"Did he talk about me?" she asked.

"All the time."

"What did he say?"

"How much he loved you."

"Was he looking forward to the wedding?"

"He was counting the days, Zann," I said. "No groom was more anxious to rush down the aisle. Except that there wasn't an aisle in this case, was there?"

Her face crumpled. "Did he tell you where it would be?"

"No, no. He refused to let me in on the secret."

"We agreed to say nothing until the very last minute."

"Somebody must have known," I suggested. "The man who was about to marry you, for instance. The caterers."

"Mom was doing the catering. We were going to take all the food with us—and everything else that was needed." She bit her lip. "Are you sure that Donald didn't give you a clue?"

"Not so much as the tiniest hint, I swear it."

"Then he kept his word," she said, relaxing. "I knew he would. Tell me what he really said about me, Alan. His exact words. How did he describe me?"

"Donald couldn't get over the fact that you'd agreed to share your life with him. The mere thought of it made him grin as if he was getting paid to do it. There was no doubt that he loved you. He was glowing with joy. His exact words?" I said. "Get a dictionary of synonyms and look up the word 'gorgeous.' I'm sure that that's what Donald did."

She almost laughed. "He was such a precious man. He used to say the most wonderful things to me. Most guys just want to make a move on you so they go into their usual routine. Not Donald. When we first met, he was practically tongue-tied. I had to take the initiative."

"Lucky man!"

She reached for the framed photograph of him that stood on her bedside table, gazing at it lovingly as pleasant memories came rushing back. I noted the stark contrast. While Donald watched over her bed from a silver frame, it was not Zann who was concealed in billfold. As she spoke, she hugged the photograph to her breast.

"I was doing a presentation at a hotel in Houston. Donald was staying there while he played in a golf tournament. He drifted into the conference room by mistake and heard me speak. So he stayed."

"Who can blame him?"

"The funny thing was," she went on, brightening as she did so, "that I didn't recognize him at first. He looked vaguely familiar but I couldn't put a name to a face. So, of course, I assumed he was a potential client. Afterwards, as the session was breaking up, I sidled over and went into my sales pitch."

"You didn't need to sell yourself to Donald, I can tell you."

Tears welled up in her eyes. She reached for a tissue in the box on the bedside table but she didn't use it. Instead, she went off into a private reverie about her love affair with Donald, looking at the photograph of him once more. It was a few minutes before she shook herself out of her daydream. Zann was contrite.

"Oh, I'm so sorry," she said. "That was very selfish of me."

"At a time like this, you're entitled to be selfish."

"Donald has left me so many terrific memories."

"Cherish them," I counseled. "But why did everything have to be so secretive? You and Donald had so much to celebrate. Why not do it in the eyes of the world?"

"If only we could have!" she sighed, setting the photograph back on the bedside table. "It was never an option, I'm afraid. When I was getting to know Donald, I didn't dare to mention his existence to my family. They'd have been horrified."

"Because he was a *haole?*"

"That was the root of it, Alan. When you throw in the fact that Donald was still married, had a very shaky record as a husband, and was much older than me, you can see what we were up against. With all my experience at selling, I couldn't market a product like that. So," she confided with a shrug, "we had to do everything in the strictest secrecy. Secret meetings, secret phone calls, secret letters, secret e-mails. It made it so much more exciting somehow."

"And it also became a habit."

"It did, Alan. Even after his divorce, Donald and I went on having furtive weekends in quiet hotels while I worked out how to break it to Mom and Dad." She became somber. "The last time I took someone home and introduced him as the man in my life, my family held up their hands in horror. My father didn't spare my blushes. He told me straight out why I should split up with Mark. How could I even consider marrying a damn *haole* who was fifteen years older than me?"

"I can see why you kept Donald under wraps."

"I had to bide my time."

"So did he," I noted. "Having met his mother, I understand why he couldn't just roll up on her doorstep with you on his arm. Her objections would have been loudly voiced."

"I was too young and too Hawaiian."

"Yet you won her over when she actually met you."

Hope flowered in her face. "Is that what she said?"

"Yes, Zann. You overcame her objections."

"Donald didn't manage to do that," she recalled, sadly. "When he told his mother about me, they had a ferocious row. Mrs. Dukelow can be very forthright."

"Oh, I can vouch for that," I said with feeling.

I could also vouch for the fact that it was Heidi—and not Donald—who took on the awesome task of explaining to the old woman that her son was about to marry someone she would deem entirely unsuitable. It would have been cruel to disillusion Zann so I held my peace. She was entitled to memories in which Heidi Dukelow had absolutely no part. It was the least I could do for her.

"I'm still in the dark, you know," I pointed out.

"About what?"

"Where this wedding was going to be. Donald told me you'd gone for something romantic but corny." She nodded. "You don't have to tell me, if you don't want to, Zann."

"I've no reason to hide it any more," she said, wistfully. "Oddly enough, it was Nick who gave me the idea."

"Nick? I didn't have your brother down as the romantic type."

"Oh, he didn't suggest it himself. Nick wasn't altogether happy about my choice of husband. He tried to talk me out of it. No," she went on, "it was his helicopter. He has a pilot's license, you see, and flies off to Kauai every weekend to see his wife and family."

"Really?" I said, pretending to be hearing the information for the first time. "So you wanted him to ferry the wedding party to Kauai."

"No, Alan. There's a tiny island, much closer than that. No more than an atoll, really. Completely uninhabited. My father got permission for us to use it for the ceremony. Donald and I would have been the first and only couple to get married there." She gave her dazzling smile. "That seemed so romantic to us."

"It was also very private."

"That was part of its appeal."

"Why?" I wondered. "You had no cause to keep it so secret."

"It was what we wanted."

"You and Donald?"

"Mom and Dad went along with the idea as well."

I could guess why. Since he was patently under attack from an unseen enemy, Jimmy Kaheiki would not have been eager to see his daughter married in a lavish ceremony that was bound to attract intense media attention. It might also attract sabotage. What better way to embarrass him than by somehow wrecking the wedding of his most valuable piece of property—his favorite daughter? As it was, details of the secret wedding had been leaked. By removing Donald Dukelow, someone had made sure that the event would never take place.

I tried to wrest some more details from the distraught bride.

"You say that your brother tried to talk you out of it?"

"Yes, Alan."

"How did he do that?"

"Oh, he just kept pestering me," she said, clicking her tongue. "Nick told me that I'd be letting everyone down. It was one thing to have a relationship with Donald—that would soon burn itself out, he said. But to *marry* him, to make the ultimate commitment, to link his name to the Kaheiki family—that was unacceptable."

"But you nevertheless went ahead?"

"Of course."

"How did your brother react to that?"

Zann was about to answer when the door opened and her mother came bustling in to see how we were getting on. Grace Kaheiki's sudden arrival gave the game away. She'd been listening to everything that was said, making sure that Zann divulged nothing too revealing about the inner workings of the family. There was muted anger in her eyes. My visit was over. In probing for information, I'd brought it to an abrupt end.

"Thank you for coming, Alan," said Zann, touching my arm.

"If you need to talk to me again, you know where I am."

"Can we offer you some refreshment before you go?" asked Grace.

"That's very kind of you," I replied, "but I'd better be getting back. Could the chauffeur run me to the hotel, please?"

"Oh, we can do better than that. Nick will take you."

I was caught off guard. "Nick?"

"Yes, Alan—he insists."

Instead of the stretch limo, I was to return in a gleaming Maserati. It was going to be an uncomfortable journey. The moment I got into the car, I could sense my chauffeur's hostility. Without even glancing at me, he gunned the engine and we shot off. Nick Kaheiki liked speed. He raced through the estate as if we were on a Grand Prix circuit and I offered up a silent prayer of thanks to the man who'd invented car safety belts. When we surged through the gates to join the main road, the Maserati slowed as

Nick began to take notice of speed limits and the presence of other vehicles. It made conversation possible.

"What did you say to Zann?" he asked.

"Your sister did most of the talking."

"This has hurt her bad. I hope you said nothing to upset her."

"I did my best not to, Nick."

"Zann is very precious to me," he warned. "She's my sister."

"So is Melissa."

"We're not talking about her."

Seeing a chance to overtake a large truck, he jabbed his foot down on the accelerator and we leapt forward. He didn't need to ask about my visit to Zann. I was certain that he'd heard every word that was spoken between us. Nick had probably told his mother when to interrupt us. Once past the truck, he reduced speed again. After festering in silence for a minute or so, he glanced across at me.

"Don't get too interested in our family, will you?"

"What do you mean?"

"You've been asking too many questions about us."

"Ah," I said. "You've obviously spoken to Captain Rapoza."

"Things always get back to us in the end."

"I never doubted it for a second."

"So who fed you all that stuff about us?" he demanded. "Melissa?"

"No," I replied, determined to protect her. "All that your sister is interested in talking about is the Pineapple Theater. You ought to go along there some time. Those women put on quite a show."

"Only they're not the kind of women I like—and it's certainly not the sort of show I'd want to watch. All that urgent breast-beating from a gaggle of dykes. Give me a break, will you?"

"So much for family solidarity!"

"You don't know the first thing about us," he snarled.

"I know that you never go to your sister's theater. Melissa said that you'd be too restless. Pity. If I had a sister with talent like that, I'd be proud of her—whatever her sexual orientation."

"Let's forget Melissa."

"You brought her name up."

"If it wasn't her," he said, shooting me another look, "who told you about the problems we been having?"

"I never reveal my sources."

"I want to know."

"Then you're in for a disappointment, I'm afraid. I picked up a snippet here, a snippet there and a snippet somewhere else. String them all together and it seems that your family is virtually under siege."

"That's not true."

"No?" I retorted. "Then why this sequence of crimes?"

"They may not be connected."

"It looks like it to me, Nick, and I have more than a passing interest here. Did Captain Rapoza tell you what was left in my bathroom? A meat skewer. Just like the one that Donald somehow acquired. It's not the kind of souvenir I envisaged when I came to Oahu."

"You'll be safe now. Hotel security has been tightened."

"I'll believe it when I see it."

"Stay in your room and nothing will happen to you."

"Is that suggestion or a command?"

"Take it any way you wish," he said, crisply.

For the next couple of miles, there was a bruised silence. I was glad that I hadn't given Melissa away. She was strong enough to stand up to her brother but I didn't want to land her in trouble with her father. Nick's gaze kept flicking to the rear-view mirror.

"Somebody following us?" I asked.

"Why should they?"

"You tell me. I know you had someone on your tail when you drove Heidi back from your factory."

"She was mistaken about that."

"Heidi's not the kind of lady that makes mistakes."

He sniggered. "She married Donald Duck, didn't she?"

"His name was Dukelow," I said, firmly, "and I won't have anyone making fun of him. Thanks to his unfortunate connection with your family, he was murdered. You ought to feel guilty about that. But if you want to talk about marriage," I went on, wanting to strike back, "why not touch on the one you forgot to mention to Heidi—your own."

"Shut up!" he ordered.

"Then you stop sneering at my friend."

"You're just asking for trouble, aren't you?"

"All I want is to see the killer caught and convicted."

"You think that we don't?"

"Of course not," I said, turning to him. "In case you hadn't noticed, that puts us on the same side. So why don't we help each other?"

"That's not the way it works."

"You've got your own methods, I suppose."

"Yes."

"So do I. They're called survival skills."

"Upset the wrong people and you're going to need them."

"The wrong people?" I echoed. "Your father? Captain Rapoza? Or are those two names interchangeable? Upset one and I upset both. They're as thick as thieves, aren't they?"

"Clay Rapoza is a family friend."

"Nothing more?"

"Nothing more," he repeated with emphasis.

They were the last words he uttered for the rest of the journey.

Officer Broderick had been replaced by a black policeman who stood outside the scene of the crime with arms folded and legs apart. As I walked past him, I gave him a friendly nod. Face impassive, he nodded back then checked his watch. My movements in and out of my room were being timed. That unsettled me. There were no unpleasant surprises waiting for me on this occasion. Someone had come in to turn down the bed but that was the only visible change in the room. The windows were still locked, the balcony empty. I felt secure.

My attention went straight to the desk. Sealed in an envelope was a nude photograph of Heidi Dukelow and I felt a strong urge to look at it again. Studying it while Emily Tenno was standing beside me had prevented me from appreciating its finer points and searching for clues as to when and where it had been taken. I'd not even turned it over to see if anything was written on it. I opened the drawer and stared at the envelope, questioning my motive. Curiosity or prurience? What was impelling me to look? Did I really think it might reveal something that was relevant to the investigation or was I merely in search of a cheap voyeuristic thrill?

Deciding that it might be both, I closed the drawer again. Someone rapped on my door. When I looked through the spy-hole, I was shaken to see that it was the very woman I'd just been thinking about. I felt a blush reddening my cheeks. Heidi knocked on the door again. I took a moment to compose myself. Opening the door, I gave her a welcoming smile.

"Hello, Alan," she said. "Mind if I come in?"

"Of course," I replied, standing aside so that she could walk past me. "Your timing is perfect. I've only just got back."

"That's what Officer Regan told me."

"Who?"

"The man on duty outside Donald's room. I asked him to let me know when you returned to your room." I closed the door. "It's okay. Cora knows I'm here. In fact, it was her idea that I should come. She wants some time on her own."

"That's only natural. As you know," I said, "I spoke to her earlier and I was astonished at the way she held up. She must have wonderful powers of recovery."

"Oh, Cora has hidden depths."

Heidi was standing with her back to the desk in which the photograph was kept. I was finding it difficult to meet her gaze when I really wanted to run my eyes over her body. She sensed my unease.

"Is something wrong, Alan?"

"No, no. Nothing at all."

"You seem uncomfortable."

"I've just got back from an unpleasant ride with Nick Kaheiki."

"What were you doing with him?"

"It's a long story."

"I'd like to hear it," she said with interest, "however long. Listen, let me tell you why I came. I don't know about you but I'm starving. I've hardly touched a thing since this morning. I guess you must be in the same boat."

"I am," I confessed. "Very hungry and very thirsty."

"Shall we grab a bite to eat?"

"Yes, please."

"Where shall we go? They've got three restaurants here."

"But they'll all be filled with other hotel guests," I protested. "Many of them will have seen me on TV this evening or picked up the rumors about the crime. They'll know. It'll be like eating in a goldfish bowl."

"We could always slip out somewhere, I suppose."

"Perhaps not, Heidi."

"What's the problem?"

"In a nutshell—fear. After what happened last night, I've rather gone off the restaurants of Honolulu."

"That fixes it," she said. "We eat here."

It was exactly what I hoped she'd say and yet I was still hesitant. The existence of that photograph was a stumbling block. If I said nothing about it, I'd be keeping her there under false pretences yet, if I gave it to her, Heidi might be overcome with embarrassment and disappear. She mistook my lack of enthusiasm for something else.

"Sorry. That was presumptuous of me. I can't just barge in here and take over like that." She raised both palms. "Forgive me, Alan. I was only trying to be sociable."

"I'd love to eat here with you," I said, "but there's something you should know first of all. Sergeant Tenno called here earlier on."

"Yes, she introduced herself to us when she returned Donald's billfold to Cora. I liked her. She struck me as a very capable woman."

"Capable and discreet."

"I'm not with you."

"There was something in that billfold that she thought might upset Donald's mother. She discussed it with me and we decided that it might be best if we removed it." I cleared my throat. "It was a photo of you, Heidi. A rather special one."

Coloring slightly, she put a hand to her mouth to stifle a gasp.

"Where is it now?" she murmured.

"In the drawer behind you," I said. "In an envelope. Sergeant Tenno asked me to return it to you in private." Heidi turned round, opened the drawer and took out the envelope. "And before you ask, it wasn't passed around at police headquarters for the men to look at. Sergeant Tenno made sure of that."

Gratitude in her eyes, Heidi turned back to face me. All discomfort had faded away. Slipping the envelope into her purse, she gave me a warm smile.

"Let's look at the room service menu, shall we?" she said.

Chapter Ten

We both made quick decisions about the food and agreed on a bottle of Californian white wine to wash it down. When I'd rung through our order, I opened the drink cabinet for a much-needed aperitif. Heidi asked for vodka and tonic but I preferred a stiff whisky. Flopping down on the sofa, we clinked our glasses then took a first long, slow, satisfying sip.

"I needed that," I said.

"It's been one hell of a day for you."

"And for you, Heidi. As well as coping with your own grief, you had to prop up Mrs. Dukelow. That must've taken some doing."

"It's not the first time we had to console each other."

"Your divorce?"

She gave a nod. "Let's talk about something else."

"That's fine by me," I said, still savoring the restorative taste of the whisky. "Tell me about your work as a lawyer."

"I'd bore you to death."

"You could never do that. Go on. I'm interested. What drew you to the law in the first place? Someone in the family?"

"No, Alan," she confessed. "It was the realization that I'd never make it in the profession that really appealed to me. Looking back, it was a crazy ambition for a twelve-year-old kid but I had the fire of youth inside me in those days."

"What did you want to be?"

"Promise you won't laugh?"

"Cross my heart."

"An opera singer."

"What's wrong with that?"

"An insurmountable handicap—I'm tone deaf."

"That doesn't seem to hold back pop singers," I said, cheerfully. "Perhaps you should have gone down-market. Formed your own group. Heidi and the Hurricanes—yes, that has a ring to it."

"It was opera or nothing, Alan," she explained. "In going to law school, I settled for second best. Mind you, there were compensations. I might not get to perform at the Met in New York but at least I knew that I'd have a regular income."

"And there's always the bath. I sing arias in there all the time."

"Tenor or baritone?"

"A horrible mixture of both, I'm afraid."

She grinned. "Then you're in my league. I'm a kind of occasional mezzo-soprano. Occasionally—just occasionally—I hit the right note."

"What branch of the law are you involved in?"

"The worst kind—contract law."

"Dull?"

"Quite the opposite," she said. "I deal with partnerships that have come unstuck. It gives you a terrible insight into human depravity. You wouldn't believe some of the things that one partner will do to another. It's a case of Nature red in tooth and claw. It makes me cringe sometimes. But it's a job."

"And it will do until you get that offer from La Scala."

"Why—are they looking for a program seller?"

We traded a smile and sipped our drinks. It was the first time since I'd spoken to Melissa Kaheiki that I felt able to relax. Heidi seemed to be happy with the situation as well. There was a definite *frisson* between us. She acknowledged it with a twitch of an eyebrow. Then she remembered something.

"How come you met up with Nick again?"

"He gave me a lift back from the house."

She was astonished. "You mean, you went out there this evening?"

"I had no choice, Heidi," I told her. "I was summoned. They even sent the limo. Zann was anxious to talk to me."

I gave her an abbreviated account of what had happened to me since we'd last met, excising all mention of my chat with Melissa or my discovery of the meat skewer in my bathroom. When I talked about my appearance on television, Heidi said that she and Cora Dukelow had watched it and thought I did extremely well, even though I looked so tired and harassed. After I told her about the arrangements for the secret wedding, she seized on one detail.

"Did you say that Nick was *married?*"

"That's what he uses the helicopter for," I told her. "To fly back to Kauai at the weekends. The rest of the time, his wife doesn't exist."

"You don't need to tell me that."

"A lot of women would be pulled by that Maserati of his."

"Well, I'm not one of them, Alan. That guy is a sleaze-ball."

"Yet he might've ended up as Donald's brother-in-law."

"Yes, Donald has been spared that fate. But I'm glad that Zann felt able to see you," she said. "That's a healthy sign. I was afraid she'd just shut herself away. I'm sure that your visit gave her some comfort."

"I hope so."

Room service arrived. It was wheeled in on a trolley whose sides opened up to form a table. The wine was in an ice bucket. After signing for the meal, I slipped the waiter a couple of dollars and sent him on his way. We sat either side of the trolley on upright chairs and examined what we'd ordered. The aroma was enticing. Uncorking the wine, I filled the two glasses, then addressed myself to the food. Heidi was as ravenous as I was. Whisky on an empty stomach had not been a wise choice for me. My steak was. Every bite was joyous sensation.

We talked about everything but the circumstances that had brought us together. Heidi asked about the golf course I'd helped to design in San Diego and I wanted to know more about her family background. She was an ideal dinner guest. Though we'd only met a couple of days ago, I was totally at ease with her. It was like having a first date with someone I felt I'd known for years. All the excitement of novelty tempered with a sense of familiarity. It was only when the meal was over that Heidi brought us back to cold reality.

"Thank you, Alan," she said, setting her napkin aside.

"I should thank you for suggesting it. I was famished."

"I wasn't talking about the meal."

"Oh."

"Thanks for not even asking about the photograph."

"Why should I?"

"Because you must have been shocked to find it where it was."

"It's none of my business, Heidi," I assured her. "Besides, I didn't actually find it. Sergeant Tenno did that. Another detective might simply have left it in the billfold and handed it back to Mrs. Dukelow. That could have been disconcerting for both of you."

"Disastrous!"

"I'm glad you were spared that."

"Me, too."

"And I'm glad that Donald's mother was spared it as well. I'm not quite sure what she'd have made of it."

"Look," she said, quietly, "do you think could we move to somewhere more comfortable? I feel that I owe you an explanation but I don't really want to give it across the remains of dinner like this." She rose to her feet. "Do you mind?"

"No, no," I said. "But you owe me nothing, believe me."

I got up and moved the trolley over to the door. There was still some wine left in the bottle so I shared it between the two glasses then took them across to her. Handing a glass to Heidi, I sat beside her on the sofa. She had another sip before speaking.

"That photograph was taken some time ago," she said.

"I'd never have guessed."

"Donald had bought this Polaroid camera and he caught me as I was getting out of bed. Well, you must have seen the look of surprise on my face."

"I only had the merest glance at the photo, Heidi."

"What I'm trying to say is that I didn't pose for it."

"It wouldn't matter if you did," I said. "I daresay that most husbands get an impulse to take a nude picture of their wife at some stage. I know that I did. Rosemary had such a marvelous body."

"Did she let you photograph her?"

"She did, actually," I recalled. "On our first wedding anniversary. After two bottles of champagne, even her famous reserve had wilted a bit. So I pointed the Polaroid at her while I had the opportunity."

"Did you keep the photograph?"

"There was no possibility of that, Heidi."

"Why not?"

"Because Rosemary destroyed it with a vengeance," I said. "After we'd celebrated our anniversary in the traditional way, she was overcome with an attack of post-coital virginity. She not only tore the photograph up and called me rude names for taking it. Rosemary then set fire to the bits before flushing the ashes down the toilet. I never saw that Polaroid camera again. She must've thrown it out."

"Our relationship was very different."

"Heidi, you don't have to tell me this."

"I think that I do," she said, quietly. "I just hope that it won't change your good opinion of me. I'd hate to lose that, Alan."

"No chance."

"You haven't heard what I'm going to say yet."

"After what I've been through today, nothing on God's earth is going to faze me. I don't care if you were a stripper in Las Vegas or posed for girlie magazines to pay your way through law school." I beamed at her. "I'm quite unshockable."

"We'll see." She sipped her wine. "When that photograph was taken, Donald was still living with Esmeralda." My jaw dropped. "You see, you *can* still be surprised."

"He and Esmeralda always seemed so, well...so *involved.*"

"This wasn't long before he broke up with her. We spent the weekend together." She looked at me quizzically. "You ever make love to your wife after the divorce?"

"To Rosemary?" I said in disbelief. "We hardly ever made love while we were *married.* Not after our daughter was born, anyway. Since the divorce, Rosemary would never even think of it—she'd rather stick hot needles in her eyes than go to bed with me again. I was the Filthy Beast with the Polaroid Camera, remember. No disrespect to Mrs. Dukelow, but I'd stand a better chance with her."

She was amused by the notion. "You might at that," she said with a laugh. "Cora hasn't given up altogether on passion, I assure you. She has a gentleman admirer."

"Really?"

"He's been around for some years."

"Did Donald know about it?"

"Of course not. He'd have disapproved."

"Why? Is she in love with some twenty-year-old Hawaiian surfer?"

"No, he's from Boston and very age-appropriate. However," she went on, "we're not talking about her. We're talking about Donald's inability to make a decision and stick by it."

"His endless quest for difference."

"That's why he went off with Esmeralda. Her problem was that the things that made her so different eventually became hideously familiar. Whereas I, who'd vanished from his life for a while, was suddenly different again. He rang me, we talked, we were drawn together." She put her glass on the coffee table. "I wasn't trying to get my revenge on the woman who'd replaced me, Alan. I did it because I still loved him."

"Did you hope to get back together again?"

"I wasn't that stupid."

"How did you feel when he married again?"

"It was exactly what I'd expected. Janine was right for him so he went for her. I had no quarrel with that. Inevitably, of course, the frost got into that little set-up as well."

"So Donald turned to you again."

"He never stopped turning to me, Alan. That's what I mean about going down in your estimation. The simple truth is that, after that first weekend when he took the photograph of me, there were others. Or, to put it another way," she said, watching my reaction, "I became his mistress. From time to time, anyway."

"I see," I said, doing my utmost not to show my disappointment. "Donald was obviously a dark horse."

"It wasn't always easy to meet up when he was on the road so much. Ironic, isn't it?" she said with a hollow laugh. "The dispossessed wife turns into the Other Woman. Not that I saw it that way at the time. I just had this bond with Donald that nothing could break."

"Not even his marriage to Zann?"

"Whose photograph did he have in his billfold?"

"Yours."

"Donald used to call me his emotional insurance policy."

"That wasn't very flattering."

"He thought it was. In times of crisis, he said, I always paid out. As for this latest romance, he'd probably have given me a call one day."

"Supposing he didn't?"

"Then I'd have been thrilled that he was happy at last."

"Even if it was with someone else?"

"I told you. I loved him."

"Enough to see him happily married to Zann?"

"More than enough."

"Supposing things hadn't worked out for them?" I asked. "If Donald had got in touch with you again, what would you have done?"

She gave a shrug. "We'll never know."

Heidi was right. I was deeply shocked. Mrs. Dukelow believed that Heidi was there for her benefit whereas, in fact, it was Donald who needed his first wife beside him. My sympathy went out to Zann Kaheiki. She would have married a man who seemed programmed to betray her. I began to see why he was so confused during our meal together, wrestling with the competing demands of a new wife and an old mistress, wondering if he really could be faithful to a woman at long last. What surprised me about Heidi was that she'd settled for so little. All she had was a tiny piece of Donald Dukelow.

"I didn't just sit by the phone and wait," she explained. "I had a busy life of my own—and it didn't involve a vow of chastity."

"But you never found a man like Donald."

"He doesn't exist."

I was forced to readjust my view of Donald Dukelow completely. Having put him down as a serial monogamist—and a hopeless romantic, to boot—I had to factor in the information that he promoted his first wife to the status of best friend so that he could sleep with her whenever his current relationship was starting to falter. My problem was that I'd liked the other women in his life and I was particularly fond of Zann. They deserved better.

"Would you like me to go?" asked Heidi.

"Why should I do that?"

"I can see that I've disgusted you."

"Not at all," I said, raising a hand. "I'm just bemused, that's all. I always thought of Donald as the Invisible Man. He's starting to taking on a more definite shape now." I looked down at her left hand. "Why did you wear a wedding ring the other night?"

"I'm still Mrs. Dukelow."

"What did Donald's mother say?"

"She was all for it.

"Didn't she see it as a provocative gesture?"

"It gave us both some comfort."

"Why did you need any comfort?" I challenged. "A moment ago, you said you'd be delighted if he could be happy with someone at last. Yet you felt the urge to remind yourself that you'd once been married to him. You can't have it both ways, Heidi."

"I discovered that. Halfway through the meal, I took it off."

"I didn't notice."

"You were too busy looking at Zann—she was the star attraction."

"Not to me."

The compliment slipped out involuntarily. It was weird. After what she'd told me, I was both repelled and attracted by Heidi. She'd conspired with Donald to deceive three women who adored him enough to share their lives with him Then there was his mother, another victim of gross deception. Heidi had no right to be sitting at a table with Zann Kaheiki and wearing a wedding ring given to her by Donald. Yet, even as I saw her in an unfavorable new light, I was strangely aroused by her, curious, tempted, filled with something that went beyond mere desire. I kept thinking about the photograph in her purse.

"Right," I said, putting my drink down, "now that you've explained the real reason why *you're* here, perhaps you can tell me why I was invited to Hawaii?"

"You already know, Alan. It was because of me."

"I don't believe that."

"Donald knew that we'd get on and—as I think you found out at Ko Olina—I do have a genuine love of golf. We needed a man, you see. So why not pick one that I'd always wanted to meet—Alan Saxon?" She saw my consternation. "Don't you understand? You were another of Donald's insurance policies. With you around, he'd have obligations. He wouldn't be able to give me sidelong glances. Did you never ask yourself why I chose to share a room with Cora?"

"I never dreamed that it was to keep out of harm's way."

"I *wanted* it to work this time," she said with obvious sincerity. "I really did. Much as I loved him, I couldn't bear the thought of

Donald knocking on the door of my hotel room days before he was about to marry someone else. That's not what I came for."

I was hurt. "And there was I, thinking I was here as his friend."

"You *were*, Alan."

"No," I said, angrily, "I was just wheeled in as a diversion for you and a safety device for Donald. No wonder he called me his bodyguard. Only it wasn't *his* body that I was guarding—it was yours."

"I can see that I shouldn't have come here this evening."

"I'm glad you did. I'd rather know the truth."

She put a hand on my arm. "Then the truth is that you're the only person who's kept me sane on this trip," she said. "Frankly, it's been an ordeal for me—playing at nursemaid with Cora, pretending that I'd got over Donald long ago. I thought that I could manage it but I couldn't."

"Everything seemed fine on the surface."

"Well, it certainly wasn't underneath."

"You put yourself in an impossible situation, Heidi."

"I paid for it, I can tell you. Without you there, I'd have gone crazy."

"Me?" I said, bewildered. "What did I do?"

"I'll tell you afterward."

We both knew that it was a mistake but that didn't stop us. We started on the sofa, rolled to the floor and ended up on the bed. Clothing was scattered everywhere. I'd like to say that we were driven by a mutual desire to do something life-affirming in the wake of Donald's death, but that would dignify it with an excuse it didn't merit. For my part, it was a combination of lust, weakness, and sheer desperation, a release from all the pressures that I'd been under, an irresistible means to escape.

The photograph hadn't misled me. Heidi was every bit as gorgeous when naked as I'd already seen. Her skin felt like silk, her nipples tasted like honey and her fragrance was captivating. Under more propitious circumstances, we'd have had a night to remember. Instead, it was all over in a matter of minutes, rushed, clumsy, ridiculously over-eager. We were like sex-starved teenagers in the back of a car, groping and slobbering, grabbing each other wildly when soft caresses were needed, missing all the preliminaries, threshing about as if our lives depended on it, racing each other to the moment of ecstasy. Panting for breath and covered in sweat, we eventually rolled away from each other.

Without saying a word, Heidi got up, retrieved her clothing and went into the bathroom. I heard the shower being switched on. Overcome with sudden remorse, I also discovered a modesty that I hoped I'd lost decades ago. It was absurd. Though I'd just made love to a beautiful woman, I somehow didn't want her to see me naked. Gathering up my things, I dressed with my back to the bathroom in case she should come in. I was doing up my shoelaces when the shower was switched off.

There was still some wine left in my glass. I drank it gratefully and tried to work out what I was going to say when she emerged. What was the appropriate behavior when you'd just been to bed with the first wife of a murdered friend? How was I to control my embarrassment? Was an apology in order or should I expect one from her? The truth of it was that we were both one hundred per cent volunteers. Any guilt was mutual. I didn't believe that Heidi came to my room for the express purpose of seducing me. She'd suggested that we go to one of the restaurants in the hotel. I now wished that I'd agreed.

By the time she reappeared, Heidi had recovered her poise.

"Sorry to keep you waiting, Alan."

"No problem," I muttered.

She indicated the bathroom. "All yours."

"Thanks."

I plunged in gratefully, as anxious as she'd been to wash the stain of what had happened off my body. Stripping swiftly, I let the water run cold at first so that it gave me a well-deserved jolt. Unlike Heidi, I reached for the shampoo as well, working it into my hair and massaging my scalp. I might not be able to cleanse my mind of self-reproach but I could at least get rid of all visible signs of our brief time in bed. As I dried and dressed myself, I rehearsed what I was going to say to her but it was a waste of time. I opened the door to find that Heidi had gone. She'd left me a souvenir. On the pillow of the bed in which we'd shared those few frantic minutes was an envelope that I thought I recognized.

Had I inherited the photograph that had once belonged to Donald?

Darting across to the bed, I snatched up the envelope and tore it open. The nude photograph, however, was not inside. In its place was a sheet of hotel stationery on which Heidi had written three words in capital letters.

IT NEVER HAPPENED.

Against all the odds, I slept extremely well that night. Choosing the other bed, I dozed off almost immediately. No regrets, no protracted agonizing and no nightmares. I not only awoke refreshed, I was able to think straight again. What the previous day had told me was that I was on my own. I could look for no help from the Kaheiki family—except, perhaps, from Melissa. Jimmy was suspicious of me and Nick had not even bothered to hide his enmity. As for the police, Captain Rapoza had unexplained loyalties that hampered his judgement. Emily Tenno might be more amenable but she was part of the system.

Cora Dukelow could offer me no practical assistance and, in spite of the fact that it never happened, Heidi and I would keep out of each other's way from now on. If I wanted answers to some of the questions that were plaguing me, I had to find them for myself. Locking myself in my hotel room would achieve nothing and I didn't want to be around in case someone delivered another meat skewer. Action was needed.

I made myself a black coffee then settled down with the Yellow Pages. The Kaheiki name was everywhere. Factories, supermarkets, gas stations, warehouses, timber yards, limousine hire, printing, travel, food imports and funeral services—they were involved in an endless array of commercial activities. I could never look into all of them or single out rivals who might have sufficient grudge against Jimmy Kaheiki to kill his designated son-in-law. My best bet was to begin with the man whose name had started us on the downward path—Gabriel Mahalona.

Thumbing to the section on manufacturers of swimming pools, I saw his half-page advertisement. The artwork was naive but eye-catching. Under the headline Pools of Paradise was a series of cartoons showing delighted families swimming in their different-sized pools. A speech balloon came out of the mouth of a boy who'd been snorkeling at the bottom of one pool—"It's true, Dad. No rust, no rot, no leaks, no lining. It must be a Mahalona product." I felt a stab of anguish. The man who had placed the advertisement was no longer alive to satisfy his customers.

But his wife would be. I needed to meet her. That was my starting-point. The problem was that I wanted to find her without anyone else knowing about it. It wasn't just Rapoza who had to be avoided. I was still wary of the person who'd followed us around the golf course. I had no intention of speaking to Mahalona's widow with a pair of binoculars trained on me. Going back to the directory, I looked up the number of the Pineapple Theater and rang it. It was still early but Melissa Kaheiki had told me to keep in touch. After a lengthy wait, I heard her gruff voice come on the line.

"I'm still in bed," she growled. "Who the hell is this?"

"Alan Saxon."

"Alan? What's wrong with you, man?"

"Nothing, Melissa—now that I hear your dulcet tones."

"It's only seven o'clock."

"I'm an early riser."

"Well, I'm fucking well not!" she howled.

"You are now."

"This had better be important, Alan. Why ring the theater?"

"I had an idea that you might live there."

"We *all* live here. That's what a cooperative is."

"You've obviously got the courage of your convictions."

"I've also got a headache," she said, yawning. "What do you want?"

"A very special favor."

"I don't do favors at this time of the morning."

"Not even for me?"

Fran Mahalona was not pleased to see a stranger riding up to her house on a motorcycle. Even when I'd removed the crash helmet, she was still very suspicious. She bore little resemblance to the happy wife and mother I'd seen in the photograph at police headquarters. Robbed of her husband and forced to bring up two small children alone, she had aged noticeably and lost weight. Deep lines were etched into her face. It took several minutes of patient explanation before she invited me into a house that was almost a mansion. She took me into the kitchen at the rear of the building. Through the window, I could see the swimming pool at the bottom of the garden. It was empty and forlorn.

"I don't see how I can help you, Mr. Saxon," she said.

"Tell me about your husband."

"They killed him. What else is there to say?"

"A lot, Mrs. Mahalona," I argued. "He loved his family. I saw a snapshot of the four of you. Gabriel looked so contented."

She sighed wistfully. "Yes, he was. Everything was going well. The company was making a healthy profit and we'd not long moved in here," she said, gesturing with both hands. "It was the place we'd always wanted. Gabe had so much to live for, Mr. Saxon. He was negotiating the take-over of another firm. That would have made him one of the biggest independent manufacturers in the whole of Hawaii. Then suddenly," she went on, snapping her fingers, "it was all gone. Gabe was murdered in his own pool."

"I'm so sorry for you."

"We'll never get over it—never!"

"Do you know why he was killed?"

"No, Mr. Saxon. I just can't understand it."

"Did he have any enemies?"

"None that I knew of. Gabe was such a friendly man."

"He must have had rivals."

"Yes, but they don't do *that* sort of thing."

"What do the police think?"

"That he must have upset someone who bore a grudge," she said. "They made two arrests but the suspects were released without charge. They tell me it's an on-going investigation but I'm losing heart. I don't think they'll ever find the killer."

"Don't give up hope, Mrs. Mahalona."

"Captain Rapoza fears that he may not be on the island."

"Rapoza? Was he in charge?"

"Yes," she said. "He's been very considerate to me. I was away with the children when it happened, you see, so it was days before the body was discovered. That would have given the killer plenty of time to disappear from Oahu."

"Oh, I have a feeling that he may still be around."

"Why do you say that?"

"Because there's a similarity between your husband's death and the case in which I'm involved. The murder weapon was identical."

"Don't remind me," she said, putting both hands to her face.

There was another long wait while she tried to rid herself of some traumatic memories. Fran Mahalona had been the person who'd found the dead body in the swimming pool, and changed instantly from a loving wife into a grieving widow. I could understand why she'd drained all the water out of the pool. Taking a dip would bring it all back to her.

She looked up at me. "I think I'd like you to go now, please."

"Yes, yes, of course," I said, moving to the door. "Just tell me one thing. You mentioned a firm that your husband was hoping to take over."

"That's right."

"What happened to it?"

"It was sold to another bidder."

"Do you happen to know who it was, Mrs. Mahalona?"

"I don't see why you should be interested in that."

"Humor me. It might be important."

"I'm not sure that I can remember the name."

"Try. Please."

Brow furrowed in thought, she opened the front door to show me out. It was a beautiful house in a pleasant setting but its charms were lost on her now. I wondered how soon it would be before she moved away from the empty swimming pool. As I watched her trying to cudgel her brain, I felt an upsurge of sympathy for her.

"The truth is that I've tried to put it out of my mind," she said.

"Was it a major company or an independent?"

"Oh, a major company. I do recall that." She concentrated again. "Lewin," she decided, snapping her fingers again. "Yes, that was it. The Lewin Group. I believe that they bought the firm that Gabe was after. He had first option, you see. It should have gone to him."

"Can you tell me anything about this Lewin Group?"

"Only what everyone knows, Mr. Saxon."

"And what's that?"

"They're a subsidiary of the Kaheiki Corporation."

The motorcycle was worth its weight in gold. It not only got me out to the Mahalona residence in the outer suburbs of Honolulu, it enabled me to shake off any potential pursuit by zigzagging through the streets. In fact, I was fairly certain that nobody tried to follow me but I'd taken no chances. Melissa's crash helmet was on the large side for me but it did its job. As I sped along the main road, I looked just like any other motorcyclist. The rush of air against my body was exhilarating. I got back to find Melissa smoking a cigarette as she fixed a poster for *Together* on the front wall of the theater.

"How did you get on, Alan?" she asked.

"Great—I'm thinking of buying myself a Harley."

"Worthwhile trip?"

"I think so. I owe you, Melissa. I'll buy you dinner some time."

She grinned. "I never go out with strange men."

"I'm not that strange, am I?"

"You are in that crash helmet. Positively *alien*."

"What do you expect from a Howlie?" She guffawed. I handed her the helmet. "By the way, I forgot to tell you. I saw your sister yesterday."

"Zann?" She was concerned. "How is she?"

"Still wondering what hit her."

"I'll try to get out there myself—now that I have my wheels back."

"Nick gave me a lift back to the hotel in his Maserati," I said. "He'd heard that I had a row with Captain Rapoza about his close links with your family. That, in itself, was proof that there *was* a link, of course. I just wanted you to know that I didn't reveal my sources."

"He must've thought it was me."

"He did, Melissa, but I'm a very convincing liar."

"Thanks. I can do without any hassle from Nick. I don't want him coming down here to stir up trouble. He's not welcome at the Pineapple."

"But he's your brother."

"Oh, he remembered that, did he?"

"I can't pretend that he sent you his undying love but, yes, he did know that he had two sisters—even though he's preoccupied with only one of them at the moment."

"Nothing new in that," she said, bitterly.

"Yet he was very pleased to see you the other night."

"Only because I conformed. I played Happy Families for once."

"It meant a lot to your sister, Melissa."

"Yeah, I know. That's the reason I showed up."

"What about the wedding? Would you have attended that?"

"In spirit, but not in body."

"Too conventional for you?"

"That's only the start of it, Alan."

"Tell me the rest when I buy you that meal."

"Better go," she said as someone yelled her name from inside the theater. "They're getting fractious. Want to stop and watch?"

"No thanks," I replied, giving her a kiss. "Another time."

It was well over a mile to the hotel but I felt that a walk would do me good. After getting directions from Melissa, I set off at a brisk pace, mulling over what I'd learned from Fran Mahalona. There was a connection between the two murders, after all, and it was provided by the name of Jimmy Kaheiki. I could see why Captain Rapoza had omitted to mention it to me. Sergeant Tenno, apparently, had been part of the conspiracy of silence.

Schooling myself not to jump to any conclusions, I examined all the facts at my disposal. In accepting an invitation from a man I considered to be a good friend, I'd walked headfirst into a hornet's nest. Now that I had a clearer idea of why I was there, I was troubled. I'd been used. I'd been selected with care by Donald and his first wife to fulfil a specific function. Small wonder that he'd not turned to one of his American friends in the golfing fraternity. They'd know too much. I didn't. It was galling. While he was alive, Donald really was the Invisible Man to me and I wished I could have kept my illusions about him.

Thanks to Heidi's revelations, I'd lost some respect for the man but my determination to help in the search for his killer hadn't been lessened as a result. If anything, it had been intensified. I wanted to know who had given him that warning in Rochester and what drove him to ignore it. I wanted the murder to be solved as soon as possible so that I could leave that gorgeous sunshine and fly back to a country with gray skies and freezing cold, where I didn't have to fear for my life. Most of all, I wished to get well away from Heidi Dukelow.

It never happened? Oh, yes it did. I was there.

As I got nearer to the hotel, I passed a string of shops selling the usual souvenirs for tourists. I was given a sharp reminder.

In clogging up my mental airwaves with details of the Dukelow and the Kaheiki families, I'd forgotten all about my own. I might not want a memento of Hawaii—I already had too many of those—but my daughter certainly would. The least I could do was to buy Lynette a couple of T-shirts with garish designs on them. I turned into a store and began to browse. It was a providential move. Had I continued on my way with my brain focussed on the murder, I might not have noticed that I was being followed.

The mirror gave him away. Hanging from a wall, it allowed those who wanted to buy hats or sunglasses to see what they looked like. It also enabled me to get my first glimpse of him. He was pretending to look at some post cards but I knew that he was shadowing me. When I moved deeper into the store, he ambled in the same direction. The advantage had now shifted to me. I knew he was there but he was unaware of the fact. That meant I could shake him off before he realized that I'd gone. Crowds were thick and the area was full of hiding places, even for a tall Englishman. A quick dash through the rear door and I'd be away.

Yet I didn't want to make a run for it. That would be too easy. It would also leave me wondering who the man was and why he was on my tail. Had he watched us on the golf course or left a meat skewer in my bathroom? Who was paying him? I wanted answers and there was only one way to get them. I worked up sufficient anger to put my personal safety aside. It was time to strike back.

Leaving the store, I strolled along the sidewalk and glanced in the windows of adjacent shops, occasionally pausing to examine some of the items that hung from beneath the awnings. I then came to a narrow lane on my left. Here was my chance. Though I turned into it at a leisurely pace, I then sprinted along it until I found a doorway in which I could hide. I didn't have long to wait. When he reached the alleyway, the man must have seen that he'd been rumbled so he broke into a run. The footsteps sounded heavy but I wasn't deterred. I was too fired up.

As soon as he reached my hiding place, I stuck out an arm and tightened it around his throat, using my other arm to grab his shoulder so that I could twist him round. Giving him a sudden push, I slammed him against the opposite wall, drawing a grunt of pain from him. He was also spurred into action. His elbows pummeled my ribs until I was forced to let him go. Spinning round, he grappled with me. It was my turn to be slammed against the wall now and it took all the breath out of me.

He was a powerful man of middle height with muscled forearms that were matted with dark hair. His movements were lithe and he was far more experienced at brawling than I was. Blood was trickling down his craggy face from where he'd made contact with the wall. His eyes were whirlpools of fury. I tried to push him away but he was far too quick for me. Slipping a hand under his shirt, he produced a snub-nosed revolver that he held so hard against my temple that I feared he was going to bore his way into my skull. I froze instantly.

"You fucking idiot!" he snapped. "I'm here to protect you."

Lance Perellini was not the sort of man I'd ever have chosen to spend time with in a café but I had no choice. When he'd stemmed the bleeding from his forehead and cleaned up his face in the washroom, he sat opposite me and slurped his coffee. Keeping me alive, it was clear, was not a labor of love for him.

"Next time you jump me like that," he warned, "I'll kill you."

"What will Jimmy Kaheiki say to that?"

"He'd probably cheer. Jimmy don't belong to your fan club."

"I gathered that."

"Nick might be upset, though. He'd prefer to whack you himself."

"Charming!"

"You shouldn't upset them."

"What did I do?"

"Poked your nose in where it wasn't wanted."

"This doesn't make sense," I said. "If they're happy to see me bumped off, why did they employ you as a bodyguard?"

"I'm much more than that," boasted Perellini. "I come expensive but I always earn my dough. Jimmy knows that. That's why he called me. I flew in from San Francisco coupla days before you got here. Jimmy filled me in. His daughter was getting married. He wanted no trouble. I was hired to protect you all."

"Well, you didn't do a very good job of it, Mr. Perellini," I argued. "It may have escaped your notice, but the groom won't be able to make the ceremony."

"Don't get me riled up, mister. I turn ugly."

"It's a fair point."

"Night your friend got killed, Jimmy had me doing my real job. I find people, see. I pick up a trail." He put both arms on the table. "Know what a bail enforcement agent is?"

"A bounty hunter."

"I prefer the other name. I hunt down fugitives for a living. That's the real reason I'm here. As a tracker. Jimmy Kaheiki wants me to find the guys who are putting the squeeze on him."

"Can't he rely on the police to do that?"

"They've got nowhere so far."

"How can you possibly succeed where they failed?" I asked. "They have enormous resources at their disposal. You're a one-man show."

"I got this nose," he said, tapping the side of it.

"Yes, I almost broke it for you. Sorry about that."

"People see the cops coming, they clam up. You wanna dig out the truth, you gotta come from the other side of the law. Like me."

"I had the feeling you'd never win a Best Behavior Award."

Perellini grinned. "You're a funny guy, you know that?" He downed his coffee in a gulp. "When I was a lot younger, I did some serious jail time for armed robbery. Taught me a lot. I know how bad guys think, what they do, where they hide. I always find them in the end."

"Why didn't Jimmy Kaheiki simply hire police protection during the build-up to the wedding?"

"Because nobody was supposed to know it was taking place. Hire a bunch of cops to patrol the house and you give the game away." He put a hand on his barrel chest. "I'm more discreet. I got better camouflage."

"Yet I picked you out."

"Only by accident," he said. "You had no idea that I waited for you to get back to the Pineapple Theater."

I was astounded. "How did you know I'd been there?"

"Easy. You borrow some wheels, you'll bring 'em back. I followed you in my car from the hotel to the theater. When you rode off, I stuck with you till I lost you at a red light. So," he said, with an expressive gesture, "I went back to the theater."

"And that's today's assignment, is it? To act as my bodyguard."

"Yes and no."

"What do you mean?"

"I told you, Mr. Saxon. I find people. Easiest way to do that is to make them come to you. Get me?"

"I'm not sure that I do."

"Your friend was iced because he was about to marry into the Kaheiki family," he explained, "and the murder was set up by the guy you met in the restaurant."

"That's right. He called himself Gabe Mahalona."

"And you got a good look at him. He wants to feel safer, he has to take you out as well. Plus, he gets in another strike at Jimmy Kaheiki because you're only here as his guest. Follow me now?"

"Only too well," I said, breaking out into a cold sweat. "You don't really care whether I live or die. I'm just the bait on the hook. Follow me and you may get the man you're really after."

"You figured it out at last. Clever?"

"Very clever, Mr. Perellini. However, there's one small snag."

"Yeah?"

"I'm no fisherman but I do know this. Before you actually catch anything," I stressed, "the bait has to be swallowed whole. Where does that leave me?"

"Wriggling on the hook till it's all over," he said with a chuckle. "Can I get you another cup of coffee while you're still able to drink it?"

Chapter Eleven

Officer Broderick was back on duty and, in spite of my aversion to police uniforms, I was pleased to see his burly figure in the corridor on the third floor. As well as barring access to the crime scene, he was also keeping a friendly eye on my room and I had far more trust in him as a bodyguard than I could ever muster for Lance Perellini. To begin with, he was on the same side of the law as me. Needless to say, I'd refused Perellini's offer of a second cup of coffee and I'd shot back to the hotel to consider my position in relative safety. I greeted Liam Broderick with a grateful smile.

"Good morning," I said. "You're doing a great job."

"How long you staying, sir?"

"Why?"

"Make sure you call Sergeant Tenno before you leave."

"Does she have any news for me?"

"All I know is that you got to ring her."

"Thanks, officer.

"And, in case you're worried about your room," he said, "it's okay to go in there. They changed the sheets on the bed half an hour ago. I checked that everything was alright. Nobody's in there now—and the windows to the *lanai* are locked."

"*Lanai?*" My memory was jogged. "Oh, yes. The word for balcony."

"We call them verandahs, sir. *Lanai*."

"When in Rome...."

"But this ain't Rome," he said, doggedly, "it's Honolulu."

"I can't fault your eyesight, officer."

"Don't get smart with me, sir."

"I'd never dream of it," I promised him.

The light was flashing on my telephone when I let myself into the room so I retrieved my voice messages. Two were from Emily Tenno, giving me a number to call. Three were from reporters who wanted to grill me about my relationship with Donald Dukelow. One was from Clive Phelps, golf writer and best friend, who'd picked up news of the murder while in Morocco, and the last was from Donald's mother. She sounded anxious to speak to me. I rang her room number immediately but, to my dismay, it was Heidi who picked up the receiver.

"Alan," she said, pleasantly, "how are you?"

"Fine, thanks."

"I did enjoy that meal last night. It was kind of you to let me stay."

"Excellent food."

"And good company," she said. "It was just what I needed. Oh, I'm getting a signal to wind up. Cora wants to talk to you. Bye."

I was relieved to hear the other woman's voice. Heidi had been too intent on conveying by her bland manner that all we had done the previous night was to enjoy a meal together, but I could not forget our ill-judged moment of intimacy as easily as that. It still embarrassed me. I tried to listen to what Cora Dukelow had to say.

"I just wanted to tell you my decision," she began.

"Decision?"

"I'm flying home this afternoon."

"Oh, I see."

"There's really not much point in staying, Alan. It would be far too distressing. The police won't be able to release the body for some time and there's absolutely nothing I can do if I hang on here. Every time I step into the corridor," she said, apprehensively, "I'm reminded of what happened to Donald. It's too much to bear. Heidi managed to find a flight out this afternoon."

"It's probably the most sensible thing to do, Mrs. Dukelow."

"I didn't want to disappear without explaining it to you."

"Forget me," I said. "I understand your feelings perfectly."

"I can't mourn Donald properly until I'm in my own house. And, as soon as Captain Rapoza gets in touch, we can have the body flown to Rochester. Mr. Kaheiki is going to arrange that," she went on. "He's been so kind to me. Did you know that the family owns funeral parlors?"

"I did, actually."

"They'll take care of everything."

"That's good to hear."

"They're such lovely people."

"Yes," I said, pretending to agree.

"That's one advantage of this trip, I suppose. It did help me to lose some of my silly prejudices. I'd have been proud to have Suzanne as my daughter-in-law. But it was not to be."

"Alas, no."

"Thank you, Alan. I'm so grateful to you."

"For what?"

"Helping me through it. You and Heidi have been my saviors."

"I only did what anyone else would have done, Mrs. Dukelow."

It was heartening to know that I'd been able to offer her some comfort but I felt sorry that she'd been so easily deceived by Heidi. Her former daughter-in-law had worked assiduously to win the old woman's trust while having a hidden agenda. It would be too cruel to tell Cora Dukelow what that agenda had been. Besides, I was getting rid of Heidi and that was a real bonus. Once she'd left the island, perhaps I could start to believe that it never happened.

"Goodbye," said Cora Dukelow.

"Goodbye."

"When this is all over, I'll write to you to express my gratitude properly. You were such a good friend to Donald. I'll not forget you."

"Thank you."

"Take care, Alan. Take great care."

"I will. Safe journey to both of you."

"Both of us?"

"Well, isn't Heidi going with you?"

"Oh, no," she replied. "Heidi felt that she'd like to stay on for a while in case there are any developments. With me out of the way, you'll probably be seeing a lot of her."

"Yes," I murmured, wincing at the prospect. "I daresay that I will."

When I put the phone down, I needed a moment to absorb what I'd just heard. For her sake, I was glad that Cora Dukelow was leaving. She needed to be in familiar surroundings, not stuck in a hotel room only twenty yards away from where her son was murdered. When the media had got fed up with badgering me, they'd have turned their attention on her and she'd be escaping all that. The fact that Heidi was staying, however, was not so welcome. Clearly, she had her own motives for doing so. I just hoped that I wasn't one of them.

I remembered the rest of my voice mail. I had no intention of giving private interviews to any reporters and I didn't really feel up to talking to Clive Phelps at that point. He, too, would want the story so that he could write it up in his column. Even though he was on vacation, his paper would have contacted him to write an obituary of Donald. My ambition was to make sure that they didn't run my obituary alongside it. Knowing Clive's style, I could almost write the first sentence for him—"Donald Dukelow beat Alan Saxon in a tournament once again, getting to heaven first in a sudden death play-off that was far too sudden for any golfing fans…."

Replaying the first message from Emily Tenno, I jotted down the number she'd left, then rang it. She came on the line immediately. Her voice had a crisp authority.

"Sergeant Tenno," she announced.

"It's me," I said. "Checking in to let you know I'm still alive."

"Glad to hear that, Mr. Saxon."

"I'm not ready for one of Jimmy Kaheiki's coffins just yet."

"You shouldn't joke about such things."

"Think I'm tempting Providence?"

"You know the score, sir. That's why there's a cop outside your door. You're a precious commodity—we aim to look after you."

I wasn't reassured. "Any developments?"

"Quite a few," she said. "We've not been sitting on our hands. First off, that Asian guy you saw going past you in the corridor on the night of the murder did exist."

"I know. Did you think I invented him?"

"It was late and you'd had a few drinks."

"I saw him as clear as day, Sergeant—he was leading two pink elephants along on a rein." I heard her give a dry laugh. "Have you run him to earth yet?"

"No, but we had other sightings at the hotel. He definitely wasn't visiting any guests on the third floor. We know that now. But he was seen by the receptionist, entering the lobby roughly half an hour before you got back to the hotel. The bell captain saw him go up in the elevator," she added, "and he confirms the time. But here's the funny thing. Nobody saw him leave the building."

"Surprise, surprise!"

"That still doesn't tie him into the murder, of course."

"It doesn't put him in the clear either," I insisted. "If you ask me to rely on *manao* here, I'd say he's involved in some way. The man who put us in the taxi at Reuben's could have rung him to warn him that we were on the way back."

"Pure supposition, sir."

"We need to find him."

"Of course."

"Have you got men out there searching for him?"

"You know anything about ethnicity on this island?" she asked. "We got all the colors of the rainbow here and a dozen more besides. The biggest group is Caucasian, then Japanese, then Filipinos, then Hawaiian and then Chinese. There's also a sizeable number of Asians, some of whom have been here a couple of generations."

"I get the message, Sergeant. Needles and haystacks."

"We got 400,000 people in greater Honolulu alone."

"That man is one of them, I'm certain of it."

"We'll keep looking," she said. "As for the guy who picked you up at the restaurant, I'm afraid that Reuben wasn't able to identify him from any of our records. Also, the lighting is very dim in his club. You probably got a better look at him than Reuben. When we release a photofit to the press, we'll go with your version."

"Artistic success at last!"

Even though the results were largely negative, Emily Tenno listed all the other things the police had done in order to persuade me that they were pursuing the investigation with vigor. The skewer from my bathroom had yielded no DNA but, because of its unusual design, they'd been able to trace it—and the matching one extracted from Donald's brain—to the manufacturer. Police were contacting the retailers whom he supplied in Honolulu to see if there'd been any recent purchases of the item.

"What about the skewer in Gabe Mahalona's ear?" I asked.

"It's not relevant to this investigation."

"Do you mean that it's not the same design?"

"I mean that I can't discuss another case with you."

"But the two crimes must be linked, Sergeant. Solve one murder and you solve them both. Doesn't that idea appeal to you?"

"For someone who doesn't like policemen, Mr. Saxon," she said, coldly, "you have an alarming tendency to tell us how to do our jobs. Next time you're about to hit a tricky putt in a tournament, maybe I'll step out of the crowd and give *you* some advice."

"Point taken."

"Good."

"But while you're on the line," I said, recalling my earlier scare, "do you happen to know a man by the name of Lance Perellini?"

There was an audible grunt of displeasure. "We know *of* him, sir," she admitted. "Difficult not to, I'm afraid. He's a bail bondsman."

"One of the best, according to him."

"He's been lucky enough to make a couple of high-profile arrests, that's all. And Mr. Perellini knows how to get publicity. Why do you ask?"

"Jimmy Kaheiki has hired him."

"Yes, we know that," she said with a hint of exasperation. "Lance Perellini was supposed to make sure that the wedding went off without any interruption. He failed."

"He's got a new job now—looking after me."

"Oh?"

"When I was shopping earlier, I realized that I was being followed so I hid in a doorway and ambushed him."

"That was a very stupid thing to do."

"I discovered that," I said, rubbing my temple. "He almost shot my head off. Is he licensed to carry a gun on the island?"

"Yes, sir."

"Thanks for the warning."

"Then here's another, Mr. Saxon," she said, raising her voice. "Don't put yourself in jeopardy like that again. And let us know where you go. You plan any more outings, check in with me or Captain Rapoza first."

"Oh, I will," I said.

And the conversation was over.

The bath was just what I needed. It gave me the opportunity to wallow in deep, frothy, comforting warm water, to wash off any vestigial traces of Heidi Dukelow and to address my mind to the murder investigation. Unfortunately, I wasn't alone for long. The telephone on the wall beside me rang so insistently that I had to pick it up.

"Saxon?" asked a voice through a distant crackle. "Is that you?"

It was Clive Phelps, ringing from Morocco on a dodgy line.

"Hello, Clive," I said. "What do you want?"

"What do I want, he asks! You're up to your hairy armpits in the murder of Donald Dukelow and you want to know what I want? Well, it's not to ask you about the weather in Hawaii, I'll tell you that for nothing." He had a quick drink. "Where are you?"

"In the bath."

"Alone?"

"No," I quipped, "I've got three plastic ducks in here as well."

"Is that all?" he replied. "I prefer to get into a bath with something much more exciting than a plastic duck, and I don't mean a loofah. You never had underwater sex? It's magical! As long as you know your geometry, that is—all a question of angles, you see, or you can cause yourself some damage. Perfect way to stimulate the phagocytes, old son."

"Spare me your memoirs, Clive."

"Then tell me what I want to know."

"Which is?"

"Every-bloody-thing, you bastard!" he yelled in my ear. "I shouldn't be ringing you, Saxon. You should have been on the blower to *me*. Let's face it, I was the one who got you that free holiday in Hawaii. If I hadn't told Donald that you were in San Diego, it would never have happened."

"So I've got you to blame, have I?"

"I always do a favor for a friend—but I expect a *quid pro quo*. As it happens," he continued, bitterly, "every pro in Morocco costs a lot more than a quid so I'm glad I brought Cressida with me to keep my spirits up."

"Cressida?"

"Our new switchboard girl. She's not exactly the Brain of Britain but at least she doesn't charge me when she drops her drawers. I'm speaking metaphorically, mind you, because Cressida never actually wears any. Not when I'm around, anyway."

"Is this conversation about me or you?" I complained.

"I thought you'd be interested."

"I'm never interested in your sordid sex life, Clive, especially when I've got more pressing things on my mind. This has been the holiday from hell so far. Donald was a good friend and a terrific golfer."

"That's why I rang you. Tell me what happened."

"Now?" I said, wearily.

"I'll let you play with the plastic ducks while you're doing it."

For all his routine lechery, I was glad to hear Clive's voice. It was crude but reassuringly familiar. I had no idea what time it was in Morocco and I didn't care. Neither did Clive Phelps. Night or day, he was always the same—chirpy, half-drunk, and highly irreverent. His call had one supreme advantage. It enabled me to describe what had happened to someone who actually believed me. Though I had to put up with his usual inane interruptions, I got out all of the relevant facts. But I never even mentioned Heidi Dukelow. If Clive knew that we'd ended up in bed together, he'd have hounded me for every lubricious detail.

His immediate concern was the obituary he was writing. Clive wanted some anecdotes about Donald and I was able to enjoy some pleasant memories of my friend for a while. There were plenty of them. I made sure, however, that I said nothing whatsoever about his private life or about the photograph he carried around with him. By the time I'd finished, Clive had enough material to write a short biography of him.

"Always remember him beating you in that play-off at Merion."

"Thanks for reminding me, Clive," I protested.

"I had twenty quid on you to win that day. Then Donald got that fluke putt on the third hole and I lost my money. Hey," he went on, lowering his voice to a confiding whisper. "What's she like? This Suzanne Kaheiki, I mean. Donald always went for class in his women. Esmeralda was my favorite. When she batted those long, black eyelashes of hers, she made my castanets click like mad. Ole! Come on, Saxon. Tell me about Suzanne."

"She's a lovely girl, Clive, and that's all I'm saying."

"Details. I must have details."

"Then go back to Cressida. I'm sure she'll let you see hers."

"Man to man—what's this Polynesian beauty like?"

"The poor woman is in mourning, Clive. Leave her be."

"How does she compare with Esmeralda?"

"I have to go," I said.

"Wait, wait!" he yelled in my ear, "there's something I haven't told you yet. Something important."

"If it's about what you and Cressida get up to in the bath, forget it."

"Listen, will you? I'm serious."

"You've got five seconds, Clive."

"I had this weird phone call about you."

I was checked. "Oh?"

"It was a few days ago. Just before we set off for Morocco. This man wanted to ask about Alan Saxon. And while we're on the subject," he said, testily, "don't you think it's high time you got yourself an agent or something? I'm fed up with being your unpaid secretary. Whenever someone needs to track you down, they get on to me."

"Only because you do the job so well, Clive."

"Piss off!"

"Who was this man?"

"He claimed to be something to do with the Koolau Golf Course. Said he'd heard a rumor that you were coming to Oahu and was it true? At that point, I didn't know," he went on, taking another drink. "When Donald rang me to confirm where you were, he didn't tell me anything about a secret wedding in Hawaii."

"Maybe because he wanted to keep it secret."

"Never thought of that," he replied with a cackle. "Anyway, I wasn't able to tell this man where you were going. All I knew at that point was that you were still in San Diego, whooping it up with Peter Fullard."

I laughed. "Fat chance of that!"

"I was only joking. Peter's idea of whooping it up is a cup of cocoa and an early night with a good book—the encyclopaedia of tropical grasses."

"Tell me more about this phone call."

"Nothing more to tell."

"You said that it was weird."

"Yes," he recalled. "There was something odd about the man's voice. He had an American accent that sounded a bit phony to me. The moment I told him I couldn't help him, he hung up on me. Not even so much as a thank you."

"Did he happen to give you a name?"

"Oh, yes. I never talk to strangers—unless they're female, very sexy and between the ages of eighteen and twenty-nine. This man failed on all three counts."

"So who was he, Clive?"

"I knew you'd ask that, so I wrote his name down."

"And what was it?"

"Gabe Mahalona."

The bath no longer held any appeal for me. Disturbed by what Clive Phelps had told me, I got out at once and dried myself with a towel. Someone knew that I was heading for the island before I even got there. The secret wedding was not as secret as Donald Dukelow and Jimmy Kaheiki had wanted it to be. We were expected. I relied implicitly on Clive's judgement. If he thought that the man who rang him had a fake American accent, then I believed him. That meant the caller could not possibly have been the Gabe Mahalona who conned us into going to the nightclub. His accent had been quite authentic.

It was confusing. The real Gabe Mahalona was dead yet there were at least two people posing as him. How many more were there? Enough to form a society? Mahalona was a successful businessman but he was hardly Elvis Presley. Why were people drawn to imitate him?

Clive's phone call may have jolted me but it had the virtue of concentrating my mind. In going through the bare facts of the case once again, I began to see them in a slightly different light. I was also reminded of two things that I didn't tell Clive, details that I hadn't even divulged to the police. While still at his mother's home, Donald had received a warning to stay away from Hawaii. He must have known at that point that the secrecy had been breached. Why did he press on with the arrangements? Why did he deliberately lead us into danger?

The second piece of information I'd kept to myself had seemed so trivial at the time that it was hardly worth mentioning. I now revised that opinion. Donald and I did not go to that particular restaurant by chance. It had been recommended by Zann Kaheiki as a place where discerning locals chose to eat. Because of that, it was vital to reserve a table. In the course of a meal, we were tricked by a little scenario that enabled the bogus Gabe Mahalona to make our acquaintance. How did he know we'd be there? If he'd followed us from the hotel, he and his accomplices would never have been able to secure tables at the restaurant at such short notice. They must have booked in advance.

I needed to speak to Zann Kaheiki—without eavesdroppers this time—but I saw how difficult that would be. If I rang, I probably wouldn't be allowed to talk to her, and if I turned up on the doorstep, I wouldn't even be permitted to see her. It was frustrating. Without realizing it, she might hold a vital nugget of information. I had to reach her somehow and there was only one way left open to me.

Dropping the towel on the floor, I padded into the room and looked up one of the numbers I'd written on the pad beside the telephone. When I rang the Pineapple Theater, I got through to the Australian girl with the whining voice. I had to tussle with her for a full minute before she let me speak to Melissa. I already had my opening line ready.

"Me again, Melissa," I said, cheerily. "How would you like to oblige a naked man for a change?

Having had my bath and recovered from my meeting with Lance Perellini, I wanted to get out of the hotel again. Staying in my room was only making me restless and, in time, when Cora Dukelow had been driven off to the airport, I'd be open to an unwanted visit from Heidi. Once I was dressed, I gave

Emily Tenno a courtesy call to say that I was going out to do some shopping nearby. It was partly true and it would give her the feeling that I was doing what I was told.

Donning my floppy hat and my sunglasses, I slipped out of the room, gave Officer Broderick a wave of farewell, took the elevator to the second floor, then got out and used the emergency exit instead. I was soon swallowed up in the blazing enormity of Waikiki Beach. It was like being a child again, playing hide and seek among the sunshades and the loungers, twisting, turning, dodging, diving and taking refuge behind cover from time to time to make sure that I was not being followed. There was not even a fleeting glimpse of Lance Perellini. I'd either shaken him off or that much-vaunted nose of his had picked up a trail elsewhere.

Since I'd had nothing to eat that day apart from a biscuit, I was feeling peckish. I made for the largest restaurant I could find on the principle that there was safety in numbers, and chose a table in the corner that allowed me to sit with my back to the wall. Somebody had left a morning paper on the table so I used it to hide behind, pretending to read it while keeping one eye on the entrance. The young waitress who took my order was of Asian origin.

"Which part of India did you come from?" I asked her.

"I was born here in Honolulu, sir."

"What about your parents?"

"Delhi, sir," she said with a smile. "You've been to India?"

"In a sense."

I saw no point in telling her about Leicester. She'd probably never heard of it. Growing up in a city with a strong racial mix had been an education for me. It was the only thing about my childhood that I'd liked. Needless to say, my father had tried to rob me of that one small enjoyment by sneering at the immigrant communities whenever he could. I'd never dared to take any of my Indian or Pakistani friends home with me. Inspector Tom Saxon would have reviled them openly. As long as he was living in Leicester, the warped values of the Ku Klux Klan had a spokesman. I could imagine what he'd say if he saw me at that moment.

The hamburger was delicious, the French fries too soggy, and the cold beer a positive tonic. With the paper lying beside me, it was impossible not to glance at it. We were on the front page. Donald stared up at me from a photograph that had been taken a few years ago when he won the Masters at Augusta National. It was the supreme moment of his golfing career and he was justifiably proud of his green jacket. My throat went dry as I realized that I'd never see that happy smile of his again. Fortunately, there was no photograph of me though my name was mentioned in the article. I couldn't bear to read it.

Fortified by lunch and certain that I'd escaped surveillance, I did what I told Sergeant Tenno I was going to do and explored the shops. Red and blue were my daughter's favorite colors so I bought her a red T-shirt with a parrot on the front of it and a blue one with a set of palm trees. Other souvenirs quickly followed, including a watch with a hula dancer on the face, moving to and fro in time to each second. I soon had a full bag to carry out of the store. It was so easy to buy for Lynette. All I had to do was to make sure that I survived to give her the presents.

As I wandered in and out of other stores, I used every available mirror to see if anyone was behind me. I spotted nobody. If Perellini was still dogging my footsteps, he was doing it with remarkable skill and deserved to take over Donald's title as the Invisible Man. It was when I turned off the main road that I hit trouble. There was absolutely no warning of it. Strolling along the street with my bag of souvenirs, I was watching a young Japanese boy threading his way along the sidewalk towards me on his in-line skates. I stepped off the kerb to let him go past, then tried to cross the road diagonally.

The screech of tires alerted me to the danger. From somewhere behind me, a car suddenly accelerated forward and headed straight for me. Looking over my shoulder, I had only a split second to make a decision. If the vehicle had hit me, I'd have ended up in the police morgue with Donald, but I somehow had the presence of mind to leap up on to the hood, rolling along it until I hit the windscreen. Through the glass, I got a momentary look at the man in the passenger seat but there was no time for introductions. As the car surged on, I was thrown violently to the ground and almost run over by a taxi coming in the opposite direction.

When I'd seen this kind of thing happen in movies, the hero always knew how to fall properly and ended up with little more than ruffled hair. Rolling over expertly, he'd jump up in time to produce a gun and shoot out the tires of the disappearing car. At the very least, he'd get the make, color and license plate number. That wasn't the case with me. I felt a searing pain as my shoulder hit the tarmac, then my head seemed to split in two. The last thing I remembered before I passed out was the face I'd seen behind the windscreen. It was the man who'd walked past me in the corridor that night when I was trying to open the door to Donald's room.

He was back.

When I finally came to, I was lying on a gurney at a hospital, wearing nothing but a flimsy gown and having the last few stitches inserted into my scalp. My whole body seemed to be on fire. The doctor finished his work and gave me a smile of sympathy, but the man beside him was running low on compassion.

"Satisfied now?" asked Captain Rapoza, leaning over me. "You got a death wish or something?"

"What happened?" I mumbled.

"What happened is that you almost got yourself killed. When you crossed the road, an automobile tried to run you down. You're lucky you're still in one piece, Mr. Saxon."

"*Am* I still in one piece? I don't feel it."

"You've got sutures in your scalp, your shoulder and your left arm," explained the doctor, a fresh-faced young Hawaiian. "We thought you'd broken your left wrist but the X-ray showed that it was just badly sprained. That's why it's bound up. For the rest, you've got multiple bruises and abrasions. If you hadn't been wearing those trousers, sir, your legs would have been skinned."

"Can I have him now, doctor?" said Rapoza.

"Yes, Captain. When you're through, the nurse can put a bandage on his head. Then Mr. Saxon will be as good as new."

"I don't feel it," I said, aching all over.

"Just try to get some rest," advised the doctor. "Excuse me."

He pulled back the curtain to step out of the bay in which I was stretched out. Memory was slowly coming back to me. My first thought was for my daughter's presents.

"I was carrying a plastic bag," I recalled.

"Right here," said Rapoza, holding it up. "Bad news, sir. One of the tires ran over it." He pulled out the watch I'd bought. The hula dancer was now motionless. "At least we know the exact time you were hit."

"That's a big consolation."

"Witnesses say you leapt up on to the hood."

"It seemed like the best idea at the time, Captain."

"Saved your life."

"Did anyone get the number of the car?"

"Coupla people," he said. "We traced it to a guy in Pearl City. It was stolen during the night. Daresay we'll find it abandoned before too long. You probably left a dent in the hood."

"Not as bad as the dent it left in me," I protested, moving my arms and legs very slowly to test them out. "I did manage to see the passenger, though. It was that Asian man from the hotel."

"You sure about that?"

"I'd stake my life on it."

"That's exactly what you did do, sir."

"How was I to know someone would try to run me down?"

"You were warned."

"Yes, but I took such precautions to make sure that I wasn't being followed. How on earth did they know I'd be walking along that particular street at that particular time?"

"Ever hear of a cell phone, sir?"

"Of course."

"The guy who must have trailed you from the hotel bided his time. When he saw you shopping, all he had to do was to call up the driver of the automobile and it came looking for you. When the chance came in that side street, the vehicle suddenly turned into a murder weapon."

"Attempted murder, Captain."

"It got one victim," he pointed out, showing me the battered watch. "The hula dancer."

"I'll buy another watch for my daughter."

"Her father can't be so easily replaced. Remember that."

"I've got such a headache," I said, putting a hand to my forehead.

"So have I—his name is Alan Saxon. You've been snooping, sir, haven't you?" he went on, wagging a finger. "Why didn't you tell us that you'd been bothering Mrs. Mahalona?"

"How did you find that out?"

"She rang to tell me."

"I was looking for a connection between the two murders—beyond the fact that both victims ended up with a skewer in their ear, that is."

"And?"

"I found one. I think you know what it is, Captain."

"Yeah," he said. "The company that Mahalona was about to take over is now part of the Kaheiki empire. So what?"

"The only way they could have acquired it is by getting rid of Gabe Mahalona. He had first option."

His eyes flashed. "You accusing Jimmy Kaheiki?"

"I feel that the matter needs looking into, that's all."

"It *has* been looked into, sir, I assure you."

"How?" I asked, trying to needle him. "Did you discuss it with Mr. Kaheiki over a friendly drink?"

"You know nothing at all about the background to the case."

"I know enough to make me suspicious, Captain."

"You were born suspicious." He tried to rein in his temper. "Now, why don't you let us do the detective work while you stay here and recover?"

"I don't want to stay here."

"You've been concussed. The doctor advises a night in hospital. I agree with that. Unfortunately, he doesn't have a straitjacket he could put you in or I'd feel really happy."

"They can't keep me here against my will, Captain."

"True."

"I want to get out there to look for the people who did this to me."

"That's our job, sir."

"Swear me in as your deputy," I suggested, grinning at him. "Like in a western—get the horses and we'll head 'em off at the pass." He was fuming with anger. "And don't worry. I'm police-trained. Ask my father."

Melissa Kaheiki was horrified when we met at the agreed place early that evening. I'd had time to take a taxi back to the hotel so that I could change out of the torn and sullied clothing in which I'd arrived at the hospital, but I still looked as if I'd taken a battering. My head and my wrist were bandaged, my face had a huge bruise down one side of it and my forearms were a network of cuts and grazes. My floppy hat hid very little of the damage.

"What happened?" gasped Melissa.

"Hit and run accident."

"You look like something out of a Pearl Harbor movie."

"Any chance of a part in your play?"

"Not a hope—you'd frighten the audience."

I told her about the incident in the street and she listened with alarm. At my request, she'd been back to the house to see her sister and to find out what I wanted to know. Making light of the dull ache in my head and the itching all over my body, I asked her how she'd got on.

"Zann was pleased to see me," she said, "even though she knew that I disapproved of her marriage. She talked a lot about Donald. He was everything she'd always wanted. Even I came to see his good points after a while."

"There were lots of those, Melissa."

"You never know. It may have worked out for them."

For a while, I thought, aware of Donald's track record.

"He treated Zann well—unlike that fink from the travel agency. She made me feel guilty for not making the effort to get to know him a little better. After all, he was going to be my brother-in-law."

"But you didn't want a Howlie in the family."

"I made no bones about that."

"That must have upset Zann."

"It did, Alan," she admitted. "A lot. First thing I did when I got out there was to apologize. I felt closer to my sister than I've done for years. Pity of it is we needed a murder to bring us together." She peered at me. "You sure you're okay?"

"Apart from the land mines going off in my head."

"You ought to be in bed."

"Too much to do, Melissa."

"Don't take any more chances, Alan. Someone's after you."

"I'm fairly safe in public like this," I argued, "and I'll be more careful when I cross the road from now on. In any case, the driver of that car probably thinks he put me out of action for a while."

"You're still a marked man," she said. "And much as I want to help you, I do have to knock the show into shape. The women were a bit tetchy when I took the afternoon off to visit my family."

"That Australian girl is always tetchy."

"Fern?"

"She gave me a really hard time over the phone."

"Fern doesn't like male voices."

"Just as well I'm not a Welsh choir then."

"She's done assertiveness training. Fern is difficult enough with women. Always trying to win points against you. With men, she doesn't even bother with the civilities."

"I noticed. When you tried to introduce me at the theater, she had a sudden urge to go to the loo. Anyway," I said, "putting

Fern aside, did you manage to ask Zann those two questions I suggested?"

"Yes, Alan."

"And did she know that Donald was warned by an anonymous caller to keep away from Honolulu?"

"No, she didn't."

"Was she upset?"

"Very. Upset by the warning and upset he hadn't told her."

"Donald was probably trying to shield her."

"Mistake."

"What about that restaurant where we dined?"

"I asked her about that," she said. "Zann remembers advising Donald to go there because of the quality of their food. But she told only one other person where you were going."

"Oh? Who was that?"

"Our brother—Nick."

Waikiki Beach was still covered in people but they were too busy oiling, sunning or admiring their own bodies to notice the injuries to mine. I limped back towards the hotel, feeling as if I needed about three days' sleep but knowing that I could not give in now. It was inconceivable that Zann had set us up at the restaurant but I couldn't absolve her brother of suspicion so easily. Was Nick the missing link between the two murders? Had he been involved in the killing of Gabriel Mahalona in order to further the family's business interests? It was a plausible explanation. To tie him into Donald's death, however, was much more difficult. Why would he want to cause his sister such grief by assisting in the murder of her future husband?

Nick Kaheiki had had little affection for Donald. That was clear. Even after the man's death, he was still calling him Donald Duck. His own wife was a native Hawaiian and, like the rest of the family, he had wanted Zann to marry one of her own kind. Was his hatred of Howlies enough to drive him to such a desperate measure or could that merely be a secondary motive? I remembered what Heidi had told me. During the tour of the factory, Nick had tried to impress her by telling her that he would rule one day over the Kaheiki family. Was he trying to bring that day much closer?

The only way that he could succeed his father was to wait until the old man retired or died, and Jimmy Kaheiki appeared to be in rude health. Systematic attacks on the corporation he had built up over the years were bound to take their toll, however, and nobody was better placed to know where and when to strike than the heir-apparent. Could Nick be orchestrating a campaign to force his father out? He was ambitious enough and, judging by his earlier brushes with the law, he was reckless enough as well. I wondered if he was clever enough.

In the wake of Donald's murder, he'd seemed angry and vengeful but that might just have been feigned. Melissa was not the only actor in the family. Nick had some talent, too. He'd managed to convince me and Heidi that he was single, yet he had a wife and family in Kauai. The speed with which he tried to pounce on Heidi suggested that he was used to making a conquest without too much effort. The other women, too, I felt certain, would have been led to believe that he was a bachelor. Had Jimmy Kaheiki been fooled into thinking he had a loving son when Nick was secretly planning to depose him?

He may not stop at Donald Dukelow. That's what Nick had said at police headquarters when he and his father had questioned me. Jimmy Kaheiki had tried to shut him up but his son had insisted on issuing the warning. *Watch your back*. It was sound advice. If I'd done that a few hours earlier, I wouldn't have been knocked for six by a car. There was no genuine concern for me in Nick's caution. He wanted me to go to ground until the police had finished with me and I could vanish from the island. That way, I wouldn't be in a position to make inquiries on my own account. I'd cease to be a problem to Nick Kaheiki—if, that is, he really was somehow implicated.

It gave me plenty to think about on my slow walk back. On first acquaintance, the Kaheiki family had seemed happy and close-knit but that was an illusion. Melissa had effectively opted out of it, Zann had moved to the mainland and, in agreeing to marry a *haole*, had betrayed her birthright. And until he had learned self-control, Nick had got himself into trouble time and again, causing his parents untold angst. So much for togetherness—it was all on the surface. Donald Dukelow would have been marrying into a highly dysfunctional family.

Lost as I was in thought, I didn't forget the advice I'd been given. In the course of my journey, I must have looked over my shoulder dozens of times, regardless of the stabbing pain it gave my neck. Though I saw nobody behind me, I knew that I nevertheless might be followed. Reaching the hotel, I climbed the steps to the patio and looked behind me once again.

"I'm over here," said a man's voice.

I turned to see Lance Perellini, reclining on a lounger with a pair of binoculars in his lap. He took the small cigar from his mouth.

"Watched you all the way," he boasted. "You're easier to pick out now you're one of the walking wounded. How you feeling?"

"Rotten."

"Good. Teach you a lesson."

"I thought you were hired to protect me."

"Got called away. Tracking duties."

"So what are you doing here now?"

"Delivering a message."

"From whom?"

"Jimmy Kaheiki," he said, getting up. "You're to come with me."

"And supposing I'm not in the mood?"

"Oh, I think you'll find that you are, Mr. Saxon. If I go back to Jimmy and tell him you're playing hard to get, he won't like it. And when he doesn't like something, there are nasty consequences."

"Don't try to strong-arm me, Mr. Perellini," I warned.

"I'm just a messenger here. And the message is quite simple," he said, stubbing out the cigar with his foot. "Do as you're told or you may have to put up with something far worse than an automobile hitting you in the ass." He took my arm. "Message received?"

Chapter Twelve

When we joined him in the rear of the stretch limo, Jimmy Kaheiki was stone-faced and tight-lipped. He used a finger to indicate that I should sit opposite him with Lance Perellini beside me. I obeyed resentfully. The vehicle was in the hotel car park with its air conditioning purring away. Kaheiki spoke to the chauffeur.

"Drive us around, Tony."

"Yes, Mr. Kaheiki," replied the other.

"Slowly."

"Right, sir."

We pulled away and Kaheiki studied me with an amalgam of interest and disappointment. I detected no sign of pity.

"You seem to go looking for trouble," he observed.

"There's no shortage of it on Oahu," I replied. "I'll say that."

"Why did you visit Gabriel Mahalona's house yesterday?"

"I just happened to be passing."

"Cut out the wisecracks," said Perellini, nudging my shoulder. "Mr. Kaheiki don't like them."

"Well, I don't like being driven around in a car against my will," I said, "so I was trying to lighten the atmosphere. Besides, isn't it obvious why I went there? The murder weapon that killed Donald Dukelow was identical to the one that was pushed into Gabe Mahalona's ear. Death by meat skewer must be pretty unusual on an island where almost everyone is able to carry a gun." I looked at Perellini. "Even tourists."

"I'm a legitimate employee here," he retorted.

"Employed to track, threaten and intimidate."

"All part of the service, Mr. Saxon."

"Did you think we wouldn't find out?" resumed Kaheiki. "You were followed to the Pineapple Theater, where you borrowed my daughter's motorbike so that you could lose any pursuit."

"And I did," I said, proudly.

"Only for a while. We soon caught up with your movements."

"I know. Mrs. Mahalona rang the police and Captain Rapoza passed on the information to you—like another legitimate employee."

He smiled. "You're not a businessman, obviously."

"No, I prefer to have a clear conscience."

"The best way to keep that in business is to have friends in the right places. They can bring influence to bear. Clay Rapoza thinks you're being a nuisance, Alan—only that wasn't the word he used."

"I know the one *I'd* use," muttered Perellini.

"Leave this to me, Lance."

"Yes, Mr. Kaheiki."

"I think that Alan knows your opinion of him."

"He tried to jump me. Only a maniac would do that."

"It was your fault for shadowing me," I said. "I was determined to find out who you are."

"Now you know," said Kaheiki. "What you don't understand is that there's a lot more to the Gabriel Mahalona case than you could possibly imagine. It's rooted in the business community here and you don't even begin to speak our language."

"I can recognize the smell of corruption, Mr. Kaheiki."

"Watch that mouth of yours," ordered Perellini.

"It smells the same in any language."

"I hope that you're not accusing *me* of corruption," warned Kaheiki, glaring at me. "Are you, Alan?"

"If the cap fits."

"That's not a nice thing to say. If it wasn't for the fact that you're a guest of mine, I might get very annoyed with you. Why can't you accept that you're out of your depth and just give up?"

"Give up what?"

"Pretending that you're Sherlock Holmes."

"In this climate?" I returned. "What use is a deerstalker and a cape on Waikiki Beach? I'd die of heat stroke. And don't forget that Sherlock Holmes smoked a pipe. I never touch tobacco."

"You know what I mean, Alan."

"Look, Donald was a mate of mine. I must do *something*."

"Then try to stay alive for his funeral," said Perellini.

"I want to see his killer brought to justice."

"Do you think we *don't?*" exploded Kaheiki, slapping his thigh. "You saw the state my daughter was in. Zann is devastated. She finally finds a man she wishes to marry and he's murdered only days before the wedding. How do you think that makes *me* feel? I don't only want the killer brought to justice. I want to throttle the bastard with my own hands." He made a conscious effort to calm down. "Why are we bickering like this, Alan?" he asked, manufacturing a smile. "Basically we're on the same side."

"And which side of the law is that, Mr. Kaheiki?"

It was not the most diplomatic remark, but I didn't regret it. Under duress, I was stuck in the back of a car with a wealthy businessman who'd made his money by cutthroat tactics and a bail bondsman who'd served time for armed robbery. I had to stand up for myself. Perellini was almost ready to hit me. Jimmy Kaheiki scrutinized me for a long time before speaking.

"I'm beginning to wish that the driver of that automobile had done a better job," he said, coolly. "I'm fed up with your insinuations."

"Then take me back to my hotel," I suggested, "and you won't hear any more of them. Yes," I added, before he could speak, "I know you're going to remind me that you're paying the bill for my stay but I'll insist on doing it myself now. That way, I won't feel indebted to you."

"As you wish."

"I do wish, Mr. Kaheiki."

"Fair enough." He raised his voice. "Back to the hotel, Tony."

"Yes, sir," said the chauffeur.

The old man's gaze settled on me again. "Tell me one thing, Alan," he asked. "Why did you meet my daughter earlier on?"

"Melissa and I are friends."

"I wouldn't have thought you had anything in common."

"A shared interest in theater. I watched them rehearsing."

"There's more to it than that."

"I'm not going to ask for her hand in marriage, if that's what you think. She wouldn't have me, for a start."

"Don't you dare use my daughter against us."

"Nobody could use Melissa," I replied. "She's her own woman."

"She's still part of the family."

"I realize that, Mr. Kaheiki," I said. "What separates Melissa from you and, I suspect, from your son, is that she actually had some sympathy for what happened to me today. I didn't ask to come here, you know," I went on, gathering pace. "I didn't go in search of a hit and run driver to spice up the visit for me. I was only on the island as a favor to a friend. A late friend now, alas. Donald wanted me to witness his marriage to Zann. But for her—but for the Kaheiki family, in general—I'd be somewhere safe and sound."

He was chastened. "You're right, Alan. We've been poor hosts."

"My complaint is against the security arrangements," I said, giving Perellini a sidelong glance. "Someone blundered."

"You blaming me?" demanded Perellini.

"One dead body, one wounded man. I'm sorry, but I wouldn't call that an unblemished record of success."

"I told you, I was here as a tracker."

"Ah, yes. That famous nose of yours."

"It did its job this afternoon," he said. "Tell him, Mr. Kaheiki."

"Tell me what—that it managed to sniff out Melissa and me in a café? That's hardly worthy of a Bloodhound of the Year Award."

"You're being very unkind to him," said Kaheiki.

"Am I?"

"You should be very grateful to him, Alan."

"Why?"

"Thanks to Lance," he explained, pointing to his employee, "one of the suspects is now in custody. An elderly man from Pakistan. I believe that he may have been in the car when it hit you."

"He certainly was," I said, vehemently. "I *knew* that he was mixed up in this somehow. He's been caught?"

"Lance handed him over to the cops."

"How do you know you've got the right man?"

"I know," said Perellini, complacently.

"I want to talk to him."

Kaheiki shook his head. "Captain Rapoza won't let you near him."

"He must. I have a right."

"You've interfered enough," he declared. "Now, why don't you thank Lance for making the first real breakthrough in the investigation? You owe him some respect for that."

He was correct. Perellini had done what neither the police nor I had so far managed to do. Using his own unorthodox methods, he'd apprehended someone. It was cheering news. With minimal intelligence to go on, he'd somehow captured the man I'd first seen in a hotel corridor. Instead of working in the complete dark, we now had a single beam of light.

"Congratulations, Mr. Perellini!" I said without sarcasm.

He basked in my praise. "I always get there in the end."

"Was he alone when you tracked him down?"

"Yes."

"Did he give you any trouble?"

"Not after I'd disarmed him."

"How on earth did you find the man?"

"By following a scent."

"How could you possibly pick one up?"

"Experience."

"It's incredible," I said. "I'm the only person who's ever seen the man, yet you manage to locate and arrest him. How did you do it?"

Perellini beamed. "That would be telling, wouldn't it?"

Back in my hotel room, I made straight for the telephone. There was some delay getting through to Emily Tenno at police headquarters but her voice eventually came on the line. I wanted confirmation.

"Is it true that you've made an arrest?" I asked.

"Yes, sir. Mr. Perellini brought in a suspect."

"What condition was he in?"

"Mr. Perellini or the suspect?"

"The latter. I get the feeling that Lance likes to rough up his captives—just to let them know who's in charge."

"He used reasonable force," she said, easily, "that's all. The man was fit enough to be interviewed. Captain Rapoza and I will be having another crack at him later on."

"And what have you found out so far, Sergeant?"

"That's confidential information."

"Come on," I pleaded. "You must be able to tell me something."

"Frankly, there's very little to tell."

"Are you certain that you've got the right man?"

"Oh, yes. No doubting that."

"Let me see him."

"That won't be necessary."

"But I'll be able to identify him."

"If we need you, Captain Rapoza will be in touch."

"How ever did Perellini manage to nab him?"

"He has contacts on Oahu," she admitted, reluctantly. "He received a tip-off and accosted the suspect in his rented apartment."

"Where was that?"

"About three blocks from where you're staying, sir."

"He was right under our noses all the time!"

"We weren't to know that."

"Has he given you the names of his accomplices?"

"I'm sorry," she said. "I can't tell you anything else."

"But the case is more or less cracked now."

"Hardly, sir."

"You have a prime suspect in custody."

"The burden of proof still lies with us," she reminded me. "All we have so far is your word that he walked past you in the corridor on the night of the murder, and your more dubious claim that he was sitting in the passenger seat of the car that tried to run you down."

"He was, Sergeant!" I affirmed. "I saw him."

"But only in a flash. That's not enough for you to make a positive identification. And even if he was in the vehicle, there's no proof that he was a willing accomplice in the attempted murder. We need hard evidence, Mr. Saxon," she stressed, "and we still don't have it."

"Why not let Perellini beat a confession out of him?" I joked.

"Interviews of suspects are governed by strict rules."

"Can't you bend them when you know someone is guilty?"

"Guilty of what?" she asked. "Walking down a hotel corridor late at night? Being given a lift by someone who turned out to be a hit and run driver? We can't charge him on either of those counts, I fear."

I was aghast. "You're not going to release him, surely?"

"He's being held for further questioning."

"You can't do that indefinitely."

"Goodbye, sir."

"Wait—there's something you're not telling me."

"I have to go," she said. "Do excuse me."

The phone went dead. I was utterly deflated. Having rushed back to my room with excitement, I felt as if I'd just run into a brick wall. The arrest of the suspect was not as yet the promised breakthrough. There was still a long way to go. And even if the police did make headway, they wouldn't update me on developments. It was obvious that they had their own reasons for holding the man and they were not about to divulge them to me. Emily Tenno's tone was explicit. I was being deliberately excluded from the investigation.

What baffled me was how Lance Perellini had manage to track down and overpower the suspect when he had no clues on which to work. Unlike me, he'd never even seen him. The search was narrowed somewhat by the age and ethnicity of the man, but he was by no means the only Asian of advanced years in Honolulu. Yet, miraculously, he'd been found by Lance Perellini. Who was he? On what charge had he been arrested? Nobody would tell me.

Disappointment sent me straight to the drink cabinet. I grabbed a beer, poured it into a glass, then added a few ice cubes from the small freezer compartment. Dropping into an armchair, I brooded. There were four of them. If, as I was convinced, the Pakistani was an accomplice, then he had at least three colleagues. Two of them had performed the little charade at the restaurant for our benefit, the third had been the ostensible business client who had dined with the fraudulent Gabe Mahalona. They were still at liberty. And so, I realized, was a fifth possible suspect—Nick Kaheiki. Had he been pulling the strings behind the crimes? Was he making a bid to take over his father's business empire? I reserved my judgement.

Until all the culprits had been rounded up, I couldn't rest. They were involved in the conspiracy to murder Donald Dukelow. With or without police assistance, I simply had to know who they were and why they'd killed my friend and done their best to dispatch me after them. Filled with a desire for retribution, I no longer felt the aches and pains from the car accident. Vengeance has medicinal properties.

The telephone rang. I studiously ignored it. After my conversation with Emily Tenno, I was wary. I didn't wish to be further depressed. The caller might be Heidi, trying to persuade me that it never happened; or Clive Phelps, wanting to pump me for more details about the murder; or Perellini, unable to resist the urge to crow over me; or one of the reporters who'd left voice messages earlier. At that moment, I didn't want to speak to anybody. But the caller wouldn't give up. As if knowing that I was in the room, the telephone rang and rang until my resolve finally caved in. I lifted the receiver.

"Hello," I said, tentatively.

"Alan?" she asked.

It was Suzanne Kaheiki. I was overcome with remorse.

"Yes," I replied. "I'm so sorry I didn't pick up the phone at once."

"They told me you'd been hit by an automobile."

"A glancing blow, Zann, that's all. I'll live."

She was agitated. "Did someone really try to kill you?" she said.

"Put it down as a near miss."

"This is dreadful!"

"It is a bit extreme," I agreed. "I mean, we all have enemies but they don't usually express their dislike so violently. My problem is that I know too much. I pose a threat."

"I want to see you, Alan," she decided. "Can I come to the hotel?"

"Well, yes. I suppose so."

"You don't sound as if you're happy with the idea."

"I'd love to see you, Zann," I said, earnestly. "I just don't want you to be upset. Looking like this, I can't really meet you in one of the public rooms. You'd have to come here and my room is close to the one that Donald used to occupy."

"I can handle that."

"Then there's no problem."

"I'll drive myself over."

"Are you sure that your father would approve?"

"There's no reason why he should know, is there?"

"He has a way of finding these things out, Zann."

"So?" she said. "He can't stop me. And we need to talk."

"I'm in Room 324."

"I'll get there as quick as I can."

◇◇◇

Since I wasn't able to luxuriate in a bubble bath for as long as I wanted, I settled for a shower to freshen myself up, using the plastic shower cap to protect the bandaging around my head. When I'd dried myself gingerly, I came back into the room to look in the full-length mirror. It was a daunting sight. Ugly bruises covered all parts of my body and there were far too many lacerations to count. In the short term at least, a dip in the hotel swimming pool had to be ruled out. Angry parents would complain that I was scaring their kids.

To hide some of the injuries, I put on a long-sleeved shirt and a pair of slacks. Short of wearing a mask, however, there was nothing I could do about my face and head. Zann would have to know the worst. The ice had melted in my beer by now so I drank it then put the glass on the cabinet. Opening the doors to let in a sea breeze, I stepped out onto the *lanai* and surveyed the scene. For the first time, I envied the guests who were lolling beside the pool in their swimsuits. Some of them were monstrously overweight, others were dangerously thin, but all felt able to expose their bodies in public. It would be a week before I even dared to look at myself in a full-length mirror again. My misadventure was something else that I couldn't put on a post card to my daughter.

When there was a knock on my door, I was taken aback. Zann could not possibly have reached me yet. Even her brother's Maserati wouldn't have got from the house to the hotel in so short a time. Through the spyhole, I saw that it was not my expected guest. It was an unwanted one. Heidi Dukelow was standing outside with her arms folded. She obviously knew that I was there so I had to open the door.

"Alan!" she exclaimed, appalled by my wounds. "Look at you!"

"I'd rather not, Heidi."

"Officer Broderick told me as we were leaving for the airport. He said you'd been in an accident."

"Except that there was nothing accidental about it."

"Tell me what happened," she said. "Can I come in?"

It would be too inhospitable to keep her standing in the corridor and I didn't want to be seen by any passing guests. Reluctant to let her into the room, I issued a proviso.

"You can't stay long, I'm afraid. I'm expecting someone."

"I just want to know the details. Are you still in pain?"

"Only when I laugh."

"I'd have come sooner but I've only just got back from seeing Cora off. Her flight was delayed so we had to kick our heels for hours. I was so relieved when it was time for her to go."

"How was she?"

"Putting on a brave face to hide the anguish."

While she sat on the sofa, I was careful to choose one of the armchairs. Proximity to Heidi was no longer advisable, especially in my delicate condition. I told her about my near-escape from death but not about my exchange with Captain Rapoza at the hospital, nor about my meeting with Melissa Kaheiki. Somehow, I no longer felt able to confide in her. Heidi exuded sympathy throughout.

"You should have stayed in hospital, Alan," she said.

"Too much to do."

"Don't take any more risks."

"I can't help it," I said. "Simply being on this island is a risk. Last time I was in Honolulu, I filled in this long questionnaire from the Tourist Board, asking me how much I enjoyed my stay. I gave them full marks on every count. Not this time. It's been downhill all the way."

"You're forgetting our round of golf."

"And you're forgetting the man who spoiled it by trailing us."

"You enjoyed that meal with the Kaheiki family, didn't you?"

"At the time," I conceded, "but not in retrospect. It was the same as the meal I had with Donald. Everything went well at first. Then we met the man who called himself Gabe Mahalona. What happened after that poisoned my memory of the whole evening."

"Yes, I can understand that." She lowered her head. "Listen, Alan. There's something I've been meaning to say. I owe you an apology."

"Not at all. It never happened."

"I didn't mean that," she said, lifting her head again. "You asked me something earlier and I lied to you."

"I know."

"Do you?"

"I asked if you'd seen anything odd about Donald's behavior," I recalled, "but you denied it. I didn't believe you."

"At that point, I didn't want you to know just how close Donald and I still were. His behavior was odd," she confessed. "When we were staying with his mother, he went into defensive mode, keeping his head down while Cora bombarded him with reasons to call the marriage off. All at once, his mood changed."

"In what way?"

"He became uncertain and irritable. That wasn't like Donald."

"Anything else?"

"Yes," she said, "he did something he'd never done before. He stopped confiding in me. Given all that had happened between us, I found that very hurtful."

"He didn't want to alarm you, Heidi."

"What do you mean?"

"According to his mother, he had an anonymous phone call when he was staying with her in Rochester. She only heard his side of the conversation but she had a strong impression that he was being warned to stay away from here."

"Why didn't he tell *me?*" she protested.

"Why didn't Cora Dukelow tell you?" I asked. "When they caught the plane to come here, they must both have known there was an element of danger. I wish one of them had mentioned it to me. It was the least that Donald could have done."

"He'd refuse to acknowledge it, Alan. If there were a real threat, Donald would have ignored it." She pulled a face. "One of the penalties of achieving celebrity status in any field is that you attract crazies from time to time. Well," she said, indicating me, "you must have come up against this problem."

"Frequently."

"Donald dealt with it by withdrawing into his shell and pretending it wasn't there. That's why he valued his privacy so much. He hated people trying to ingratiate themselves with him, to cash in on his celebrity. Then there were the others," she sighed. "Those who envied him and wanted to hit back out of spite. Hate mail merchants."

"I've met a few of those in my time as well.

"What did you do?"

"Tear the letters up and throw them away."

"Donald had the same reaction," she said. "The year that he won the Masters, he had a death threat before the last round. Most golfers would at least have shown it to the cops. Not Donald. He was determined to win that green jacket or to die in the attempt. So he destroyed the letter. If the crazy who wrote it was trying to put him off his game, his plan backfired. Donald went out and shot the best round of his life."

"I know, Heidi. I was three shots behind him that day."

"Warnings just never frightened him off. He came here to marry Zann and nobody was going to prevent him." She got up from the sofa. "But I've taken up too much of your time," she said, moving to the door. "If you've got company, I'll make myself scarce."

"Thanks for coming," I said, following her across the room.

"You want a nurse, just give me a call."

"There's really no need for you to stay on the island."

"I think there is," she said, casually. "Don't you?"

I was unequivocal. "No, Heidi. I don't."

I opened the door and let her out. Though I'd been unwilling to talk to her at first, our chat had given me some valuable insights. I now understood why Donald Dukelow had refused to change his plans in the wake of an anonymous phone call. In his shoes, I'd have done the same. I was given scant time to reflect on what I'd learned during Heidi's visit. Minutes after one woman had gone, another was knocking on my door. I let Zann Kaheiki in with far more enthusiasm.

"Dear God!" she cried, hands to her mouth. "You poor man!"

"It's not as bad as it looks."

"Was anything broken?"

"Only the watch I'd bought for my daughter. Come and sit down," I invited. "Can I offer you a drink? Tea, coffee, alcohol of some sort?"

"No, thanks," she said, moving to the sofa.

"Then I won't either," I decided. "How are you, Zann?"

"Recovering slowly."

"You look wonderful."

It was no idle compliment. She was wearing a sleeveless blue dress of the finest silk with a floral pattern that seemed to wind itself around her body like a convolvulus. Her hair was brushed back and held in place by a silk bow that complemented the dress. Expensive sandals of the perfect color and style completed the outfit. The effect was startling. Zann would never have been taken for a woman who was in mourning though I could see that extra make-up had been used to conceal the slight puffiness around her eyes. I sat beside her.

"I simply had to get out of the house," she said, restlessly. "I've been locked in my bedroom for over thirty-six hours and it's not healthy. Mom wanted to come with me but I told her I'd rather be on my own."

"Why did you want to see me?"

"To tell you something in person. Melissa asked me some questions on your behalf and I wasn't entirely honest with her."

"Oh?"

"There are some things I find it very hard to talk about."

"Well, you don't have to say anything you don't want to, Zann," I assured her. "This is not a cross-examination. The reason I asked Melissa to speak to you is that I didn't think I'd be welcome in the house. Also, to be frank, when I did come to see you, someone was listening in on our conversation."

"Mom and Nick. I was livid when I realized that."

"Did you challenge your mother?"

"Of course. She said that they wanted to make sure you didn't upset me in any way. I was very fragile yesterday."

"Was anyone eavesdropping on your conversation with Melissa?"

"Oh, no. I made sure of that." She laughed. "They wouldn't dare do that sort of thing to Melissa. My sister can be very confrontational."

"I've seen her in action at the theater. She's a streetfighter."

"Melissa's also a pussycat when she wants to be."

"Were you pleased to see her?"

"Very. We were starting to lose touch."

"Melissa regrets that," I said, quietly. "What was it you told her that might have been misleading?"

"I pretended that Donald had received no warnings to stay away."

I was surprised. "You *knew* about that phone call?"

"We had no secrets. Donald told me everything."

Apart from the role that Heidi played in his life, I thought.

"Weren't you worried by the threat?"

"No. Once we'd made our plans, we weren't going to let anybody rearrange them for us. I belong to the Kaheiki family, Alan," she said, tilting her chin. "Nobody—but *nobody*—pushes us around."

"Defiant to the end. You and Donald were well-matched."

"A hundred warnings wouldn't have stopped us."

"But it wasn't really a warning for Donald to stay away from here," I said as the truth slowly dawned on me. "In fact, it was quite the opposite. Whoever made that phone call knew the sort of man Donald Dukelow was. In telling him to keep away from Oahu, he was instead guaranteeing that Donald would be here."

She was disturbed. "I never thought of that," she admitted.

"The worst thing that could happen for the people who were out to get you was for the wedding to be shifted at the last moment. It *had* to be in Hawaii or it couldn't be sabotaged in the way that it was."

"But how did they know that the wedding was even taking place?"

"It only needed a slip of the tongue from someone in the family."

"They swore to keep it secret—so did the minister."

"It leaked out somehow, Zann. Like the name of that restaurant."

"The one person I mentioned that to was my brother."

"That's what worries me," I said.

There was no point in holding back now, even though I had to broach a difficult subject. Melissa had told me enough to make me highly suspicious of Nick Kaheiki. I wondered what his other sister had to say. I chose a roundabout approach.

"Why did you decide to work on the mainland?" I asked.

"Why not?"

"Because it would have been so much easier for you to slot into one of the family enterprises. They have a stake in the travel business. You could have helped to run the operation in Oahu and develop it."

"I was more interested in developing myself, Alan," she explained. "If I was parachuted into a top executive post, I'd be viewed and resented as Daddy's Little Girl. I couldn't bear that. So I fled to the mainland, graduated from U.C.L.A., then landed a job under my own steam."

"All credit to you."

"I can't say that my parents were entirely pleased."

"They were afraid you'd meet too many *haoles*."

"My father saw it as a rejection of the family," she said, "whereas it was just a desire to make it on my own. It also kept me away from home quite a lot. That was the other big strike against it."

"How much did you know of family affairs?"

"Lots. Mom would e-mail me almost every day."

"Did she tell you about any difficulties they were having?"

"Sure. I read it in the papers, anyway. The Kaheiki name causes a tiny ripple even in L.A. When one of our gas stations was torched, for instance, there was a quite a feature on the problems here. Listen," she went on, "Donald and I did take it all into account, you know. That's why everything was so secret. If we'd gone for a big wedding, it would have been asking for trouble."

"Your family has reservations about Donald, didn't they?"

"Mom and Dad came round in the end."

"What about your brother?"

"Nick found it more difficult to accept. Tried to talk me out of it. He even set his wife onto me at one point, but I knew what I wanted. After all the guys who'd tried to make a move on me just because I was there," she said, ruefully, "it was a joy to meet someone like Donald. He was a true gentleman."

"Yet married at the time."

"Things were already winding up between him and Janine."

"And you were ready to take him on?"

"With two or twenty broken marriages behind him. I loved Donald. When your feelings are as strong as mine, nothing else matters."

"It does to the rest of your family." I changed tack. "Your brother showed Heidi around the factory. She was very impressed."

"Nick's a good manager. Keeps everyone on their toes."

"Is he ambitious?"

"Very."

"How soon does he want to take over the reins from your father?"

"As soon as possible," she said, smiling. "Tomorrow, if need be."

"Even though the Kaheiki empire is under attack?"

"Nick relishes a fight."

"But he can't fight an invisible enemy, Zann. There's been vandalism, theft, arson—and now murder. This is heavy stuff."

"You don't need to tell me that, Alan," she said.

"Who do you blame for it all?"

"Blame?"

"If your name wasn't Kaheiki, it's a safe bet that Donald would still be alive and the pair of you would have gone on to be happily married. But you didn't," I reminded her. "You came from the wrong family."

"I wouldn't change it for the world," she declared, proudly. Her face then clouded and she chewed her lip. "Having said that, I won't deny that there have been tensions. It's one of the reasons I decided to leave the island. My father's got amazing energy. He worked around the clock to get where he is and I admire him for that, even though I couldn't always approve of his methods."

"You mean, he sailed too close to the wind?"

"You have to do that sometimes, Alan."

"Not if other people get badly hurt."

"It's a competitive world," she said, blithely. "You're either a winner or a loser. Heavens, nothing is more competitive than the professional golf circuit. Do you care about hurting other people's feelings when you beat them in a tournament?"

"Of course not."

"There you are then."

"It's not a fair comparison, Zann," I argued. "You can keep losing in golf and still make a reasonable living if you squeeze onto the fringes of the leader board often enough. In business—if someone gobbles you up and spits you out—that's it. You're dead and buried."

"I hear what you're telling me, Alan," she said, gravely. "You believe that Donald was killed because of the way that my family does business. He was a scapegoat."

"I might be the next."

She grabbed my arm. "No," she protested, "that would be too much to bear. I feel guilty enough already. Why don't you simply take the next flight out of here?"

"Captain Rapoza wants me to stick around—and so do I."

"In spite of the danger?"

"Maybe I have some of the Dukelow spirit in me as well."

"Look where it got Donald."

"He wasn't expecting trouble. I am."

"What you really need is some sort of protection."

"Your father arranged it for me," I told her. "Without bothering to tell me, he assigned a bodyguard to look after me. Lance Perellini."

"Yes, I've met him."

"So have I, Zann. We didn't really hit it off. He introduced himself by sticking a gun to my head. Mr. Perellini and I will never be bosom friends, I fear."

"My father's used him in the past."

I was curious. "Oh? In what capacity?"

"You'd have to ask Daddy that—or Nick. All I know is that Lance Perellini is very good at what he does."

"So he keeps telling me."

"I've seen articles about him and his triumphs," she recalled. "He catches big-name fugitives. A bounty hunter."

"I certainly wouldn't like to have him stalking me," I said. "Did you know that he's turned someone over to the police?"

She sat up. "Someone involved in the murder?"

"Probably."

"Who is he? When was he arrested?"

"Perellini brought him in this afternoon. I don't know his name."

She swallowed hard. "Was he the man who killed Donald?"

"I don't know, Zann."

"What do the police say?"

"They're still working on him right now—not that they'll tell me anything. I'm not on Captain Rapoza's Christmas card list any more. He's taken against me."

"Why?"

"I think he's worked out that I don't trust policemen."

"Captain Rapoza has a good reputation."

"For what, though?" I asked. "That's the question." I raised an apologetic hand. "Forgive my cynicism. I have a rather warped view of law enforcement officers. They're usually much more interested in enforcement than in the law. That's what gives them their buzz."

"You really are cynical, aren't you?" she said.

"Blame it on my unhappy childhood."

"What's Captain Rapoza done to upset you so much?"

"Ask your father."

Before I could explain what I meant, there was a thunderous banging on the door. I thought at first that it might be the officer who'd replaced Liam Broderick but a glance through the keyhole told me that it was Zann's brother. He looked angry. I opened the door to him.

"Is Zann here?" he demanded.

"Yes, I am," she said, coming to the door. "What do you want?"

"To stop him using you."

"I came here of my own accord, Nick."

"Well, it's time for you to leave."

"Don't you think that's a decision you should leave to your sister?" I suggested. "Zann doesn't need your permission."

He looked at me properly for the first time, baring his teeth in amusement when he saw my injuries. His eyes darted back to his sister.

"I think you should go."

"Who says so?" she retaliated.

"I do, Zann."

"How did you even know that I was here?"

"Never you mind."

"But I *do* mind!"

"He's only trying to dig for dirt about our family."

"That's not true at all. Alan is a friend."

"And a fucking Howlie," he growled.

"Perhaps you *had* better go, Zann," I said, stifling her protest by putting a finger to her lips. "I fancy that your brother wants to have a private word with me."

"Then he'll have to do it with me here," she insisted, glaring at him, "because I'm staying until I'm ready to leave."

"In that case," I said with forced politeness, "I suppose that you'd better come in, Nick. But no wrangling with your sister, please. Zann is here as my guest. You're not."

"This won't take long," he grunted.

He stepped into the room and I closed the door. Strutting around, he sized the place up and even ran an exploratory hand over my golf bag. Zann and I resumed our seats on the sofa.

"Nice room," he observed. "Remember who's paying for it."

"I am now," I told him. "And your father knows why. I'm not on the Kaheiki payroll any more. Though it looks as if someone down at police headquarters is. Why not tell Zann how you found out she was here?"

"It's not important."

"It is to me," she asserted. "Was I followed?"

"No, Zann," I said. "You were seen coming in here. That officer outside is not only guarding the crime scene, he's keeping tabs on me. My guess is that, the moment I let you in, he contacted headquarters to report your arrival and Captain Rapoza rang your father to see if he knew that you and I were alone in here." I gestured towards her brother. "Nick is only the errand boy. Your father sent him to fetch you."

"I'm nobody's errand boy," said Nick, defiantly.

"Why don't you at least sit down? No charge."

"I prefer to stand."

"Don't be so silly, Nick," scolded his sister. "Sit down and say what you have to say. But no more bad language—or out you go."

He shifted his feet with embarrassment. Primed to berate me, he was constrained by the presence of his sister. In the end, he perched on the arm of one of the chairs and glowered at me.

"What on earth's the matter with you?" said Zann.

He pointed at me. "He is. The snooper."

"On our first night in this hotel," I informed him, "a dear friend of mine was murdered in his bed. That gives me a right to snoop. If you've got nothing to hide, you've got nothing to worry about."

Zann was mystified. "What's Alan supposed to have done?"

"He's too inquisitive about our family," said Nick. "First, it was Melissa and now, it's you. He's determined to get at us."

"I don't believe that for a second. He's been very kind to me."

"Yes," he sneered. "He's been kind to Melissa as well. That's the way he works. Winning your confidence so that he can tease information out of you." He turned on me. "I'm putting a stop to it."

"You're not your sisters' keeper," I said. "They outgrew you a long time ago. Melissa went off to do her own thing and so did Zann. They don't need your approval, Nick."

"We never did," added Zann.

"You're a Kaheiki," he said, bunching a fist. "You owe the family some loyalty, Zann. We've a right to expect that."

"I've not been disloyal in any way."

"And neither has Melissa," I said, trying to clear her of suspicion. "We became friends because I was interested in the kind of work she does at that theater. It may not have much appeal to someone who drives a Maserati and flies a helicopter, but it has an audience."

"Yeah," he scoffed, "and we know what kind!"

"Nick!" protested Zann.

"So much for brotherly love," I remarked.

"Shut up!" he snapped.

I rose to confront him. "This is my room and I'll say what I want in it. If you don't like that, I suggest you get out until somebody house-trains you properly."

"We'll both go," said Zann, getting up. "Nick's spoiled everything."

"It was lovely to see you."

"Next time, I'll make sure there are no interruptions."

"Thank you, Zann. I'd appreciate that."

I escorted her to the door, opened it then planted a farewell kiss on her cheek. She gave me a sad smile. Her brother sat resolutely on the arm of the chair. I eased her gently out.

"Leave us alone," I said. "Nick wants to do some male bonding."

I shut the door behind her, then strolled nonchalantly across to my golf bag. Nick stood up and flexed his muscles. Now that his sister had gone, he was able to show off. It was a time for preventative action. I was alone with someone who wouldn't scruple to use violence, even when there was a police officer nearby. He was confident that any charges I might bring against him would be dropped. Given my injuries, I was not able to defend myself properly so I needed a weapon. As he ambled towards me, therefore, I pulled a club out of my bag.

"That's far enough," I said, sharply. "Do you know what this is?"

He stopped in his tracks. "Yeah. It's a driver."

"No, Nick. It's my equalizer. It puts us on the same level. Come any closer and—I swear to God—I'll hit you straight down the fairway. So you can drop all that I'm-much-stronger-than-you stuff."

"I ought to take that club off you and stick it up your ass."

"Do me a favor and try."

Before he could move, I swished the club through the air a few times just to remind him that I knew how to use it. He had second thoughts. He'd been sent to threaten, not to assault me.

"Back off, Mr. Saxon," he warned. "You're causing aggravation."

"To you?"

"To the whole family."

"Zann doesn't think so. Nor does Melissa."

"Keep away from them."

"What are you afraid they might tell me?" I taunted. "That their brother can't bear the idea of running a shirt factory for another twenty years while he's waiting to inherit the crown?" He was nonplussed. "You didn't tell Heidi about the delay, did you?" I went on. "You tried to give her the impression that you'd be cock of the walk in no time at all. Master of all you surveyed.

Oh, and you somehow forgot to tell her that you were married as well."

"Be quiet!"

"You obviously have no qualms about fucking a fucking Howlie."

"Shut up, will you?"

"I thought we were going to talk. How can we do that if I shut up?"

"Keep out of our hair."

"All that I did was to talk to Mrs. Mahalona. And she told me something that made me look at Donald's death from a different angle. It seems that her husband was killed to spike a business deal he was about to close. And who were the beneficiaries?" I said with mock surprise. "Why, none other than the Kaheiki Corporation."

"So what does that tell you?"

"That it was in your interest to have Mahalona out of the way."

"And?"

"I'm wondering if Donald got on your hit list as well."

"Don't expect me to cry over that idiot," he jeered. "Donald Duck deserved what he got."

"Hey, now be careful," I said, taking a step towards him. "I'm the one with the equalizer, remember. Show some respect for Donald."

"Quack, quack!"

I raised the club and he could see that I was ready to use it. He scowled at me but there were no more jibes about my friend.

"Now," I said, "why don't you try to convince me that you were nothing to do with either of the murders?"

"Me?" He gave a harsh laugh. "You're crazy!"

"Crazy people get crazy notions sometimes."

"Talk to Captain Rapoza. He'll help you to wise up."

"He and Sergeant Tenno won't even speak to me any more. From the moment I found out that the Kaheiki name linked both murders, they started treating me like a leper. Unlike you and your father," I said, "I don't have any pull with the Police Department here. I heard about that brawl you got into one night earlier this year. You beat some poor man to a pulp, then walked away free."

"He asked for it and he was the one who attacked me."

"Why did the police drop the charge against you?"

"Because they knew who the guy was," he said, "and why he'd been riling me. I was cornered that night by Gabe Mahalona's brother."

I was shocked. "His brother? Why?"

"Because he made the same mistake as you, that's why. He made a stupid assumption about me." He eyed me with disdain. "You should have done your research more thoroughly."

"Meaning?"

"The person who killed Gabe Mahalona didn't kill your friend."

"He must have done."

"Don't bank on it."

"But it was the same weapon, the same *modus operandi*."

"A tit-for-tat crime," he said, contemptuously. "Clay Rapoza is certain of it. The meat skewer that killed Mahalona was a different make from the one they found in Donald Dukelow's ear. And there were lots of other significant differences between the two crimes. There's context here, Mr. Saxon, and you don't know a fucking thing about it."

"Is this true?" I said. "There are two different killers?"

"Yes," he replied. "Now that you've got involved, they'll both come looking for Alan Saxon. As a golfer, that should appeal to you."

"In what way?"

"It's a sort of Honolulu play-off," he said with a broad grin. "The guy who kills you first is the winner."

Chapter Thirteen

Nick Kaheiki didn't need to hit me with his fist. His revelation was a blow in itself and it made me reel. He took great pleasure from my obvious dismay. When he left the room, his derisive laughter echoed along the corridor. His father's diagnosis had been horribly accurate. I was out of my depth. In trying to find the connection between two murders, I'd been misled by sheer ignorance. The police were partly at fault. If Captain Rapoza or Sergeant Tenno had had the decency to give me full details of the Mahalona case, I wouldn't have gone so far up a blind alley.

However, the full blame couldn't be laid at their door. I'd been the victim of my own drive to find Donald's killer. Thanks to my blundering efforts, I'd annoyed the police, alienated Jimmy Kaheiki and his son, come close to having my head blown off by a bounty hunter, and been run down deliberately by a car. It would have been nice to invoke the Heidi Principle and decide that it never happened, but actions have consequences. In my case, they could be fatal ones.

Donald Dukelow and I had fallen for the same trick. That's what really disturbed me. In warning him to stay away from Hawaii, someone made sure that he would go there. In leaving the meat skewer in my room, a similar result had been achieved. Instead of forcing me into hiding, it fired me up to continue the search for the killer. In short, it got me out of the safety of the hotel into a street where I could be attacked. Donald and

I were both lured into a position where we were vulnerable. Our strength of character was, in fact, our weakness. Knowing that we would respond in a certain way, someone had applied pressure to us.

After the talk with Nick Kaheiki, I was left in no doubt as to the magnitude of the danger I was in. A golf club might have kept him at bay but it was little use against a hit and run driver or a man with a gun. I slotted the club back in the bag, then closed and locked the windows, vowing that I'd never step out so incautiously onto the *lanai* again. I was being watched, I was being hunted, I was being set up. Apart from putting one officer outside my room, the Honolulu Police Department was doing precious little to secure my safety.

I decided to take the matter up with them.

It was a fraught journey. I spent the whole of the ride looking out of the rear window in case another vehicle was following us. When we reached police headquarters, I made sure that I paid the driver inside the taxi before scurrying quickly into the building. My haste was my undoing. In making a mad dash for safety, I reawakened aches and pains that had been dormant for some time. Every gash, graze and bruise wanted to let me know its exact location on my body. I was in agony.

The desk sergeant informed me that Rapoza and Tenno might not be available for some time and, even then, there was no guarantee that they'd agree to see me. I stuck to my guns. If I had to wait until midnight, I was determined to speak to one or both of them.

In the event, I only had to sit around for an hour or so. Word came through to the desk and I was taken to Captain Rapoza's office. Emily Tenno was in consultation with him. Neither of them looked overjoyed to see me again, though Tenno did give me her pitying smile when she noted my injuries. Rapoza sat on the edge of his desk. Tenno and I each took a chair opposite him.

"Thanks for coming," said Rapoza. "Saves me ringing you."

"I thought I was *persona non grata* around here," I said.

"Oh no, sir. You're just a pain in the butt."

"I've got one of those myself, Captain, so I know how you feel."

"We've just finished our second interview with the suspect," he went on, ignoring my remark. "Not that it got us very far. He's old but very cunning. The original wily Pathan."

"What's his name?"

"According to his passport, it's Sohail Yasin but that's an alias. He's also known as Aftab Hussein but his real name is Razzaq Khan." He handed me a sheet of paper. "That was faxed through to us an hour ago. Recognize him?"

I looked at the photograph. It could well have been the man I'd encountered twice before, but I could not be absolutely certain; the photograph was taken some years ago. I remembered far more wisps of white hair than I could see now. It was the high cheekbones and the look in his eye that eventually convinced me it was the right man.

"Difficult, isn't it?" said Rapoza. "They all look the same."

"Not to me, Captain," I replied. "They're highly individual. Did you say that his real name was Razzaq Khan?"

"That's right."

"Strange. I knew a Razzaq Khan at school. Nice, happy, fun-loving kid, he was. Best cricketer in the class. Razzaq would never have been sitting in a car that tried to run me down."

"I think we've heard enough about your childhood, sir," suggested Tenno. "Can you or can you not identify the man?"

"I believe so, Sergeant. It's him."

"Good."

"That means we can let you take a peep at the guy later on," said Rapoza. "If you hadn't recognized him in the photo, there'd have been no point." He took the sheet from my hands. "I'll have that back, please."

"Who is the man?"

"We're still trying to find the full details."

"Does he have a criminal record?"

"Not in the States—only in Pakistan."

"So how do you come to have his photograph?"

"Intelligence, sir," he explained. "Didn't your father tell you that prevention is better than the cure? If you can anticipate what someone is about to do, you can sometimes stop him doing it. Our drug agencies were warned about this guy."

"Has he moved to Hawaii, then?"

"No, he works out of New York. That's where we got this pretty picture of him," he said, putting the paper down. "From the NYPD. Razzaq Khan is a drug lord. He started smuggling narcotics when he was still in his teens so we're looking at a guy with over half a century of experience behind him. That means he's very rich, very cagey, and used to giving cops the runaround."

"Yet you say he did time in Pakistan?"

"It was only a token sentence. He'd been running things from his home in Peshawar, up near the Khyber Pass. Lot of his merchandise came from Afghanistan though he had other sources as well."

"And he was only in prison for a short time?"

"Bought his way out, apparently. Part of the deal was that, if he was released, he'd quit the country."

"So he did," said Tenno. "Moved to New York."

Rapoza sighed. "Why does every country dump its shit on us?"

"He's certainly not one of the poor and huddled masses, Captain."

"No, Emily. He feeds off them."

"I don't understand," I said, hunching my shoulders. "What brought a man like that to Oahu?"

"The murder of Gabriel Mahalona."

"You mean, he was responsible for that?"

"No, Mr. Saxon," he said, looking down at the photograph. "He came to avenge it. Mahalona was one of his lieutenants, hired to run his operation in Hawaii and along the West Coast of the mainland. The swimming pools were just a front. The business was the perfect cover. Gave him the chance to travel to California regularly. When he exported pools to the mainland, they'd often have a supply of cocaine or heroin hidden away in them." He switched his gaze to me. "Who'd think of searching a swimming pool when it was unloaded off a vessel?"

I was compelled to change my opinion of Gabe Mahalona. In the picture I'd seen of him, he'd been the image of contentment, a family man through and through. But he was nothing of the kind. He was a drug baron with a wide geographical remit. I thought of the palatial house with its grieving widow and its empty swimming pool.

"And no," said Rapoza, seeing the question in my eyes, "his wife didn't know what was going on. Fran Mahalona firmly believed that their beautiful new house was bought with the profits of the business."

"She still does," added Tenno. "And so does her brother-in-law. According to Rod Mahalona, it was all a plot by Jimmy Kaheiki to blacken his brother's name. Rod was so incensed that he assaulted Nick Kaheiki in a bar—well, he tried to, anyway. I feel sorry for the Mahalona family. They just won't accept the truth."

"I'm having a job accepting it myself," I confessed. "Are you saying that this man—Razzaq Khan—came all the way from New York to find out who killed Mahalona?"

"He's a guy who protects his interests," said Rapoza, "even at his age. Millions of dollars are at stake here. When his lieutenant gets cut down in a turf war, he has to strike back. That's the way the game is played. Trouble was, he chose the wrong target."

The penny dropped at last. "Jimmy Kaheiki!" I declared.

"Got it. Whoever bumped off Mahalona made it look as if Jimmy was responsible. As it happens," he went on, "they'd locked horns a few times in the past so it wasn't difficult to signpost Jimmy as the villain. He does like to throw his weight around. But he didn't clash with Mahalona over narcotics. Jimmy has principles. He'd never touch drug money. No need to, for a start. He's got all the dough he wants."

"Why didn't you tell me all this before?" I complained.

"Confidential information."

"But it could have stopped me from going to Mahalona's house."

"We never thought you'd do a crazy thing like that, sir," said Tenno, defensively. "And, besides, you have such a low opinion of cops. Saying you don't trust us is hardly the way to make us feel well-disposed towards you."

Rapoza gave a nod of assent. "Frankly, there were times when I could have run you down in a car myself. Anyone ever tell you that you're your own worst enemy?"

"It was my father's theme song."

"That figures."

"You could have sung a duet with him, Captain," I teased. My mind was still racing. "Look, I still haven't sorted it all out yet. Everything seems to start with the first murder."

"Correct."

"So who *did* kill Gabe Mahalona?"

"We're not absolutely sure," admitted Rapoza. "Chances are it might have had nothing whatsoever to do with narcotics. Mahalona had lots of enemies in the business world. Nowhere near as many as Jimmy, though. Could be someone tried to kill two birds with one stone. They rubbed out a rival and put the blame on Jimmy Kaheiki. Using that meat skewer was such a neat trick."

"Was it?"

"You obviously haven't noticed the advertisements around here."

"I've been too busy looking over my shoulder."

"Among his many other claims to fame, Jimmy Kaheiki is one of the largest meat importers in the archipelago."

"Yes, I knew he was in the food business."

"The advertisements are everywhere," said Tenno, taking over. "You must have driven past dozens on your way here this evening. They usually feature a piece of prime Texas beef. With a meat skewer sticking out of it. Or they show some kebabs at a barbecue. Even more skewers on display. It's almost a family trademark."

"See what I meant about symbols?" asked Rapoza.

I was repelled. "So that's why Donald was killed in the same way."

"It was a message aimed directly at Jimmy. Turning his future son-in-law into dead meat, complete with skewer. That really hurt him."

"Donald Dukelow is the person I feel sorry for," I said, "and not Jimmy Kaheiki. Donald was an innocent bystander. He didn't deserve what happened to him that night."

"I agree with you there, sir."

Tenno got up. "Perhaps it's time for Mr. Saxon to see if he can identify the suspect," she said. "Shall I take him along?"

"When you've explained one thing to me," I insisted.

"If we can, sir."

"I believed, all along, that the same man killed both victims. It wasn't just the coincidence of the meat skewers," I argued. "It was the fact that someone deliberately took on Gabriel Mahalona's identity. And he did that by giving us the man's business card and showing us a photo of his children. If he *didn't* kill him," I asked, "then how could he possibly get hold of those items?"

Captain Rapoza exchanged a covert look with Tenno.

"We're still working on that, sir," he said.

It was definitely him. I had no hesitation in saying so. As I studied the man through a two-way mirror, I recognized the elderly Pakistani who had strolled past us in the corridor that night and expressed a silent disgust. I was struck by the irony of it all. Donald Dukelow, whom I'd known for almost twenty years, had the kind of indeterminate features that I forgot as soon as he walked away from me. Yet I could clearly remember the face of a man I'd glimpsed for no more than a second on the two occasions when he'd suddenly intruded into my life.

"Take as long as you like," said Tenno. "We want you to be sure."

"I am sure, Sergeant."

"That's the man you saw at the hotel?"

"And in the car. I'd know him anywhere."

"You have good eyesight, Mr. Saxon."

"I need it on this island," I said.

I looked at the man again. Seated in a chair, hands folded in his lap, he was serene and relaxed, as if he didn't have a care in the world. Behind his serenity, however, I sensed a quiet arrogance, a conviction that he could always outsmart his interrogators. He was no ordinary gangster. Here was an international drug lord with a lifetime's experience of evading capture or of wriggling out of almost all the charges brought against him. His age was part of his disguise. Looking like a benevolent old grandfather, he would never be suspected of making his fortune out of organized crime.

"How did Perellini know where he was?" I asked.

"He has friends in the drug world," replied Tenno. "Rivals of this guy who were only too ready to point the finger. Lance Perellini is a brave man. The suspect was carrying an automatic pistol and a knife when apprehended. Oh, yes," she said, "and there was another weapon in the apartment—a meat skewer. It may have been intended for you, sir."

I was horrified. "You mean that *he* was the killer?"

"That's our guess. It doesn't take all that much strength to thrust a skewer into the brain of an unconscious man. And who would suspect him? Let's face it," she reminded me. "In your first statement, you didn't even mention the man. He didn't register."

"Well, he does now. Let me go in there."

"That's out of the question, Mr. Saxon."

"But he may be the man who murdered my friend."

"All the more reason to keep you apart," she said. "You wouldn't be able to control your temper. Besides, we have to get more evidence first. And while we have him in custody, his accomplices are still at large."

"I'm aware of that, Sergeant, believe me. Someone left a meat skewer in my bathroom. I can accept that Razzaq Khan is willing and able to commit a murder," I said, "but I can't see him climbing along a series of verandahs to get to my room."

"Someone else obviously did that."

"Someone who's still out there, lying in wait for me."

"Be careful, sir," she said, touching my arm with something close to affection. "We'd hate to lose you now."

"We?" I asked. "Can you really be speaking for Captain Rapoza?"

She showed her dimples. "Maybe not."

I was in a predicament. The police station was starting to give me the usual feelings of nausea yet I was in no hurry to leave. Inside it, I was safe: once I left, I was fair game. In the end, Rapoza made the decision for me. I was in the way. He'd told me enough to give me a clearer idea of what was going on and wanted me off the premises. He even conjured up an unmarked police car to get me back to the hotel. I was grateful. When it dropped me off, I went in through the main entrance. I didn't care if my appearance shocked some of the people in the lobby. I was getting used to my disfigurement.

Someone was waiting for me. She jumped up from her seat.

"Alan!" she cried. "I was hoping you wouldn't be long."

"What are you doing here, Melissa?" I said, giving her a warm hug.

"Take me somewhere private and I'll tell you."

By the time we'd reached the elevator, we'd turned every head in the lobby. The combination of my injuries, Melissa Kaheiki's facial adornments and the fact that our arms were linked familiarly together as we strolled along created a mild scandal. I could almost hear people asking themselves what we were going to do together. Fortunately, we were soon out of earshot of the fevered speculation.

"You're such a welcome sight!" I told her in the elevator.

"I've never met a man who said that to me before."

"Yesterday was bad enough but, in some respects, today was even worse. I feel as if my head's spinning, Melissa."

She giggled throatily. "It's the effect I have on you."

"What would you say to a drink?"

"Hello, goodbye and—boy, that tasted good!"

We let ourselves into my room and raided the cabinet. Melissa drank her beer straight from the can. I sipped a whisky into which I dropped a couple of ice cubes. We sat down.

"I wanted to make sure that you were okay," she said, solicitously.

"I hoped that you'd come to tuck me in."

"No, I'll let Fern do that."

"What?" I protested. "That Aussie marsupial?"

"She did you a big favor, Alan. It was Fern who sent him packing."

"I'm not with you."

"This guy called at the theater while I was out," she said. "Wanted to know if Alan Saxon was likely to drop in again. Claimed he was a friend of yours. Tried to turn on the charm."

"Which of his balls did Fern bite off first?"

"He didn't stay long enough for that. Fern can pick out a phoney at twenty yards. She had him out of there in a flash. He was no friend of yours, Alan," she said, anxiously. "I thought I ought to warn you."

"Thanks, Melissa."

"I rang first but you weren't here, and I didn't want to leave a message. Truth is, I wanted an excuse to see you again."

I pointed to my face. "When I look like *this*?"

"I felt so sorry for you earlier."

"Sympathy doesn't run in your family, I'm afraid," I said. "Your father had none to spare and Nick almost laughed out loud when he saw me. The general consensus was that I got what I deserved. You were the honorable exception," I added. "Oh, and Zann, of course."

"You've been out to the house to see her?"

"No, Zann came here. That's why your brother descended on me."

"When was this?"

I told her about the visit of her siblings and she snorted with anger. Pleased that her sister felt able to get out of the house, she had nothing but scorn for her brother.

"Nick actually *enjoyed* the fact that you're on someone's hit list?"

"Yes, Melissa," I said. "So did Lance Perellini, now I come to think about it. He said I was like the bait, wriggling on the end of a hook. Do you know who Perellini is?"

"Vaguely," she replied. "He was staying out at the house one time when I drove over to see Mom. She said he'd been hired to do some work for Daddy and was leaving the next day."

"What did you make of him?"

"Hated the guy on sight. Perellini was too sure of himself. Never stopped grinning, like he'd done something really good and was entitled to a lap of honor."

"Yes, that's our Lance, " I agreed. "In fairness, he gets results."

I gave a highly condensed version of what I'd learned at police headquarters. Like me, she was relieved that an important arrest had been made and was ready to give Perellini his due.

"That's great news, Alan. The boss man is in custody."

"But some of his employees are still on the loose—and looking for me. At a guess, I'd say that it was one of them who called at the theater earlier on. Did he give a name?" Melissa shook her head. "Did Fern describe him to you?"

"Yeah. She said he was an ugly, fuck-faced, bullshitting bastard." She laughed. "That's Fern's opinion of most men, actually. When I pinned her down on detail, all she could say was that he was big, mid-thirties, Hawaiian. Came on to her like some cheap salesman."

It sounded like the man we'd met at the restaurant. I was worried.

"He's after me because I can identify him," I explained.

"So? Hole up here until the cops get him."

"I don't have any faith that they will, Melissa. It was Perellini who made the one arrest so far, not the police. I'd hate to pay the bill that he's going to give your father. Perellini's services cost the earth."

"Daddy can afford it."

"It must be all that meat he sells," I suggested.

"And the rest," she said with a sigh. "There's almost nothing that the Kaheiki Corporation doesn't make, import, control, or sell."

"Except peace of mind. If they did, I'd buy some of it."

"Hang in there, Alan. You'll be fine."

"Why? Are you going to lend me Fern as a guard dog?"

She grinned. "Now, that's an idea!"

"Listen," I said, mustering some resolution. "Don't worry about me. Contrary to appearances, I can look after myself."

"What did the others say when they got a load of you?"

"The others?"

"Mrs. Dukelow and Heidi."

"Oh, Donald's mother flew out earlier today. Heidi stayed behind."

"You got some company, then," she said. "And she'll be much more user-friendly than Fern. I don't think Heidi would call you an ugly, fuck-faced, bullshitting bastard, would she?"

"Not in so many words."

"Team up with her, Alan. That way, you won't feel so lonely."

Until Heidi Dukelow's name crept into the conversation, I'd been enjoying Melissa's visit immensely. Then I was reminded that there was still some unfinished business, staying in a room just down the corridor. One day, I hoped, I'd be able to outlive the shame of that little episode. Heidi seemed to have managed it in the space of a few minutes. I'd need much longer. When Melissa was there, I was sorry that she'd brought up the other woman's name. After my visitor had gone, however, I came to see that she might have done me a favor. In turning my thoughts once more to Heidi, she made me examine my relationship with Donald's first wife more carefully. It was an instructive exercise.

Offered the chance to leave with Cora Dukelow, why did Heidi elect to stay behind? The ostensible reason was to await developments, but those could have been communicated to her on the mainland in seconds. Was there a darker purpose at work? Everything that had happened so far pointed to a mole. Only a handful of people knew that the wedding was about to take place. Secrecy had somehow been compromised. Assuming that the leak had to be at the Hawaiian end, I'd never even considered that it might have occurred in Donald's camp. Who was better placed to know what was going on than Heidi?

I certainly owed my presence on the island to her manipulation. And she had no qualms about deceiving her former mother-in-law about the true nature of her dealings with Donald. Heidi was a cool customer. She was used to getting exactly what she wanted. When her passion was aroused—as I'd discovered in that very room—she could claw like a tigress. Not all of the scratches on my body had come from the accident. Had she set out deliberately to sabotage the wedding arrangements? Did his ex-wife fear that Donald had finally found someone who would make her role redundant? Was the mole, in fact, a vengeful, dispossessed woman?

I couldn't believe that Heidi would have wanted the man she loved to be killed, nor did I see her having any direct involvement with the drug dealers who were behind the murder. But she had motive, means, and plenty of opportunity to leak information about our arrival on the island, hoping, in doing so, that the marriage would not take place. She could not have foreseen that it was the removal of the groom that made the ceremony difficult to perform. To whom had she given the details? I didn't know but my suspicion of her remained.

Heidi was too glib and self-possessed. She claimed that all she wanted was Donald's happiness, but would she really let him find it in the arms of Suzanne Kaheiki without feeling at least a twinge of jealousy? I doubted it. Perhaps Donald had met the ideal partner at last. Zann really was the one. Heidi would have sensed it at once. Her role as the resident mistress was under threat. The only way that she could keep her hold on Donald was to scupper the wedding plans. Viewed in that way, Heidi was a monster. Had I really ended up in bed with a woman like that?

I tried hard to persuade myself that I was letting my imagination run away with me. Heidi Dukelow was a bright, attractive, professional woman with a life of her own that was quite independent of the Dukelow family. That being the case, why did she cling on to them? Why had she made herself available to Donald whenever he wanted her? Why did she court his mother in the way that she did? What was in it for her? The only explanation was that she loved Donald enough to let him call the tune. Until he met Suzanne Kaheiki, that is. That was the turning point. Heidi must have decided that she could never compete with Zann.

I had the awful feeling that I'd been hoodwinked. The reason I liked Melissa so much was that she was so abrasively honest. What I saw was what I got—a dynamic, talented, committed, in-your-face woman who thrived on her work and who gloried in her sexuality. Heidi Dukelow came from a very different mold. She hid behind a mask. What I saw was really an illusion. I'd befriended, eaten beside, played golf with, walked, talked, and made love to a beautiful woman, but I still knew very little about the way that her mind worked.

What was her game?

◇◇◇

I slept fitfully, waking up every so often to wrestle with my anxieties, then drifting off out of exhaustion. Rising early next morning, I had a shower with the plastic cap over my bandaged head once again. When I shaved, I tried not to look too closely at the battered face in the mirror. It brought back too many unpleasant memories. As I was dressing, I heard my complimentary copy of the morning newspaper being slipped under the door. On the previous day, I hadn't even glanced at it but I was more curious now. I walked over to pick it up.

We dominated the front page again. The banner headline told of the arrest but what caught my eye was the photofit picture of another man the police were anxious to trace. It was based on my description of the imposter with whom Donald and I had gone to the nightclub. It was a reasonable likeness. I fancied that, if Fern ever did something as conventional as reading a newspaper, she'd surely recognize the man who came looking for me at the Pineapple Theater.

A knock on my door made my muscles tighten with apprehension. Fearing that it might be Heidi, I peered through the spyhole and was relieved to see that it was room service with the Continental breakfast I'd ordered. I was soon having my first delicious cup of coffee. Chewing a croissant, I read the article about the murder investigation. Rapoza had been canny. He'd revealed enough information to give the press something to bite on without giving too much away. I saw no reference to the killing of Gabriel Mahalona. The murder of Donald Dukelow was being treated as a separate and unrelated crime.

The Honolulu Advertiser was an interesting newspaper, and I read it from cover to cover, even making a doomed attempt to do the crossword. What saddened me was that so many fascinating things were going on in the city and I wasn't able to participate in any of them. There was an item about the Pineapple Theater in the entertainment section. Beneath a photograph of Melissa and her colleagues was the predictable caption—MAGNIFICENT SEVEN IN RAID ON PEARL HARBOR. Fern was the only woman who didn't oblige with a smile for the camera.

Prompted by Emily Tenno's comments, I looked for the Kaheiki name in the advertisements. It was prominently displayed. The skewers were there in abundance in the pictorial adverts for their imported meat. One thing I wouldn't order on the island was a kebab. The last section I read was the sports pages. My envy stirred as I saw a photograph of a golf tournament being held at one of the military courses on Oahu. I wished that I had the same freedom to play the game that I loved.

It was well past eight when the telephone rang. I picked it up.

"Yes?" I said.

Lance Perellini's voice came on the line. It was disagreeably terse.

"Jimmy wants to see you," he told me.

"He knows where I am."

"The limo will be outside your hotel in fifteen minutes. Be there."

He rang off. As invitations went, it was not the most courteous that I'd received. I felt that it marked a downward shift in Jimmy Kaheiki's view of me. The previous day, his command had been delivered in person by his enforcer. All that I merited now was a curt instruction. My instinct was to ignore it but that would only inflame Kaheiki even more and I'd no wish to do that. If I disobeyed, he'd send either his son or Perellini to bang on my door. Getting out of the hotel did have some appeal and the stretch limo was a guarantee of my safety. I was certain that it would be bulletproof.

Accordingly, I was waiting in the lobby when the vehicle cruised up to the main entrance with Tony at the wheel. Jumping out, he gave me a deferential smile, then opened the rear door so that I could get in. We set off and jostled with the heavy morning traffic. Apparently, I was being driven to the Kaheiki estate. That meant the enticing possibility of seeing Zann as well. I settled back in my seat.

"What does Mr. Kaheiki want me for?" I asked the chauffeur.

"I don't know, sir," he replied.

"Did he say anything at all?"

"I just follow orders."

We were five miles out of the city limits before I realized that something was wrong. Instead of staying on the main road, we swung off to the left and accelerated.

"Where are we going?" I asked.

There was no answer from the chauffeur. Tony was clearly following orders that hadn't been issued by his employer. I was being abducted. Panic set in. Releasing my safety belt, I tried the doors but found them locked. An override button prevented me from lowering the electronically controlled windows. The screen that separated me from the driver was made of thick glass. I was trapped. I wasn't being taken to the Kaheiki estate at all. It had been a clever ruse.

My suspicion of Heidi Dukelow had been ridiculously wide of the mark. She was not the mole, after all. It was the man who was driving the car, the trusted chauffeur who was party to the private conversations of the Kaheiki family and who'd heard all that we'd had to say about our hosts when he drove us back from dinner at the estate. Hidden behind the glass screen, he was easily forgotten by passengers and could listen to their indiscreet remarks at will. Tony was the person who'd leaked details about the secret wedding. He was one of them.

Yet it was Lance Perellini who had given me my command over the phone. Was he part of the gang as well? Was he betraying Jimmy Kaheiki? It seemed unlikely. If he was in league with the enemy, why had he gone to such trouble to arrest their leader? I was bewildered. All I knew was that I was in danger at a time when I was least able to defend myself. I needed a weapon and looked desperately around for one. My only hope lay in the drink cabinet but I had to make sure I didn't signal my intentions to the chauffeur. His job was to deliver me unarmed.

Reaching forward surreptitiously, I opened the door of the cabinet and examined its contents. In front of a serried rank of bottles was a row of glasses. A broken bottle would give me some defense but not against a firearm. What I needed was a concealed weapon, something that I could hide about me until it could be used to best effect. I decided on the corkscrew, large enough to inflict real pain yet small enough to be concealed under my shirt. As I stretched forward to get it, I caught Tony's eye in the rear-view mirror so I helped myself to a bottle of tonic water instead. After removing the top, I raised it up as if toasting him, then took a long swig. He looked away.

I grabbed the corkscrew in a flash. Tucked into my belt, it dug into my flesh but it also gave me a degree of comfort. I covered it with my Ben Sherman shirt. Then I drank the tonic water slowly. At least, it would not be spiced with a drug that disabled me. Donald had been given no chance. I hoped that I might be. I concentrated on trying to control my fear. In a crisis like the one that I faced, a cool head was vital. When Tony glanced in the rear-view mirror again, I forced a smile.

Slowing down, we turned off the side road and down a bumpy path that was hardly an ideal surface for a luxurious stretch limo. As we rumbled through a wooded area, the car's suspension was put to the severest test. Eventually, we pulled up outside what looked like an abandoned hut. We came to a halt and Tony sounded the horn twice. The signal brought two figures out of the hut. One of them, a chunky, middle-aged man, was holding a gun and he covered me as the limo doors were unlocked and I was beckoned out.

"Recognize me, fucking Howlie?" he taunted.

It was the man who'd abused us at the restaurant while pretending to be drunk. He was clearly sober now. His companion had a copy of the morning paper. He held it up beside his face so that I could compare the photofit with the real thing. Chuckling happily, he beamed at me.

"Good likeness, Alan," he said. "Well done, my friend."

Then he rolled the paper up and beat me around the head with it. I put up an arm to ward off the blows but enough got through to hurt me.

"I was driving the car when it hit you," he boasted.

"I'm surprised you ever passed your test," I replied.

He struck me hard across the face with the paper. When he was impersonating Gabe Mahalona, he'd oozed geniality. There was none of it in sight now. He spoke in Hawaiian to the chauffeur, then sent him on his way. Tony backed the car into a clearing to turn it round before driving off. I wondered what excuse he had to cover his absence from the Kaheiki estate. The man with the gun prodded me with it.

"Get inside," he snapped.

"Sorry we can't offer you hula dancers this time," said the other man, giving me a shove to help me along. "Go on. In you go."

The hut was large, low and dilapidated. Most of the roof had collapsed and there was a gaping hole in one wall. Some old wooden crates lay at the far end. A piece of tarpaulin covered something that was on the floor in front of them. There was a foul stench.

"Excuse the stink," said the man with the gun. "Mike hasn't had time to do the cleaning yet."

"Is that your name?" I asked, turning to his companion. "I thought it was Gabriel Mahalona."

"Only when it suits me," he said.

"Did you kill him?"

He was offended. "Me? You're *pupule*—crazy. Gabe was my friend."

"Then how did you manage to steal his billfold?"

"I didn't. I got the business card and the photo of his kids from Gabe's office. When he got whacked," he went on, "the alarm bells rang. I had to get in his office and take away anything that might be considered to be incriminating evidence."

"What's incriminating about a business card and a family photo?"

"They were souvenirs of a guy I really liked—and I thought they might come in useful one day."

"They did, Mike," said his friend. "You sure fooled this guy and that other mother-fucker. We both did."

"Yeah, okay. Calm it down, Billy Bob."

"Shit, man! We could've been Hollywood actors."

"And stop waving that gun around," said Mike. "Put it away. He's going to give us no trouble. Are you, Alan?"

"What's the point?" I replied. "I'm in pain as soon as I move."

"Good. It'll remind you who you're up against."

"You try anything," warned Billy Bob, thrusting the gun into its holster, "and I'll tear you to pieces. I'd like that." He gave me a nudge. "Get our present?"

"What present?"

"In your bathroom."

"Yes," I said. "The meat skewer came in handy for taking the pips out of my grapefruit." I turned to Mike. "Did you put it there? You must be a hell of a gymnast, if you did."

"It wasn't me," he admitted. "Couldn't have swung down like that."

"So it *was* done from the room above."

"Maybe. Maybe not."

I relaxed slightly. Their manner was far from friendly but I didn't get the impression that they were about to kill me. The gun was back in its holster and they were regarding me with contempt rather than hostility. All that I could do was to play for time and find out as much as I could about what had actually happened.

"You do realize that you made a big mistake?" I said.

"Mistake?" echoed Mike.

"Jimmy Kaheiki had nothing to do with your friend's death."

"Don't give me that. Of course he did."

"No, Mike. The police told me."

"And you believe those fucking liars?" demanded Billy Bob.

"The murder was rigged so that the blame fell on Jimmy Kaheiki."

"Yeah, yeah. How many times we heard that?"

"Too many times," said Mike. "I heard Jimmy say it himself. Know what he did? When we started hitting his property, he offered to buy us off. Swore he had nothing to do with Gabe's death, but he'd stump up the dough anyway as a gesture of goodwill."

"Good-fucking-will!" sneered the other man.

"Fair's fair, Billy Bob. It was a generous offer—tempting enough for us to take seriously. So we sent a man in to talk terms with Jimmy," he went on. "Only there was a part of the deal he forgot to mention."

"What was that?" I asked.

"He's brought this hired gun over from the mainland."

"Lance Perellini?"

"That's the guy. Hot shot bounty hunter. Always got his man, that was his claim." His face darkened. "He certainly got *our* man. The guy we sent in there never came back. Tony reckons that Nick Kaheiki took him up in his helicopter and dropped him into the ocean." He jabbed a finger at me. "You telling me that family got no blood on their hands? Perellini was paid to take our man out."

"He shouldn't have done that," said Billy Bob. "Should he, Mike?"

"No. It made our boss angry. That's why he came here in person."

"Are you talking about Razzaq Khan?" I said.

"Yes," answered Mike. "The man they killed was his son."

I began to see why a seventy-year-old man was prepared to endure a long flight to Hawaii in order to wreak vengeance with his own hands. But I still couldn't understand why Donald Dukelow had been the chosen victim when the real target should have been someone in the family. Mike volunteered the answer.

"We wanted to make the bastard *squirm*," he told me. "We wanted to make Jimmy's life a misery. Kill him and we let him off easy. Destroy his property, harm his business, sully his reputation, keep him guessing where we'd strike next—that was our plan. Then Tony gets a first whisper of this secret wedding," he said with a chuckle, "and that proved we had Jimmy on the run. *We* were the reason for the secrecy. He was filling his pants in case we found out."

"And we did," said Billy Bob, gleefully.

"We had a guy on the inside, see," continued Mike. "Tony had his price, we met it. When the time comes, we pull him out."

"What time is that?" I asked.

"You'll see."

"So am I next in line? Is that it?"

"You, Al?" he said, patting my cheek. "Of course not."

"But you tried to kill me only yesterday."

"Luckily, you survived. We need you alive now—to trade."

"Trade?"

"We get the boss and the cops get you. Simple."

"What if they don't go for it?"

"Then you won't be needing your return ticket," said Mike, holding me by the throat. "You'd better pray that Captain Rapoza comes through. He doesn't want another dead celebrity on his hands. Your name would create more headlines around the world. Look how much bad publicity he's had so far. No," he concluded, "I reckon that Rapoza will see sense."

"It was only by a fluke that he got Mr. Khan in the first place," said Billy Bob, angrily. "We left him alone in the apartment for less than an hour."

"That's when Perellini struck," I pointed out.

"Yeah, we know."

"He tracked down your boss by getting a tip-off."

"So?"

"Aren't you afraid he'll track you down in the same way?"

Billy Bob gave a wild laugh. "No chance!"

"Don't underestimate him," I cautioned. "That's what I did."

"Oh, we had great respect for Lance Perellini," said Mike, crossing over to the tarpaulin. "That's why we both went after him." He pulled back the tarpaulin with a flourish. "I think that Mr. Khan will be very pleased with us. Don't you?"

I gaped in horror as I stared at the corpse of Lance Perellini. His assassins had been thorough. Donald Dukelow had been killed with a single meat skewer. Dozens had been used to turn Perellini's head and face into a grotesque pincushion. There were skewers in his ears, his eyes, his cheeks, his nose, his mouth and his throat. Some had even been hammered into his skull. Blood had spurted readily to cover his face and soak his shirt.

The two men jumped back as I began to retch uncontrollably.

"If you're going to throw up," ordered Mike, "get outside."

I made it just in time, lurching through the door and vomiting into some bushes nearby. When I'd finished, I wiped my mouth with a handkerchief. I was summoned back inside the hut. They'd had the grace to cover the dead body with the tarpaulin again. Billy Bob put one of the wooden boxes in the middle of the hut.

"Sit there," he said, pushing me on to the box. "We got to truss you up like a Thanksgiving turkey."

"It's for the benefit of the cops," added Mike, taking a Polaroid camera out of a leather travel bag. "They'll need visible proof that we got you. Take that strapping off your wrist."

"But it's badly sprained."

"Take it off," he ordered, "before we cut it off for you." As I unwound the bandage, he pulled some handcuffs out of the bag and held them up. "We got these off Lance. He sort of bequeathed them to us."

He tossed them to Billy Bob, who slipped them over my hands and locked them in place. My sprained wrist throbbed in protest. There was more to come. Out of his bag, Mike took two rolls of the wide sticky tape used for sealing up parcels. Giving one to Billy Bob, he used the other to bind my legs together. I was amazed how easily it was done. Billy Bob repeated the process on my upper arms, running the tape around me three times to immobilize me. I did indeed feel like a turkey, ready for the oven. Mike pointed the camera at me and pressed the switch. When the photograph was ejected, he put it on the floor so that it could develop, slipping the camera back into the bag and taking out a brown envelope instead.

"I already got one of Perellini in here," he said, "just to show that we mean business. It should speed up negotiations a lot."

"Yeah," agreed Billy Bob. "What they're getting is Before and After photographs. Lets the cops know what'll happen to you if they don't trade. The photos will give Jimmy Kaheiki another scare as well. He brought Perellini to the island to smoke us out."

Mike picked up the photograph from the floor and thrust it under my eyes. It was gathering definition now. As my face was conjured into view, I looked helpless and frightened. He waited until the Polaroid had come out completely, then popped it into the envelope and sealed the flap.

"Quick as you can, Billy Bob," he said, handing him the envelope.

"I'll ring as soon as I make the delivery. You keep an eye on him."

"Oh, Alan isn't going anywhere."

Billy Bob gave me a playful punch, then went out of the hut. A few moments later, I heard a motorcycle start up and shoot away at speed.

"I'd love to be there when Captain Rapoza opens that envelope," said Mike, gloating. "That one of Perellini will make his eyes pop out."

"He'll come after you for this," I warned. "You realize that?"

"He's been after us for months and never got so much as a sniff. We had the whole Honolulu Police Department chasing shadows. Once we get the boss out of there, we'll be off the island in no time."

"How?"

"You don't need to know."

I glanced towards the corpse. "I take it that he was killed here?"

"Right after he made that phone call to you. If he did that," said Mike with a chuckle, "I promised that we'd let him live. Trouble is, I'm the sort of guy that breaks promises now and then."

"Does that mean you can't guarantee that I'll make it?"

"Your fate is in Rapoza's hands, Alan."

"That's what worries me."

I wasn't at all confident that the police would respond so promptly to the demands made on them. They had a notorious drug lord in custody, a man who was at the hub of an international operation, and who was also facing a murder charge. If they took him out of action, they'd gain great kudos. If they let him go—and simply got me in exchange—the police might not feel they had the best of the bargain. After all the bitterness between us, Captain Rapoza would hardly rush to my rescue. I had to put my faith in Emily Tenno.

"How will you hand me over?" I asked.

"We got that all worked out."

"Your boss can't possibly go back to New York now. He'll be wanted for the murder of Donald Dukelow."

"We always have exit strategies in hand for this sort of situation."

"How many of you are there altogether?"

"Enough."

"You've been watching us since we got here, haven't you?"

"Of course, Alan," he said, "we're professionals. You had a pair of eyes on you as soon as you arrived at the airport. Tony has keen ears as well. We also had someone else staying at the hotel. He watched you have lunch with the two ladies."

"Who followed us around Ko Olina?"

"That was me. I really am a keen golfer, see. I was hoping to pick up a few tips from a master. Only problem was," he said with a chortle, "I kept the glasses on Heidi most of the time. She sure has a cute ass, that lady. Especially when she bends over to get the ball out of the cup. Well," he added. "Don't need to tell you, do I? You saw it in close-up."

I was glad that he couldn't read my mind at that point.

"So who put that skewer in my bathroom?" I wondered.

"I told you. We had a man on the spot. Another guest."

"Is he still there?"

"You're asking too many questions, Alan."

"I'm impressed with the way you've got it all stitched up."

"You're just trying to wheedle information out of me that don't concern you. So," he decided, reaching for a roll of tape. "Maybe, I ought to shut you up for a bit."

Tearing off a strip of tape, he stuck it across my mouth. All that I could do was to mumble. He was highly amused. Fetching another box, he sat down on it with the newspaper in his hands.

"Here's the way it's going to be," he explained. "When Billy Bob gets there, he keeps out of range of any security cameras. Pays some kid to deliver the envelope to the desk sergeant, then rings me here. I wait until I'm sure the envelope will have been passed on to Captain Rapoza, then I give him a courtesy call. Satisfied?" I nodded. "Good. Now keep quiet while I read the paper."

He worked his way slowly through the newspaper, letting out an occasional laugh and even quoting an item to me from time to time. I was astonished at his calm. He might have been a tourist, sitting in the sun as he leafed through a magazine. The fact that the dead body of Lance Perellini lay on the other side of the hut didn't seem to trouble him at all. It certainly troubled me. My captors were sadistic. If the police didn't obey their dictates, then I might well be given a demonstration of how easily meat skewers could be inserted into a human head.

The longer we waited, the more convinced I was that something had gone wrong. Billy Bob had been captured, the plan had to be aborted. My eye stayed on the travel bag. What else was in there apart from a Polaroid camera and a couple of rolls of tape? How many skewers did they have left? The cell phone in Mike's shirt pocket finally rang. He took it out and flicked a switch.

"Yeah?" he said.

Listening carefully, he nodded his approval before switching off the phone. He checked his watch, then gave me his broad grin.

"So far, so good," he said.

He returned to his paper and tried to describe a cartoon strip to me. Somehow I didn't find it quite as hilarious as he seemed to do. It was almost fifteen minutes before he tossed the paper at me.

"Have a read of this," he suggested. "I got a call to make and it could take a little time." He opened the door. "You stay here with that meat head of a bail bondsman."

I sprang into action. Having had ample time to work out what I had to do, I slipped my hands under my shirt to grab the corkscrew. It had been digging into me ever since I'd sat down but it might now be my salvation. My arms were bound but I could still bend them at the elbow. Bringing the corkscrew up, I used its sharp point to poke away at the tape. It was not easy but I persevered, working methodically until I slowly made progress. The handcuffs impeded me and my left wrist was in agonizing pain. I pressed on, terrified that Mike would return before I could cut myself free. I could imagine the sort of punishment he'd inflict.

The tape finally gave way, allowing the use of my arms again. Though the tape was still stuck to my back, it did not stop me from bending over to hack through the bonds holding my legs. I tore off the tape, then braced myself for more pain as I removed my gag with a sudden jerk. It stung like mad. Darting across to the tarpaulin, I lifted it so that I could feel under it without having to look at Perellini's face again. It was unlikely that my captors had left the key to the handcuffs still on him, or his gun, for that matter, but they weren't what I sought. Remembering the cigar he'd been smoking the previous day, I knew that he must have a means of igniting it. My hands groped in his pockets until they closed on a cigarette lighter. I pulled it out.

Dropping it into my shirt pocket, I scurried across to the travel bag and opened it up. There were several items inside, including a supply of meat skewers and a hammer. I seized the latter gratefully. It had already been used on Perellini with hideous results. Now it was mine. It felt good in my hand. I was empowered. I stood behind the door and waited, my heart pounding with a mixture of fear and anticipation. I heard Mike give a satisfied laugh as he switched off his telephone. Evidently, a deal had been struck with the police. I wanted no part of it.

When he came back into the hut, Mike was completely off guard. I didn't hesitate for a second. Holding the hammer with both hands, I brought it down hard on the back of his skull. It felled him to the ground. Bleeding profusely and yelling obscenities at me, he tried to get up so I hit him again, using the side of the hammer this time to deliver a blow to the temple. With a grunt of pain, he sagged to the floor and brought both hands up to his head. Dropping the hammer, I grabbed his cell phone instead. I also took the newspaper with me as I hared out of the door. Mike was badly dazed but he was a strong man. Before long, I might have a wounded bear on my trail.

Keeping to the path, I ran until I heard a roar of anger from way behind me. It was time to divert him. Diving into a clump of bushes, I crumpled the newspaper, then set light to it. Within seconds, there was a healthy blaze. It would not be long before it was visible from much further afield. An alarm would be raised. Mike had obviously seen the smoke. He staggered down the path, holding a gun in one hand and using the other to press a handkerchief to the wound at the rear of his head. I hid behind a tree and waited.

The fire was now established. Seeing that he had no chance of putting it out, he swung round and started shooting indiscriminately into the undergrowth.

"You bastard!" he yelled. "Where are you?"

I was in no mood for conversation with him, especially as one of the bullets buried itself into the tree behind which I was concealed. When the gun was empty, he let out a cry of frustration, thrusting it back into its holster. Weakened by the loss of blood, and evidently in great pain, he went down on one leg. Since his back was now facing me, I crept slowly away until I felt I was out of his earshot. I then used his cell phone to ring the police and ask for help.

Keeping my voice low while I talked, I thought that I was relatively safe. All that I had to do was to stay hidden until the police arrived. Though I couldn't provide them with precise details of my location, I gave them a rough idea where they'd find the fire that I'd started. It was now crackling merrily away, broadening its base and sending a column of smoke high into the sky. Though I'd lit it in order to summon help, it was almost my undoing. Hot sparks were scattered far and wide. When a portion of them fell on my shoulders, I let out an involuntary cry of pain.

Mike heard it clearly. Forcing himself to his feet, he came crashing towards me through the undergrowth. I didn't know whether to stay there or make a run for it.

"So *that's* where you are, you fucking Howlie," he bellowed.

"The police are on their way, Mike," I warned him.

"Then they'll be able to scrape up what's left of you."

When he caught sight of me, he paused for a moment. He looked revolting. His head, face and shoulders were covered in blood, and the handkerchief that he was holding to his skull was absolutely sodden. There was a note of sheer indignation in his voice.

"You *hit* me, Alan," he said. "You fucking well hit me."

"I had to get out of there somehow."

"I'll kill you for that!"

Forgetting that he was out of ammunition, he tore his gun from its holster and pulled the trigger. When it simply clicked, he hurled it at me with vicious force. I ducked just in time and let it whistle over my head. Mike tottered. Impeded by the handcuffs, and suffering from my own wounds, I was hardly in prime condition for a fight but he left me no option. Mike wanted revenge. I decided that attack was the best means of defense. As he moved uncertainly towards me, I flung myself at him with all the power that I could muster and knocked him to the ground.

There was a howl of anguish as his head thumped against the hard surface. It made him reach for me angrily with both hands. I dropped the cell phone. We grappled, rolled, punched, twisted and gouged, neither of us able to subdue the other. Cursing me violently, Mike then bit me on the chest. The searing pain served to give me a strength and determination that I thought had been squeezed out of me. With an upsurge of energy, I forced him over onto his back. I snatched up the cell phone and brought it down on to his head as hard as I could, hitting him repeatedly until his resistance slowly ebbed away. Both hands up in supplication, he began to bleat for mercy.

I got up, discarded the cell phone, and searched for the gun he had hurled at me. When I found it, I stood over him with the weapon raised.

"Make one move," I said, breathlessly, "and I'll give you the headache of a lifetime. It will feel as if someone is driving a dozen meat skewers into it simultaneously." He groaned in agony. "This gun is much more solid than that Nokia cell phone of yours. Remember that and stay exactly where you are."

Mike did as he was told. All the fight had been knocked out of him. When I eventually heard the approaching police siren, I almost cried with gratitude. It was over.

The chauffeur was the first person to be arrested. Tony had to face the wrath of his employer as well as the rough handling he got from the police. Mike Kamanu, the man with whom I'd fought so fiercely, was treated in hospital before being brought to the police station. He had the gall to complain that I'd damaged his cell phone. As they tried to leave the island by boat, Billy Bob Puhi was arrested by coastguards with two other men. One of the accomplices, a Japanese sailor, was, it transpired, the man who had rung Clive Phelps with the fake American accent. The other, a lithe young Hawaiian, had been staying at my hotel to keep me under observation, and had dropped down from the verandah above my room to leave the meat skewer in my bathroom.

Captain Clay Rapoza was in high spirits for once. Everyone had been rounded up. As I sat in his office with Sergeant Emily Tenno and Jimmy Kaheiki, he showered me with congratulations.

"See?" he said. "I knew we'd make a cop out of you."

"Hang on, Captain," I corrected. "I was the one with the handcuffs on, remember. Until they were cut off, I felt more like a criminal."

"You *thought* like a cop. That's what saved your life."

"Why didn't you smash that guy's brains out when you had the chance?" asked Kaheiki. "You saw what he did to Lance Perellini. In your place, I'd have kept hitting till there was no head left to hit."

"I'm not a killer, Mr. Kaheiki. All I used was necessary force."

"Just like your father was trained to do," observed Rapoza.

"He always relied on instinct."

"The main thing is," said Kaheiki, slapping me on the back, "that we caught the whole lot of them. And that's down to you, Alan. You were too smart for the assholes." He gave a deep sigh. "I'll never forgive myself for trusting my chauffeur like that. Tony had been with me for years. How could he get mixed up with those guys?"

"Ask him when you visit him in Halawa Prison," said Rapoza.

Tenno looked at me. "What are your plans, Mr. Saxon?"

"I leave on a flight tomorrow afternoon," I replied.

"Glad to go?"

"Euphoric."

"Can't we persuade you to stay a little longer?" said Kaheiki. "At my expense, of course. You did so much for our family. It won't bring Donald back, of course, but it will make Zann sleep better at nights."

"Yes," said Tenno, considerately. "There's been closure now."

"Hardly," I argued. "What about the related murder of Gabe Mahalona? It's still unsolved. Then there's the mysterious disappearance of Razzaq Khan's son. That's what really brought the father to Oahu."

"Forget the son," said Kaheiki, contemptuously. "The only person who knew what happened to him was Lance Perellini, and he took the secret to his grave. I paid him to frighten the guy off, and that was all. I had no idea he went to extremes."

"As for Mahalona," said Rapoza, "we can finally close the file on that case as well. When we applied a little pressure, Tony talked his head off. It turns out that he was in league with the drug gang who bumped off Mahalona, and made it look as if the murder had Jimmy's fingerprints all over it. Tony was real clever. First of all, he works for Razzaq Khan's rivals, then he takes a bribe from Khan's henchmen. That chauffeur of yours had big balls, Jimmy," he went on. "He was not only betraying you, he was playing one gang off against another."

"And all three of us were paying the rat!" wailed Kaheiki.

"Tony is oozing with repentance now. He gave us the name and whereabouts of the guys who did rub out Gabe Mahalona. We had them in custody within an hour."

Having been embroiled in its repercussions, I was relieved to hear that the murder had finally been solved. It would be some consolation to Mahalona's widow, though she would never accept that her husband was involved in a narcotics ring and that he had been eliminated by rivals because of his success. Mahalona had been used as a pawn to set Razzaq Khan's gang against Jimmy Kaheiki, so that they could they could get involved in a feud that would leave the field clear.

"The heat is off now, Mr. Saxon," Tenno pointed out. "You can go wherever you like without needing a bodyguard. How are you going to spend the rest of the day?"

I held up my bandaged wrist. "But for this, I'd head for the nearest golf course. That's my life support system. As it is, I'm going to do some gentle sightseeing instead. Before I go tomorrow, I'd like to have a few pleasant memories of the island."

"You're leaving quite a few behind, sir."

"Thank you, Sergeant," I said, rising to my feet. "I'd better be off."

Emily Tenno shook my hand, Jimmy Kaheiki treated my arm like a parish pump that needed robust treatment, and even Clay Rapoza felt that the occasion deserved a handshake. His eyes twinkled.

"You ever decide to become a cop," he said, "come and see me."

Kaheiki grinned. "Or me, Alan. I'll write you a reference."

"That goes for me, too," said Tenno.

"I think I'll stick to golf," I told them. "No disrespect to you, but it's a world in which you meet a better class of person."

◇◇◇

It was evening when I got back to my hotel room. A day of sightseeing had revived me and shown me some of the nicer things on the island. It also enabled me to dodge the press and to get some more presents for my daughter. There was a message from Heidi Dukelow in my voice-mail but I was in no hurry to contact her. Instead, I took a shower, removing the bandage so that I could wash my hair. When I glanced in the mirror, I saw that I looked much better without the bandage so I left it off. While I got dressed, I treated myself to a whisky on the rocks.

I'd completely forgotten about Heidi's message. She was soon knocking on my door to see if I'd got back. Letting her in, I mumbled an apology that she brushed aside with a light laugh.

"Where've you *been* all day?" she asked. "Apart from helping to catch the bad guys, that is. Did you know you were mentioned on the TV news this evening? You're a hero, Alan."

"I was simply trying to save my own skin."

"Don't be so modest."

"I did what I had to do, Heidi, that's all."

"You did much more than that. I rang Cora to tell her. She was over the moon with the news that Donald's killer is behind bars. She sends her congratulations, by the way."

"Hey, look," I said, "I can't take credit for Razzaq Khan's arrest, and he actually committed the murder. Lance Perellini turned him in."

"According to what I hear on TV, the whole gang was involved in the conspiracy to kill Donald and you helped to catch them. That deserves a Congressional Medal in my book. Since I don't happen to have one with me," she went on, "will you settle for a kiss?"

I turned my cheek to her. "As long as it's a very gentle one."

"This merits a kiss on the lips, Alan."

"I'm not up to that yet."

"What's wrong?" she complained, caressing my hand. "Have I got bad breath or something?"

"Far from it."

"So what's the problem?"

The problem was that I was alone in my room with a beautiful woman, who was wearing the gorgeous sleeveless dress I'd seen on our first night on the island, and who had the same scorpion clasp on her arm as then. She had also put on that enchanting perfume of hers. In spite of everything, desire began to stir. Then I looked at the scorpion again and saw the evening sun glinting off its tail. I knew the sort of sting that it could inflict.

"The problem is that we've come to the parting of the ways, Heidi."

"Not until we leave the island."

"Oh, I think we've reached it now."

"Don't be silly," she said, kissing me lightly on the cheek. "You had a triumph today. We must celebrate it somehow."

"No," I decided.

"Why not?"

"It never happened, remember."

She stepped in closer. "I know, Alan—but it might."

"I don't think so."

"Give it a chance."

When I took the phone call from Donald in San Diego, I was in the right place at the right time and in the right mood. Now, by contrast, I was in the wrong place, at the wrong time and in the wrong mood. But, then, whenever I met Heidi Dukelow, that would be the case. In practical terms, I was still in some physical discomfort. My ordeal that morning had only served to intensify the constant ache and the sudden twinges. The shoulder that she now decided to stroke was plagued by a distant burning sensation. Heidi might look and feel wonderful with her clothes off but I certainly wouldn't.

"I insist on buying dinner for you tonight," she announced.

"No, thank you."

"If you're feeling threatened, we'll have it in a restaurant."

"The answer's still the same, I'm afraid."

"Why?" she asked, hurt by my unexpected rejection. "What have I done? What did I say? Aren't we still friends?"

"Of course," I said, detaching her hand gently from my shoulder. "The truth is that I already have a date for tonight."

She was taken aback. "With a woman?"

"With seven of them, actually," I explained. "By way of a thank you, I'm taking out the entire Pineapple Theater Company for a meal. Melissa and the girls deserve to eat properly for once. My only worry is Fern."

"Fern?"

"A ball-breaking Australian. My guess is that Fern usually lives on raw meat pushed through the bars of her cage. One way or another, it should be an interesting evening."

"What about tomorrow?"

"I fly home to civilization."

"I see." She was downcast. "This is it, then."

"Yes, Heidi. This, I fear, is it."

She gave a wry smile, then she kissed me softly on the lips. Her perfume invaded my nostrils again. Whatever else Melissa and her fellow actors would be wearing, it would not be an expensive perfume. That didn't matter. I'd feel safe with them, as long as I didn't sit next to Fern.

"I was lying," said Heidi, wistfully. "It did happen."

"I know. I was there."

"Okay, it was a bit of a disaster, but it meant something."

"Yes," I agreed. "It meant that we're not really suited. We did the wrong thing for all the wrong reasons, Heidi. That's why it didn't work. All I can do is to apologize."

"Whatever for? It was what we both wanted."

"At the time."

"And now?"

I checked my watch. "The Magnificent Seven will be waiting."

"Why do you think I stayed on here?" she asked. "It wasn't only to see how the investigation panned out. It was for you, Alan. Didn't you realize that? I was hoping that we could start all over again with a clean slate."

"It wouldn't work out, Heidi."

"It might." She held both my hands. "I'm only talking about seeing each other from time to time. Sharing special moments. I know that you often come to the States, and I visit Europe occasionally. I thought that we might just meet up now and again." I shook my head. "Why not?"

"Because I'd be competing with Donald again," I argued. "You don't want me, you just need a replacement for him. Sorry. You'll have to look elsewhere, I'm afraid. Donald will always be the most important man in your life, Heidi."

"That's true," she admitted. "He always was and always will be."

"Don't try to involve me in a play-off for your affections," I said, walking her to the door and opening it. "I could never beat Donald when he was alive. I'd stand even less chance now."

Heidi looked crestfallen. She summoned up a wan smile, gave me another kiss on the lips, then walked out of my life for good. Her fragrance still hung in the air but it no longer had any appeal for me. I'd survived everything, including her last bid for my affections. I felt that I was at last free of all my entanglements on the island.

It was almost as if they'd never happened.

To receive a free catalog of Poisoned Pen Press titles, please contact us in one of the following ways:

Phone: 1-800-421-3976
Facsimile: 1-480-949-1707
Email: info@poisonedpenpress.com
Website: www.poisonedpenpress.com

Poisoned Pen Press
6962 E. First Ave., Suite 103
Scottsdale, AZ 85251